THE PROCESS OF MURDER

William J. and Martha Q. Schafer

"You can keep his luggage. You can have the book as well: it's a why–dunnit in q–sharp major and it has a message: never talk to the sort of girls that you wouldn't leave lying about in your drawing room for the servants to pick up."

—*Muriel Spark, The Driver's Seat*

12/2/13 8:42 PM

ISBN 978-0-9911918-0-2

Cover design: Mary Ellen Niedenfuer

www.uridesigns.com

Forward

The Process of Murder is the first book in the Richard Poole mystery series. If you have comments or corrections, please contact the publisher at amarich@notecloud.com.

The Process Of Murder

ONE HUNG HUNGARIAN

WALKING BRISKLY, RICHARD Poole left the heavier shade around Ashpole Manor and stepped into the blue open twilight of the grounds.

He was pleasantly tired—not really exhausted, as he thought he might be—from the effects of jet lag. But he wanted to see the manor's vast grounds before darkness finally descended. His sense of time was distorted, another strange effect of the Englishness that surrounded him.

He had been on English soil for almost a day, but he was still mentally across the Atlantic, and he counted on the sights and sounds of the estate to soothe him before he found his bed. Dusk was settling, so he walked briskly down the gentle slope from the house through a broad swatch of formal gardens, the brilliance of clumped roses and other flowers muted by the slanted light.

His goal was a dovecote at the base of the shallow hill, a squat tower of soft grey and yellow stone surmounted by an odd ogee-roofed cupola. He had seen it from the dining room windows and resolved to explore it. One of the staff had identified it as a dovecote when Poole enquired about the strange tower poking up through the trees. Not that he had an interest in doves, culinary or ornithological. But he knew what a dovecote was, and the peculiar beehive–shaped roof on the building intrigued him, It was another strange sight in this strange little country that reinforced his sense of being transported to a brave new (or old) world.

1

Poole had never traveled in England, though he had been stationed in Europe with the Army (Germany, France) and had made frequent trips to the Middle East in his years with the agency. He had changed planes at Heathrow and looked idly out the windows of the passenger terminal, but he had never really thought about *being* in England. Now here he was, on assignment by TransAtlas, sent out on his own for two weeks in rural England.

Poole followed the little graveled path between low hedges, across a knot garden dotted by showy roses, their colors almost luminescent in the late daylight. A bird sang in the dense shrubbery across the broad lawns of Ashpole Manor, a birdsong alien to him. Gravel shushed and clicked under his shoes. Otherwise, it was a silent world, a piece of country forty minutes from Heathrow, miles from the train he had ridden out, from the world of business and bustle which was his normal environment.

He stopped in the center of the garden, stretched, sniffed and stared around. Behind him, the immensity of Ashpole House stretched, its dozens of tall windows catching the sunset and turning blindingly bronze, like shields or tablets set into the buttery stone. Someone walked across the raised terrace, the small figure lending a sense of scale to the house, accentuating its vastness. Poole shook his head at the idea of someone calling this place "home," at the notion of a "house" larger than most hotels.

But the quiet of the scene was most important to him. He needed peace, a respite from the usual pace of his life, and the assignment to this executive training conference was almost an offer of a paid vacation. When Harvey Lewis had called him into the cavernous penthouse office at TransAtlas headquarters and laid out the assignment, Poole had restrained himself from leaping across the monstrous mahogany slab Lewis called a desk to hug the old pirate. Two weeks in England! A placid stint of executive–sitting. A few pages of perfunctory reporting on the processes of the conference. A piece of cake, solid angel food.

In the east, the sun slid behind clumps of deep–green forest, a golden ball balanced on the edge of the world. Then Poole noticed shapes on the acres of lawn between himself and the verge of the forest. He thought of statuary, but one shape moved slightly. A herd of small deer drifted out from the shadows, grazing on the rich, green grass. What next?—Robin Hood and his band come to poach the king's red deer? Poole watched the shapes for a moment. Light was failing rapidly, and he wanted to inspect the little tower of the dovecote before he returned to the house and a bed he hoped to be large, deep and soft. He continued down the hill.

The dovecote was a solidly–built stone edifice about two stories tall, a squat tower with a slate roof, the whole structure like a pepper grinder set down on the grassy quilt of the rose garden. As he approached, he read a small sign planted next to the iron–bound oak door:

DOVECOTE, BUILT 1611

England, a land of convenient, legible labels. He made a circuit around the building, looking up at it. A smooth cylinder of small stones about the size of building bricks, each stone carefully smoothed and set. The roof incorporated three small dormer windows and ended in a cupola of slatted wood—where the birds, evidently, came and went. Something moved on the dark grey roof slates. A dove—he would call it a pigeon—strutted there. A grey–and–white fancy bird with a spreading lyre–like fan tail. It marched along the verge of the roof, shook itself, glanced down with one dark eye then spread its wings and flew off toward the woods.

Stopping by the door, Poole glanced around. Then he decided to be bold, visitor or no, cheeky Yank abroad or not. He turned the big iron ring that served as a handle, and the heavy door swung inward. He stepped into the wide doorframe. Dim light fell through the windows above and through the slotted cupola, enough to outline the walls, punctured by many indentations or slots, the places where the birds rested. Poole understood the term "pigeonhole" graphically for the first time. The middle of the cylinder was occupied by a large wooden structure, a giant's ladder of oaken beams built as a helix, big steps that twisted around a massive vertical axle. Ingenious: the dove–tender could thus climb up and swing himself around the walls and harvest the squabs from their nests in the stone.

Poole pushed at the oaken steps in front of him. On an impulse, he stepped up onto the bottom rung of the ladder. And felt something hard bump his temple. He looked up into the thick shadow and saw the polished toecap of a shoe. As the structure swung slightly under his touch, the shoe also turned a little before his eyes, revealing another shoe next to it, also pointed delicately downward. Richard Poole squinted up into the darkness to make out the body that dangled there above him from the ladder, a strange harvest in an empty dovecote.

✧

In ten minutes, Poole was back with the porter's flashlight. A cock–and–bull story about a lost cigarette lighter had gotten it. Now the grounds were velvety with darkness, the tower of the dovecote only a shadow rearing above the blackness of the garden. He glanced back to see if anyone had followed him from the house. He had a strong, unsettling intuition telling him to keep his discovery to himself.

Poole reentered the dovecote, pulled the thick door nearly closed and shone the light upward. A man in a dull–grey business suit hung neatly from the top of the turning ladder by a blue–and–red–striped necktie.

The hanged man turned very slightly, hands at his sides, like a manikin in a grand guignol display. His head was twisted sideways by the noose, his face black and distorted, tongue extended rudely, eyes bulging and opaque. Richard Poole had never seen a hanged man before, but this is what he assumed a hanged man would look like, all right. Gingerly, Poole ascended the big rungs until he was level with the dangling man. The silk tie was wedged and folded into the base of the topmost rung of the ladder. It had slid around the man's neck, its knot tucked under his ear like the fat knot on a hangman's noose.

In the next minutes, Poole examined the corpse and the ladder carefully. There were scuffs in the high polish of the shoes and small marks on two rungs of the ladder, where the feet had kicked at them. Bits of waxy wood were wedged under the nails on one hand, as if the man had scrabbled at the old tarnished oak of the rungs. *Why couldn't he reach the ladder*, Poole asked himself. His hands were free. The crystal of the man's wristwatch—a cheap Swiss model worn on the left wrist—was fractured, as if he had flailed his arms wildly against the heavy central axle–beam of the ladder.

On the cold stone floor of the dovecote, Poole found a thin leather wallet. In it were twenty–five pounds and several documents in a language he could not read. A business card smudgily printed in English read *James Drus ~ Sales Representative ~ TAC Hydraulics* followed by what Poole assumed to be a telephone number. Poole slipped the wallet and its contents into his own jacket pocket, extinguished the flashlight and stepped outside. A gibbous moon had risen, and pale grey light suffused the quiet garden. The heads of the roses were now monochromatic, little clouds of paleness in the shadow. Richard Poole felt he had stepped from a mausoleum into a graveyard. All that was needed to complete the gothic feeling of the nightscape was an owl, a bat and a raven. He walked quickly up the graveled path toward the gigantic bulk of Ashpole House, now outlined by floodlights and punctuated by tall lighted windows in the staterooms on the ground floor and a few lights in the stories above.

The house was a solemn face of the night, the windows eyes.

Poole hurried toward it, nevertheless, to find haven from the horrid quiet of the dangling man in the dovecote.

The interior of Ashpole Manor house was monumental and grand, so imposing as to suppress Poole's excitement. Entering at the back, east end, he walked into a reception hall large enough to accommodate an indoor softball game. Marbled floors and staircases exuded a coldness not offset by the electric lighting. Off this hallway was another great hall and a state apartment that had once been a dining room and was now the refectory–lounge for the conferences Ashpole Institute sponsored. Chairs and sofas were spotted about the room at twenty–yard intervals, and the ceilings were tall enough to permit hang–gliding.

Poole hurried down the room to a smaller hallway and the porter's office. The porter was a small sandy–haired man in a uniform that looked to have been handed down from a small–town production of *The Student Prince*, a kind of motheaten maroon cavalryman's uniform with yellow stripes on the trousers and rows of greenish buttons on the jacket. Poole recalled some such figure appearing in *The Wizard of Oz*.

The porter looked self–conscious about his clothing or perhaps just mildly depressed. His name, Poole knew from his arrival that morning, was Fred. He was the kind of functionary who probably only had one name, perhaps had been known from birth only as Fred or as "good old Fred." He had a slight cast in one eye and an accent that sounded like someone speaking carefully through a mouthful of cake.

"Here's your flashlight, and many thanks," Poole said. Should he tip the man? If so, with which of the odd coins that weighted down his trouser pocket? Why were they of such disparate sizes and shapes, and what did 5p *mean*, anyhow?

Fred accepted the flashlight without reply. Poole scanned the empty lounge.

"Where is everyone, anyhow?" he asked.

"Ah, the evening meetings have started, haven't they?" Fred said. "The whole lot scuttled off to the meeting rooms upstairs."

Poole walked across the immense foyer, with its frescoed ceiling, ranks of marble statuary and potted plants of Amazonian size and luxuriousness. His footsteps produced rattling echoes down the halls and alcoves.

As he climbed the broad stairs, Poole reflected on how small the house made him feel and how alien he felt in England. He trudged down an apparently endless hallway lined with scowling portraits of peers peeping out of puddles of chiaroscuro.

At the end of the hallway, two men leaned together in conversation. Poole recognized one as Sir Leicester Harcourt, chief director of Cavendar Institute. The other Poole thought was an assistant director. Sir Leicester turned and grasped the handle of a door at the end of the corridor. Poole accelerated his walk, feeling trapped in one of those nightmares of ever–protracted perspective, when no amount of panicked running gets the dreamer nearer his destination. He called out, "Wait a moment—Sir Leicester…"

The large, portly man glanced toward Poole and then resumed his talk with the smaller man at his elbow. The man nodded rapidly in response to Sir Leicester's speech.

As Poole drew up, half–winded, he repeated, "Sir Leicester…" But the large man simply looked down his ample nose and slipped into the room. The smaller man glanced at Poole and followed Sir Leicester. A hand–lettered card on an easel next to the door read

CAVENDAR INSTITUTE WORKSHOP

LARGE GROUP SESSION—21:00–22:00

Poole looked back down the empty corridor and then followed the two men. It was a state meeting room, a massive double cube with gilded rococo ornamentation over every available surface. But Poole ignored the amazing decor. He was aware that half a hundred people sat in folding chairs, staring in his direction. He slithered along the wall, brushing heavy velvet drapes, bumping a huge vase on a fantastically fretworked Chinese stand, working his way around the seated phalanx of conference members. He saw Sir Leicester and his assistant seated in the group.

Aiming for the back of the room, in a kind of Groucho Marx half–crouch, Poole yearned for a convenient cloak of invisibility. His instructions, clearly reiterated by Harvey Lewis, were that he be a quiet observer of the conference and in no wise a participant. Now he seemed to have achieved unwittingly the status of a late walk–on in a baroque opera.

A meeting was in progress, though Poole could see no moderator or convener at work. Someone across the big room was speaking, in a ripple of marbled echoes: "...see the purpose of sitting here without any agenda, just wasting time in a lot of blathering..."

He lost the rest of the statement in a sound like steam rushing out of a valve, the sound usually rendered in comic strips as "Pssst!"

A woman beckoned and gestured, pointing at the vacant chair next to her on an aisle. Poole ducked around a life–size bronze Hermes, nearly impaling himself on the messenger's outthrust caduceus, and flopped into the gilt chair.

The woman whispered, "I thought they'd all catch sight of you and jump in. They're looking for any target, moving or still."

She was a compact, pert redhead, her hair a tangle of thick curls around a distinctly heart–shaped face. She was dressed in a business suit with a floppy silk tie of the sort worn by the cast in the second act of *La Boheme* instead of small placards reading "I am pretending to be a Bohemian artist." She thrust out her hand, and Poole took a strong big–business–like handshake.

"I'm Amanda," she said. The plastic tab on her lapel spelled it all out: *AMANDA EVANS ~ CONFERENCE COORDINATOR.*

Poole loosened his hand and realized he was grinning lopsidedly. Panic communicated itself to his foolish facial muscles. "Oh, yeh, " he said. "Richard Poole. I'm here as an…observer."

She leaned closer and peered at him. "Nonsense," she said. "Not possible. Where's your tab?" She tapped his lapel with a pencil.

"Ah, well—I *am* here only semi–officially…"

She picked up a clipboard and leafed through pages of photocopied lists. "Oh, yes. Poole, Richard B. Perhaps we ought to clear out of here until I can understand your story. Come along."

Her tone communicated a schoolmarmish insistence Poole could not have resisted even if he had wished. She scooted around him, and he slunk after her, as if he were being marched to the cloakroom for a half–dozen swats with a ruler, or as they would say here, "Six of the best for you, Sir!"

Following Miss or Mrs. or Ms. Evans, Poole noted how trim and compact her figure was, even inside the travesty boss's costume, how precise her movements. He concentrated then on not tripping over an edge of carpet or skating across an acre of glossy marble floor before he was out of the room. Several members of the seated congregation turned to stare or frown.

A deep voice across the room interrupted the speaker to intone, "This group seems content to be spectators at a little drama, a whole roomful of Hamlets. *Is* the play the thing to catch the conscience of the king? And who will be elected king this time?" There was a muffled snort of nervous laughter.

Then Poole collided softly with Amanda Evans, who was opening a peculiar door inset between two massive rococo picture frames, a door that looked to be covered in velvet, blending in with the acres of velvet that covered the wall. It was an exit straight from Lewis Carroll, Poole thought.

"Ex*cuse* me," Poole said, and Amanda Evans stepped nimbly aside.

"Sorry," she said. "If you're in such a dreadful hurry, go right ahead," swinging the door open wider.

"No, no," Poole said. "Ladies…you first."

She pursed her lips, frowned and then ducked through the doorway, Poole followed her into a small passageway only dimly lit by a bronze candelabra glowing with small bulbs meant to recall taper flames.

Amanda Evans turned to face him, bundling her clipboard against her chest like a shield. "Now, what is all this nonsense?"

"It's a…an emergency. I must talk with Sir Leicester right now."
"First, I must find out who you are and why you're here, doing a one–man awkward squad routine," she said. She was as deadpan as every Brit he had spoken with thus far: was it ridicule, chastisement or simple amusement?

Poole ran his hand through his hair, or what hair remained after the ravages of time. She did not seem as severe as the cut of her suit and her icy tone implied.

"I think I should only talk with Sir Leicester. Believe me, it's a genuine emergency. I'm sure he'd want to know about it first."

"I am Sir Leicester's associate," she said, "and it is absolutely impossible to speak with him now. If you are a member of the conference and understand anything about the Cavendar Process, you must realize why. Everyone feels a genuine sense of emergency at a Cavendar Conference."

She whined the vowels of "genuine" in a passable imitation of Poole's ineradicable Midwestern accent. He winced.

"I can listen to the situation and assess it, Mr. Poole. I assure you I am both qualified and empowered. Now, would you tell me exactly who you are and what your business is?"

"Can we go somewhere for a cup of tea…or coffee, or whatever it is you drink? I feel like we're huddled here plotting an assassination," Poole said, gesturing at the dim shadows in the narrow corridor.

"All right. There should be something in the common room."

Amanda Evans led Poole down the corridor. They crossed into a grand junction of marbled halls and descended the main staircase again. Poole still could not share the feeling of being trapped on an impossibly grandiose stage—set for a tragedy of blood. He recalled the Marx Brothers in *A Night at the Opera* and giggled to himself: perhaps he was cast as Harpo this time, although he usually felt he had drawn the Groucho role.

In the windy common room, about the size of a U.S. bowling alley, Poole followed Amanda Evans to a table and they sat, taking a moment to eye each other over cups of coffee.

"Mrs. Evans," he began, and she cut in, "*Miss* Evans, but please call me Amanda," with a sweet smile. When she smiled, the resemblance struck him—with the massed bronze hair, the heart–shaped face and fresh grin, she was an incarnation of one of the platoons of putti that infested the walls of Ashpole Manor, a little cupidon extracted from the high baroque, outfitted in a Marks and Spencer's skirt–suit and plunked down in the late twentieth century. He almost choked on the awful coffee, which tasted like an extract of turnip tops.

"Miss Evans—Amanda," he tried again. When he attempted to speak with a Brit, his tongue seemed to swell like a bladder. Why did he feel like a patent idiot in uttering the language he had owned and casually abused for forty years?

"Here's all I can tell you for the moment: I am a legitimate representative of TransAtlas Corporation—he thrust his ID badge toward her—"and I'm at the conference as an observer for TA's interests. A semi–official undercover observation, I suppose you could say. And there is a situation at hand which I must report to

Sir Leicester himself. Believe me, it's a real…problem."

She produced her clipboard again, copied from the ID badge and said, "Let me be the judge of the situation, Mr. Poole. I assure you I am competent to evaluate any, er, situation that might arise at Ashpole Manor. That is precisely my brief as Sir Leicester's administrative assistant. My God—this coffee is absolutely *foul*."

She smiled brightly again amidst this *non sequitur*, and Poole felt his scanty purchase on reason loosening further. A little voice back in the furthermost recesses of his cerebral cortex said, "Don't start falling in love, dolt!'

"Okay," Poole said—to her, not to his agenbite of inwit. "I don't have much choice. I'll have to trust you. I'm the gofer on this end, and my instructions are to handle things 'without resort to unnecessary communication stateside.' That was Harvey's choice phrase. Here's the situation, Amanda: There's a dead guy hanging by his necktie out in your fancy dovecote."

Poole awaited her reaction. Amanda Evans set her coffee cup down carefully and looked closely at him. Her eyes were really *green*, Poole decided. Or maybe a kind of…taupe.

Then she said carefully, "If Robin or Donovan put you up to this, I'll *kill* them. *After* I've killed *you*, Mr. Poole. I'm totally browned off at their childish ideas of humor. My work here is strenuous enough without…"

"Miss Evans—Amanda—I solemnly assure you this is no joke, and I don't know who Robin or Donovan might be. I don't know a blessed soul in England except for Fred the porter. I've been busy snooping since I arrived this afternoon. There is, I swear it, a skinny dead man hanging by a red–and–blue tie down in your fancy dovecote. Or there was, about twenty minutes ago."

"That does sound like a genuine—even a gen–you–wine— emergency. But I insist on ocular proof. Let's go down to the dovecote. We'll need an electric torch. Do you carry a gun…like

American snoopers are supposed to?"

"No. I suppose I could have gotten one into England all right, through the company, but I hate the damned things for a whole variety of reasons. And I'm not exactly a gun–toting detective, Amanda. And for God's sake, call me Richard. I don't have a title you can use, and I don't carry a magnifying glass or fingerprint kit, either."

"Finish your abominable coffee—if you can do it—and tell me about your, er, job description. You'd be surprised at what I would want to know. Especially about your mysterious TransAtlas Corporation and its devious ways."

Poole sat: was this a tactical foray, the first phase of a serious interrogation or polite conversation? TransAtlas' first and only inviolable commandment, at least according to Harvey Lewis, was simple: *need to know*. Poole's method was to listen, to observe and to give out as little information as possible. He remembered a WW II slogan—*Loose Lips Sink Ships*. His little rowboat would go down by the bow if he spoke out of turn. He recalled Buster Keaton standing solemnly at attention in his homemade rowboat as it sank into a pond. The boat had been christened the Damfino, short for damned–lf–I–know. That was where he stood now—cold water up to his ankles and the ship foundering, without even a salon orchestra to render *Nearer My God to Thee*. That had been a *British* boat, too, a Cunarder built to the exacting specifications of the Stiff Upper Lip. He was going to find himself a life preserver, and Amanda Evans looked soft and pneumatic enough to be a very comfortable one—no Mae West, but any hand is a helping hand for a drowning man.

"Okay. I think we have mutual interests to protect, if you're concerned about the conference and Sir Leicester and the reputation of the Cavendar Process. I don't think we—you—want panic or scandal on the first day here, and I presume that the dead man yonder is *not* part of your process. Right? I mean, you don't plant stiffs around to test the mental agility and social graces of these people?"

"Hardly. Unless it is some kind of stupid prank by Robin or Donovan. They're two of the younger staff, and they tend to express certain regrettable hostilities in aberrant behavior. That's a verbatim quote from Sir Leicester's last confidential staff evaluation. And that is why I want to *see* your dead man."

"We'll get to him. I don't think he'll wander away. Here's what I found on—or near—him." He flipped the worn wallet across the table. "Not much to go on, if there aren't labels or laundry marks in his clothes. "

She looked at the meager contents of the wallet. "Hmm. He's Hungarian, and he's *not* a member of the conference. At least he's not on the computer list, for what *that's* worth. Now, tell me as simply as you can why *you* are involved in the conference and have set yourself up to deal with this…situation."

"Amanda, I can only tell you I'm an over–under–in–between for TransAtlas, a Johnny–on–the–site for the corporation. You know Figaro? Rossini? I'm *that* kind of factotum. A kind of super–gofer, although Harvey Lewis hates the term."

"I thought a gopher was a small American rodent with big teeth. You don't match that description."

"Thanks a lot. Gofer–with–an–F. I go fer this and go fer that, on a fairly high level. Fred's your resident gofer here, although you'd probably call him a stoat or a weasel, except he seems harmless and noncarnivorous. I'm what you might call an all–purpose, low–rent trouble–shooter."

Poole found himself staring at Amanda, who shifted under his gaze and blushed. He wondered how far and how fast the blush spread over *all* her fair skin. He laughed and thrust the thought away. Setting his coffee cup down, he said, "Let's go out to your dovecote."

✧

The dark was denser with the finality of night, and the flashlight beam seemed weak, watery, making the dangling man in the dovecote even more an illustration from a B–grade horror movie, flinging violent shadows around the cylindrical walls as the body twisted slowly on the big ladder. Poole watched Amanda Evans more closely than the corpse. When you've seen one hung Hungarian, you've seen them all, he thought. Her reaction had been interesting: which is to say, she had betrayed no reaction at all when he opened the door and flicked on the flashlight. She was not a crier or a shrieker or an expresser–of–histrionic–attitudes. She had sucked in her breath a bit, but she had only stared for a second and then moved in to examine the cold cadaver.

Poole studied the mortal remains of James Drus more carefully: gaunt, sallow and pitiful in death, as stretched and blank as a Giacometti sculpture, he must have been marginally handsome in life, about six feet tall, thin, distinctly European—at least non–American—to Poole's eye. His face was so hideously distorted by the death–trauma that it was only a caricature in rictus of human features. But his hands, rather long and thin, Poole noticed, were roughened, the nails short and chipped, the hands of a workingman, not an idle executive. His suit was cheap, ditto the shoes. Poole found no labels or marks on the clothing.

Why such a fancy necktie? Poole asked himself.

"You were right, Mr. Poole," she said. Her voice was fainter, less controlled. "We have a very nasty situation on our hands. We'll have to think how to deal with it."

"Whoa. What's this *we*? I know *I've* got footwork to do, but who else is included? We're going to have to call the local cops in, but I'd like a running start."

"Mmmm. I'm trying to think that out," she said. "Let's get out of here, though."

15

As they backed through the door, Poole gazed once more, sadly, at the hanged man. The most mysterious card in the Tarot pack, and here it was framed up in living—or *dead*—color, 3–D, on our stage tonight. The dead man still turned slowly on his terrible axis, and his open eyes glinted greyly down at Poole, his hands turned out slightly as if in a mute gesture, imploring a little help, a little pity. Something nagged at Poole's memory in relation to the Tarot figure: *what?*

They returned to the bulk of Ashpole Manor, which seemed minatory to Poole, the giant ogre's castle in a fairy tale, the black hulk of an unknown fate. Amanda Evans led him down a narrow back corridor to a small room outfitted as an office. She turned on a desk lamp and sat behind the cluttered desk. He pulled up a wooden chair, and they huddled under the pale cone of light.

"Let's see what we know," Amanda said. "We have a man in the dovecote who may or may not be one James Drus, with a meager batch of identification in the wallet you showed me. No passport. This all may be left by his…murderer. Or planted as a false clue. I have"—she paused to flip through papers on her clipboard—"three applicants for the conference as yet unaccounted for. None named Drus. None from Hungary. You found the body—when?"

"Ten after nine," Poole said.

"And being a careful snoop, you checked your digital watch, now set at GMT, British Summertime, not at some outlandish Transatlantic time?"

"Yeh. And something else: the grounds were swarming with people this afternoon, up till suppertime—seven o'clock. I think it had to have happened between seven and nine, and unless we can find someone who was down at the dovecote later, we aren't going to be able to tell the time until a police pathologist does his tests. Which should be done, by the way, as soon as possible."

"Yes. The police," Amanda sighed, "must be brought in soon. But

I want to know more about you and how you connect with the Cavendar Conference before I ring up the locals. I don't want any surprises."

Poole pulled an ancient bulldog pipe from his jacket and banged it on his hand.

"Can I smoke this thing? I don't really smoke it so much as give it burnt offerings. A lot of matches."

Amanda Evans nodded, and Poole fiddled with the pipe. He didn't really like it, and the tobacco he had bought at the airport before the flight was made of old tennis shoes, but he had thought the pipe might blunt his American image, and it was a time–honored way of buying time in conversation. No one could ramrod or sidestep a really determined pipe–fiddler. When he had burnt up two matches and produced a small noxious cloud of beige smoke, he nodded cheerfully at Amanda Evans.

"I didn't kill our friend out there. I can't prove it to you, and I probably can't convince you that I'm not sinister enough to do it. From your perspective I am—or ought to be—the prime suspect. First, I'm the only one who knew about the dead man. Second, I'm an anomaly, a nonentity, in your scheme of things. You seem to have on your hands a stranger who has killed another stranger."

"Richard, I also see other openings. You assume that James Drus —or whoever he is—was murdered. Perhaps he died accidentally. I don't see how that could happen, but I also don't see any convincing evidence that he *must* have been hanged by someone else. Perhaps he hanged himself. But why in the Ashpole dovecote? How is he connected with this place?"

"We need that police pathologist," Poole said. The old pipe had gone out, but it still exuded a foul odor. Smoking a pipe, he recalled, was like being haunted by an evil–smelling spirit. "Perhaps he didn't even die of hanging. Maybe he was killed some other way and strung up there to cover it."

Amanda Evans and Richard Poole stared blankly at each other across the small splash of light from the desk lamp. She tapped a pencil on the desktop blotter and pursed her lips.

"From my perspective, *you're* a suspect, too, Amanda. Maybe you had some inscrutable reason for eliminating this glitch in the Cavendar Process, to erase this guy who doesn't show up on computer printouts. Maybe he's a former lover. Maybe he's a secret agent. Maybe he annoyed you with uncouth manners and a foreign accent. How do I know?"

"You'll have to trust me that none of the above apply."

"Right," Poole said. "And you'll have to trust me that I'm just what you see—a middle–level corporate watchdog who wouldn't harm a fly. Except in line of duty."

"I'm still waiting to hear what it is you do—and are going to do —about this…situation."

"Damage control," Poole said. "That's my basic job. I think that's your objective, too. I want to see that whatever's happening here doesn't gum up the large and intricate works of TransAtlas Corporation in all its many and varied…what do you say?— avatars."

"My, what big words you have," Amanda said.

"The better with which to obfuscate, my dear. To continue: your job, unless I'm really off the beam, is also to practice damage control for your boss, Sir Leicester. To keep this…incident from stinking up the place and closing the show. Right?"

"Right enough. You don't know how complicated and delicate a Cavendar Conference can be. And I must give you a short course on that before we go too far along. But yes and yes, my first task is to see that whatever we have here is contained and doesn't contaminate the Process. The conference members and staff must be kept free of extraneous confusion or distraction."

"And you don't want a lot of pointless scandal, either. Nothing to blot all the scutcheons tacked up on the walls."

"Fair enough, but I don't think that's a basic concern. We seem to have a conjunction of moral, legal and social problems right in the person of that...dead man in the dovecote."

Poole stared hopelessly at his cold pipe, shrugged and thrust it back in his pocket. "I think you've got the first move, Amanda."

"Yes. I once heard some oaf on an American movie say 'Here goes nothing.' Does that apply?"

She picked up the phone, dialed and sat staring slightly past Poole. The peculiar angle of the light, the old wood paneling close around them, the deep shadows thrown made an odd chiaroscuro portrait of this woman, an attractive but deeply mysterious picture. Poole sat back as the line clicked and Amanda Evans invented her speech for the police.

✧

A definite chill settled as Amanda and Poole stood under the huge Palladian portico waiting for the police. In a few moments, headlights flickered through the long avenue of beeches and limes, and then a black Ford rolled up, rattling the thick gravel of the drive. Two men emerged briskly, all business.

A compact black–haired man in an overcoat came around the car, and a much larger blond slipped from the driver's side (*backwards* Poole thought—*everything's a mirror–image in this damn place*). The driver was dressed in a dark–blue uniform but was capless.

The small man approached, stopped with an inclination or half–bow to Amanda. "I'm Chief Inspector Griffiths, C.I.D. This is Constable Davies. Or have you met?"

"No, no. I'm Amanda Evans. I called the station. I'm conference coordinator for Ashpole Center. This is Richard Poole. A conference member."

The little man was self–contained, diffident. He wore a small black pencil mustache he nibbled as he gazed at Amanda and

Richard. The big man beamed openly, round–faced and ruddy. Out of the serge uniform he might have been a farmer about to launch into a disquisition on the assorted joys and miseries of country life. Instead, he produced a small notepad and began writing.

"A forensics team and the medical examiner are on the way," Griffiths said. "But we need an initial peek, don't we?"

"Oh, yes," Amanda said. She glanced at Richard, and he tried to read the signal.

"Er, I found the body," Poole said. "I reported it to Miss Evans." He handed the wallet to Griffiths, saying, "I picked this up off the floor but tried not to handle it too much."

Griffiths took the wallet in his handkerchief, clucking his tongue.

"No one else has been involved now?" Davies said, his first words. His accent, Poole noted, was a broader, amplified version of Griffiths' muted voice, a peculiar ventriloquil effect.

"No. We called…directly," Amanda said.

Griffiths glanced around side–eyed at the immensity of Ashpole Manor—or at what could be seen in the lights from the windows and from the floodlights on the drive. "A fine house," he said.

It was a feeble voice, but according to Poole's Patented Personality Perception Inventory (Poole's Law No. 3), this made Griffiths a man to watch: If someone in authority reeks bozoness or wimpitude (the law read), watch out, because you're about to be blindsided.

"Very grand," Griffiths continued, his voice a sigh like a small steam leak or a slowly–deflating bicycle tire. He scuffed a shoe in the gravel and said, "Let's see your dead man."

Amanda led them around the house and down the gentle slope to the dovecote. In the close darkness of the building, Poole watched the two policemen work briskly and efficiently. They examined the body and the surroundings. Davies stood behind his superior, copying busily into his notebook as Griffiths spoke in low, clear phrases. When he stopped and stepped back from the dangling man, he declared, "Yes indeed, very dead. Our most able and loquacious forensics dogsbody will cheerfully tell us how long, why and how. I'll need your views, Mr. Poole and…"

"*Miss* Evans—Amanda."

Griffiths stared at the handkerchief–wrapped wallet he had drawn from his pocket, sighed and handed it to Davies.

They trudged silently back to the portico, where a big black police van had parked, and Davies led a team of uniformed and plainclothed men back around the house. In the room where they had taken coffee, Poole and Amanda answered brief, formulaic questions by Griffiths.

Griffiths ended the inquisition and sat tapping his Biro against his chin. He roused himself and said, "Spell your last name, please, Mr. Poole."

"That's Poole–with–a–silent–E," he said and almost bit his tongue.

He had resolved never to use that phrase, after an unfortunate episode as a freshman at Gower College. He had used it at a tea, in introducing himself to Brains Bainbridge, the dormitory head resident. His roommate, Jack Iverson, known as "I.I." (or "Aye–Aye") Iverson, for *Invincibly Ignorant*, had piped up smartly with "And it's also Rick–with–a–silent–P." For the rest of his college years, Poole had often received campus mail addressed to Prick Poole.

They followed Griffiths through the axis of Ashpole House, across the terrace and toward the dovecote. The police had strung portable lights around the building, and figures moved back and forth, silhouetted in the glare.

"This will attract a good bit of attention," Griffiths said. "I suggest you alert your staff to the situation, Miss Evans. We don't want rumors and panic flying about. I'll need to speak with Sir Leicester and other staff members as soon as possible."

"Inspector Griffiths, I've explained how disruptive this may be to the conference," Amanda said. Poole identified her tone as one of rapidly gathering stubbornness.

"I do understand. But we too have procedures to follow in case of a serious crime. I'm sure you will cooperate fully with our investigation, and we will be discreet."

Amanda read her wristwatch and said, "The evening plenary session is nearly over. I'll see Sir Leicester and...others."

"Excellent. If you can take them to a private room, please come down to the dovecote and let me know. Thanks for your cooperation. Mr. Poole, I'll need to talk with you as soon as the pathology fellows give me an inkling about the picture."

He descended from the terrace. Poole and Amanda stood watching, until she said, "Bloody officious Welshman!"

Poole looked at her curiously, and she said, "Oh, I know—I've kept my wretched husband's wretched Taffy name. I began life a Coulter, and I suppose I ought to make the effort and take the name back. Now, follow along if you like, and see how all this will wash with your bosses back in Texas or wherever you come from."

Texas? Poole thought. He trailed Amanda as she plunged back into the corridors and up the grand staircase. His knees felt gelatinous from rushing around, and Poole decided that bona fide jet–lag was about to strike him down.

Sir Leicester wore an expensive, well–tailored suit, dark blue with a faint grey stripe threaded through it. A luminous pearl–grey waistcoat, a handmade white broadcloth shirt. A necktie, dark green and red, with that paramecium pattern Poole could never recall by its proper name, knotted fatly. Poole avoided looking steadily at neckties after seeing the strung–up Hungarian.

He noticed that Sir Leicester's clothing was loose, rumpled and liberally dirty—small food stains and flecks of cigar ash spotted the considerable expanse of costly wool, perhaps as a badge of station: *I am well–born and powerful enough to look like a total slob* it announced in a modest shout. It fit in well, Poole decided, with Poole's Law No. 3. He watched Sir Leicester with wary respect and tried to decipher his rapid, high–pitched speech, which seemed mixed up with elements of a lisp, an Elmer Fudd impediment and bizarre pronunciation of simple words. The *ou* diphthong and various *o*'s somehow emerged a strangled *i*, as in "There is a fishpind arind on the grinds somewhere." Sir Leicester also laughed mirthlessly through his nose.

"Well, my dear," he said to Amanda, bending toward her but not modulating the stentorian half–shout that constituted his intimate tone, "I trust you to handle the matter in your normal, intelligent manner. At all costs, we must protect the process—yes?"

To Poole's ear this sounded like "pwotect the pwocess." He wondered if Sir Leicester could be induced to repeat "The perfectly priceless process must be protected from powerful perils."

Poole was jolted when Sir Leicester turned abruptly and pointed the extremely large cigar he held in his left hand. "And you, Mr., ah, Poole, must put me in the picture. I had some communication with your Harvey Lewis prior to the beginning of the conference. The difficulty is that you are here on…ambiguous status. Until we resolve that, I must trust our Miss Evans to do all the…liaising." With the last nonce–word, he made a sketchy, Prospero–like gesture of blessing with the giant cigar and turned away.

Poole started forward, but Amanda caught his arm. Sir Leicester moved down the corridor with amazing speed, considering his bulk, girth and stumpiness, his smallish feet twinkling beneath him, unbuttoned suitcoat billowing.

"Richard," Amanda said, "that's *all* you'll get from him now. He can't say anything else, and he'll simply cut you—ignore you—if you persist."

"How the hell do I proceed, then? Which assistant can I talk to?"

"None, I'm afraid. They're all involved in the process now—assigned to groups and tasks. You'll have to follow my lead. I think this is all going to be distressing for you."

"Can you at least cue me in on who people are? I got a few names and faces this afternoon when I went to the check–in meeting. But I can't just hang around and let you baby–sit me."

Amanda tapped her fingers on the clipboard and sighed.

"I'll give you a copy of the registration list and show you the biographies conference members submitted. But you *must* gain some perspective on the Cavendar Process and what you'll see here. Since Sir Leicester's father founded the Institute in the nineteen–thirties, we have conducted about five hundred conferences by the Process. We have had nervous breakdowns, sexual intrigue, physical assaults and maimings, attempted blackmail, drunkenness and general disorderly conduct. But never a murder. And before the Process even *began*! The mind boggles."

They descended again to Amanda's cubbyhole of an office, and Poole felt spavined from walking. Amanda found a small blue book on an overflowing shelf and handed it to him. It was titled in gilt–stamped letters: *An Introduction to Group–Process Conduct*, and below that, *Sir Alfred L. Harcourt, O.B.E.* It was battered, and gilting on the page edges gave it the look of a well–used missal or prayerbook.

"It *is* a kind of Bible for the Cavendar Method," Amanda said presciently. "And you should give it your full attention—not to say devotion."

Poole flipped the book's thin pages and thought glumly, *Small type, big words, no pictures.*

✧

Inspector Griffiths stood waiting in the great hall, with his hat in his hands behind his back, his head tipped to take in the huge expanse of a Verrio mural that lapped across the ceiling and a third of the way down the walls in the central rotunda. It was a colorful procession of mystical allegory—the entire pantheon of Greek gods, goddesses, demigods, daemons, monsters, entangled with mortals armored in bronze or stripped to the pinkly glowing buff. It told some kind of story, but Poole thought it looked less like a classicizing narrative than an aerial photograph of a full–fledged riot at an especially drug–drenched rock concert. Larger–than–life bodies in every posture of disarray and activity flung themselves through acres of *trompe l'oiel* Vitruvian architecture with impossible energy. Poole felt tired just looking at it.

Griffiths muttered "Very grand" again. Then he turned to Poole and Amanda and said rapidly, as if issuing instructions, "The forensics laddies say our fellow was indeed hanged dead. Death by strangulation. Don't see how he could plan to do it, however. Our Mr. Coghill—he's the top pathologist wallah—says the tie was nearly torn through with the strain on it. Also says he doesn't know of a competent hangman outside South Africa, since we stopped turning them off. Who would know about hanging as a form of execution? You, Mr. Poole?"

Poole shook his head. "I've never seen a hanging."

"Don't they still do the, er, deed in Texas?"

"Why the hell do you all think I'm from Texas?" Poole asked, and Griffiths made a placating gesture. Poole had bounced his words off the Verrio and all around the marble lantern of the rotunda. Marble echoes jeered down at him, "Exas, exas, exas."

"Sorry," Griffiths said, "Just a silly assumption. Too much telly, I expect. The wife watches *Dallas* with religious fervor. Something must have rubbed off."

Amanda giggled, and Poole glared at her.

"It's the generally corrupting influence of your Yank media," she said. "Now, we'd never think any such thing if we'd all stuck with *The Archers* or *Coronation Street*."

Poole sat with the computer list and tried to absorb the names and addresses. Conference members were sent by TransAtlas—employees of the many subsidiary companies or executives or civil servants who worked as liaison for TransAtlas operations. Poole made check–marks next to names he recognized. A few people here he had met fleetingly. The list ran to forty–seven names, and Amanda Evans had starred the three no–shows. That left forty–four potential suspects, excluding the staff of Cavendar Institute and the battalion of workers who maintained the house and grounds. Poole groaned, wishing for a principle like Maxwell's Demon to help him sort real from imaginary prospects.

He looked up to see a small, thin man approaching—the one Sir Leicester had been addressing before he plunged into the Plenary Session meeting. A fortyish fellow, Poole guessed (though all English men he had met thus far looked oddly boyish, even when grey and withered). Wearing a rumpled taupe suit, a faintly pink shirt, a tie the color of boiled carrots and brown tasseled loafers, he looked slightly uncomfortable or embarrassed. Poole stood and extended his hand.

"Richard Poole. TransAtlas," he said.

"Yes. John Walker. Delighted," the man said. "Amanda Evans sent me along to brief you a bit. May I—?"

"Sure. Sit. I need someone to sort out the roll call."

"Oh, I can't be of much aid there. It'll be days before the members sort themselves out in my mind's eye."

"How long have you worked here?"

"It seems forever and a day. Actually, a bit more than twenty years—since I came down from Oxford."

"Can you explain to me about the, er, process of the Process? How were these people accepted for the conference, and how much do you know about their backgrounds?"

"That's fairly easily described, but I thought you were TransAtlas' man on the spot. Weren't you briefed on the scheme?"

Poole shrugged. "My boss is a great believer in rugged individualism and empirical observation. He tends to throw me headfirst into ponds and stand on the shore yelling, 'Swim, damn you, or die!'"

"You have the new authorized version of holy writ," Walker said, nodding toward the book on the table. "Your best course is to absorb all of Sir Alfred's dreadful prose you can stomach. To be fair, the ideas are quite fascinating. It's just that Sir Alfred was an admirer of Walter Pater, and something terrible happened to his ability to write a simple sentence. Everything is coated with a layer of late–Victorian marmalade and treacle. All ideas are described as 'shining' or 'evanescent' or some such. All art aspires to the condition of music, you know. I believe Sir Alfred thought he was playing a magnificent pipe organ, when it was really just a hurdy-gurdy."

"What I need, I think," Poole said, mopping at his brow—he seemed to alternate periods of chill with periods of fever, some kind of transatlantic hot flashes—"is a way to group these people, along with the conference staff. They can't all be equally significant."

"See page one–ten, I think it is, in the Book of Alfred. On leaders and followers and the sociobiological psychic pathology of small–group units," Walker said. He put a little smirky twist on every phrase referring to the Founder of the Cavendar Process.

"Conference members are accepted," Walker said, as if reciting a well–known but venerated text, "on the basis of a simple application, without regard to status or background. The usual member, our records show, is in his—or her—mid-to-late thirties, established in an occupation, paid above the norm, firmly middle–class, ambitious but not overtly creeping. Most have arrived at a point of decision in their work–lives, when they must go up and on or opt for stasis. They come to the Cavendar Process seeking help in choosing. Or they are sent by an organization because they are elemental in decision–making and personnel development. They are forced into self–analysis by the Cavendar Process, which for a period of a week or two plunges them into group participation. Their task is to study the activity of their group here—and they are in groups ranging from small—eight or ten members—to large—twenty or so—to a plenary or whole group—the forty–five or so members, plus consultants. Along the way, staff consultants observe them and help push them in the process, by means of commentary—not explicit instruction. There—that's about as condensed a summary as I could muster."

Walker glanced at his watch. "Good God!" he said. "Gone eleven and the pubs are all bolted. Pity. Well, not to worry—I can always creep back to my lonely bottle of malt whiskey. Where was I? Ah, yes: We create a clearly structured organizational and social hierarchy at the Institute, to which conference members must adapt themselves. This brings out latent fears, phobias, desires and tendencies, according to the Word of Alfred. Of course, describing it is all theory, when the terrific thing about the Process is that it's all practice. Theory doesn't really count for bugger–all. It's like your boss's idea—sink or swim. It only takes a few days for this stark fact to make itself a shining manifestation, as the Prophet might say."

"So," Poole said, "none of these people—the members—is prepared for the Process ahead of time?"

"Oh, we always have a few who have done some mini–course or other in group dynamics or organizational theory or leadership training. And from your side of the herring pond, we get refugees from EST or some other damn fool Californian mumbo–jumbo. Those saved and sanctified by Kahlil Gibran or Billy Graham or TA." Walker abruptly assumed an eerily accurate burlesque accent of an American radio/TV announcer: "Hey, fellah—I'm OK. Are you OK? Shit, yes—we're all OK. Ever'body ah know is one OK guy."

"I hope *you* don't think I'm from Texas or California—" Poole began, when he was interrupted by the abrupt entrance of a very large man followed by two women. The enormous man plunged into and across the room, a large belly preceding him like the blunt prow of a great ship. He wore an old, grey double–breasted suit, but even its wide cut would not close over the swell of abdomen. He moved in a smooth, unswerving waddle, reminding Poole of Sidney Greenstreet about to commit an unspeakable act with great suavity.

"You—little man!" he bellowed at Walker, who flinched, cast a glance of dismay at Poole and half–rose.

"Just what the hell is going on now?" the man–mountain said. Poole detected a European cast to his accent, which projected over a small toothbrush mustache, which made Poole also think of Oliver Hardy about to pitch a monumental tantrum, ending with the pronouncement, "Well, this is *another* fine mess you've gotten us into!"

"Er, let me—" Walker began, but the big man flung out a hand like a bunch of over–ripe bananas.

"None of your ever–so–smooth excuses, you...you...*punk*!"

The women had caught up with the man and were arrayed on either side like caryatids supporting the central figure in a grotesque sculptural group, a gigantic Laocoon without python. Poole examined them: leftie was slender and young, dressed in a sweater-set of muted elegance, and rightie was not slender but downright skinny, fragile, birdlike and much older. She wore a kind of business–suit rig–out like Amanda's only less successful, in various browns. She was a watery blonde, her opposite a lustrous brunette. They both froze for a second at the man's elbows, in a supporting posture. Then he threw out both his massive arms and almost bowled them over.

"Every time we begin, it is the same stupid story. Someone manages to bugger up even the simplest details!" The big man glared first at Walker and then at Poole, who felt a twinge of irrational guilt. The giant seemed a virtuoso at projecting blame.

Walker said rapidly, "Felix—let me introduce you to a conference member. Richard Poole—he's a kind of facilitator, observer, for TransAtlas Corporation."

The big man drew himself even further up. "And now we have you consorting, fraternizing, with members?" he bawled. "My God, the whole world is...collapsing." As if moved by suggestion, he stepped backward and descended into a small settee which visibly contracted under his avoirdupois. If a bit of Sheraton furniture could cry in pain, it would have shrieked.

"Richard, this is Felix Schwann. And Marcia and Marion. They are our small–group coordinators this session," Walker said. The women supplied last names—Marcia Draper and Marion Halley. Felix Schwann glowered at Poole and yanked a handkerchief from his sleeve, with which he sponged his wide brow.

"Walker—I must lodge yet another strong protest. The room assignments are intolerable," Schwann bellowed. "I refuse to be treated like...cattle." He pulled a crushed box from his jacket pocket and from the box a small cigar. He stared sulkily off to the side.

"It *is* a bit much", Marion began, and Marcia made it a contrapuntal duet, with, "*More* than a bit. I've been shunted down into the pits again, in the East Wing."

Marion took up the refrain: "It's everlasting cold, the rooms all smell like drains, there are no proper chairs, and half the lights are out."

"That's not the point," Schwann interjected, creating a full trio. He rose between the women, and it was suddenly *Rigoletto*, at the moment when the big quartet commences. Schwann, Poole thought, was certainly stout enough to haul a woman around in a sack, and each companion was small enough to qualify as a conveniently portable Gilda.

"The point about your so-called management of this so-called Institute," Schwann continued, in full voice, "is that it gets bloody worse from one conference to the next bloody conference. I am..."

Marcia disrupted the flow with, "Oh, yes—poor Felix has been working so hard to..."

Then Marion entered the canon with, "We've all put our shoulders to the wheel this week, and..."

Then the three voices knotted unintelligibly, all three mouths moving, a stream of language battering Poole and Walker. Schwann threw up his big hands and outgunned the small women, a bass howl emerging from the *stretto* with "For the love of Christ, shut your mouths, you fucking hyenas!"

Echoes rattled around the room like ricochet shot. Then the younger and prettier woman—Poole thought she was Marcia—screwed up her face as if to cry, Marion quickly threw an arm around her, glaring at Schwann, who subsided and stared with satisfaction at the coal on his cigar.

Walker leaned forward and said rapidly, "Look here, Felix—you can't go into your hysteric mode this early in the conference. It becomes more and more premature."

Schwann shifted his bulk and leaned eye-to-eye with Walker. "And you, my fine-feathered lounge-reptile friend, can kiss my..." His voice throttled.

Walker stepped back and said, "One would think that thirty years in England would give you at least a passing knowledge of simple idioms, Felix. I've always thought it was a mistake to involve foreigners on the staff. The dam began to crumble when Sir Leicester imported those awful Poles and Czechs and Hungarians. But I've never understood why we must match them with half-bred *mittel–Europan* staff members."

Marcia and Marion had crumpled onto a settee twinned with Schwann's, and Marcia looked up and said, "You don't have to be so racialist and bloody–minded, John."

Schwann shrugged expansively and ground his cigar butt into a small porcelain ashtray on the table at his elbow. "I demand to bring this to the staff session," he said to Walker. "Tomorrow morning, before we go on with the small–group meetings. I made a position paper on the inefficiency of your scheduling after the last conference, and no one even sent an acknowledgement. That is my ultimate word."

He rose with dignity and moved away with the same hull–down speed Sir Leicester had shown. Marcia blew her nose loudly into a tiny hanky and called after him, "Don't fret yourself, Felix. We'll have it all nicely sorted out in the morning."

Felix waved one big hand carelessly and exited loudly through the swinging doors at the end of the room. Walker stood, and both women jumped up.

Marion said with rigid dignity, "I had hoped you could treat Dr. Schwann with simple courtesy, Jack. We have to bear the brunt of his anger, you know. It's becoming impossible to keep our minds on the Process, with all this dissension and pettiness among the staff. While I certainly wouldn't take Felix's part on every issue— especially those bearing on theory—I do think Sir Leicester ought to chair a procedural meeting, with *all* staff present."

Marcia dabbed at her eyes and said, "I support Marion completely on the matter. *You* don't have to work day in and out with Felix, so you can indulge yourself with spiteful comments and actions. It goes so contrary to the spirit of the conference."

Poole caught Walker's sleeve to forestall his answer and interjected, "Were you, er, ladies with Dr. Schwann all evening? At the plenary session?"

They looked at him, and he saw that neither was certain whether or not to answer.

Walker stepped smoothly between Poole and the women and said, "I'll make certain the matter is on an agenda. And I'll alert Amanda to the room–assignment cock–up. As for Herr Schwann's complaints about my organizing abilities—well, he can go hang."

Poole stared at Walker, who began to blush, slowly, deeply. He bit his lip and muttered, "Damn it, man—a figure of speech. That fool Hun always gets my idioms tangled when I listen to him for a half–minute."

The women stared, uncomprehending, and Walker turned back to them: "I assure you, dear ladies, I will put my tiny mind to the problems of working with the gigantic Felix."

Marcia and Marion departed, stiff with muted anger. Walker turned to Poole. "The head policeman put me a bit in the picture," he said. "About the hanging, I mean. And no, I haven't a clue about the affair. And yes, I was in the plenary session, as I think you saw."

"Before that?" Poole asked.

"Before that, supper, innumerable little chats with innumerable staff members, all at about the same pitch as the one you just witnessed. Even earlier, a chin–wag with our Amanda. I don't know if I'm covered for every second of the day. Would you care to give me more facts about this to–do?"

"Umm," Poole said. "No—I'll come back to you tomorrow. At this instant, I don't think I could organize a simple sentence. I prefer you don't talk with others about what you know."

He and Walker moved toward the door. "Knowledge is power," Walker said abstractedly. "All power tends to corrupt, and absolute power tends to corrupt absolutely. You could engrave that motto over the main gate here, instead of 'Abandon hope, all ye—' and have the Cavendar Conference reduced to its essentials. But you will discover all this *experientially*, as Felix might say."

In the vast space of the main hall, under the rotunda again, Poole left Walker. The small man trotted away, leather soles clattering on the marble floor. The house was still brightly lighted, and the space felt to Poole like a waiting room, a train station, a place of departure from which travelers might go in any direction into the darkness. Fatigue hung on him like an old suit of clothes. He found the stairway to the residential wing and trudged up to rediscover his cramped room, once probably living space for a junior maid or minor servant.

As he crossed the long, dim hall that bridged the wings of the house, he passed an open doorway, heavy dark–wood doors thrown back on a small baroque chapel, sumptuously decorated in more dark paneling, festoons of heavy gilt, splashes of muraled walls and tall stained–glass windows, now opaque with night. The small space contained a dozen benches, choir stalls at the side, a tall pulpit, an altar with a broad table, rails, a vibrantly bright Assumption painted on the end wall. It was lighted by more dim mock–candle bulbs in wall sconces, which threw dagger–shaped shadows in crisscrosses.

Poole started to enter, when he saw a figure in front, in the pew directly before the pulpit. Darkness shaded the shape, but from its bulk, Poole guessed it was Felix Schwann, slumped in meditation or dejection.

For an instant, Poole stood on the threshold. Then he backed quietly away. The man seemed bent in prayer, deeply quiet. Poole had no need to disrupt him. The dark scene, with the faintly gothic touches of altar, crucifix, emblems of devotion in brilliant style, stirred something in Poole's memory. He had watched such a scene before, and he felt an unpleasant quiver of something like *deja vu*: *I have been here before.*

He shook his head and observed a small squadron of black spots in his vision—jet–lag was about to embrace him like a succubus. Tomorrow would give him time to catch up with his other self, the elusive *doppelganger* he had outdistanced above the Atlantic, courtesy of British Airways. He continued along the dim corridor, found the room with 221B stenciled on the door and entered. Without turning on the light, he undressed and fell onto the small, narrow and—it at once transpired—lumpy bed. He opened his mouth to yawn and fell instantly asleep.

An observer might have imagined that Richard Poole struggled to cry out in his deep sleep.

CAVENDAR RULES OK

ASHPOLE MANOR SPREADS across 3200 acres of field and woodland in northeastern Buckinghamshire. A large house of some sort has stood there since before Domesday, associated with the Cavendar family. The present pile looks from a distance like a college of Oxford or Cambridge weirdly transported into a gigantic pasture and left there as a prank, a sprawling collection of buildings welded together by brute force in disregard of style or reason. The main house is a hollow square fused by the implacable will of Jeffrey Wyattville between 1814 and 1820 from several earlier buildings and wings. At a cusp in architectural history, when various fads and fashions were dying and birthing, Wyattville had trouble deciding from month to month the direction his massive project was taking. The house, therefore, seems *grown*, not built, in some exuberant mitosis, an uncontrolled multiplication of living cells.

The south front is a grand Palladian structure built in 1735 by the twelfth earl to teach that surly pup Burlington a thing or two about English classicism. To this noble stone structure, with its superbly balanced porch and pediment, Wyattville grafted two rebuilt wings—the west wing (the so–called "Turkish facade") and the north wing, a slightly restored Jacobean block that had been a servants' quarters for a century. To this, Wyattville added a balancing east front in a neogothic style that would have made Horace Walpole blanch with envy, complete with pointed turrets, narrow dart–shaped windows, cupolas, bow–windowed bays and other odd excrescences. Wyattville finished his unification of the house by decorating the roofline with dozens of luring gargoyles, twisty chimneys and strange pyramids, obelisks and other bizarre scrimshaw.

The effect of Ashpole House is one of crazy–quilt heterogeneity, so when a visitor walks all the long circuit around the house, he is likely to return feeling disoriented. Nothing looks the same from different perspectives, and at varied times of the day the house may look sinister, reposeful or merely profoundly silly. Wyattville told the fifteenth earl that he aimed at an "effect of wildly playful Nature at Her sportive best."

The vast park around the house had been developed by Charles Bridgman and William Kent, who were shouldered aside by Lancelot Brown, who made his stock comment about the landskip's great "capability" for improvement and then went on to lay out rides and vistas and to plant 400 oaks, limes and beeches and a handful of sequoias from savage America. Humphrey Repton arrived shortly and drew up a careful Red Book of the park {still preserved in the archives in the Old Kitchen), which improved on the improvements of Mr. Brown, further decorating the Nature abundant in the parkland. Repton added a serpentine canal and three lakes at different levels in the grounds, connected by ingenious conduits, pipelines and waterfalls, all further powering a half–dozen fountains. Scattered around the grounds were a herd of red deer estimated at 90 head, a smaller herd of Highland cattle, a stable block built by William Kent in 1732 but extensively revised by Sir John Soane (at about the time the fourteenth earl was being shot to death in the Peninsula on campaign with the Iron Duke), a long water and a Palladian bridge designed by Brown but appropriated by Repton, an Aegyptian Tomb from a sketch by Sir John Van Brugh (discarded from the first drawings for Blenheim), the Vale of Ida (dominated by the Nelson Column), a gothick eyecatcher by

William Kent, which looks like a giant, ruinous pocket comb inserted in a large meadow, a Gothick Temple cobbled up from hints by Alexander Pope to James Gibbs, the Duke's Hunting Lodge, an odd, capless tower like a colliery smokestack perched on a distant ridge. There are also a handful of lesser follies, quincunxes, cascades, knot gardens, mazes, temples, etc. Vistas shoot in all directions, and a ha–ha approximately four miles long wiggles like a serpent around the landscape and is as effective a deterrent against poachers as were any of the seventeenth earl's patent humane mantraps.

In short, Ashpole Manor is a supreme example of the architecture of egotism and power from about 1650 to 1850, and only its status as a privately managed institute for industrial management training prevents it from being overrun by mobs of tourists or turned into a menagerie–cum–carnival stocked with mangy lions, spavined camels and molting ostriches.

South of the estate, just outside the majestic Ramillies Gate, stands the ancient village of Ashpole Norton, in medieval times an important market town, noted for the quality of sheep traded there. In the late nineteenth century, the seventeenth countess was smitten, after poring through the works of Mr. Ruskin and Mr. Morris, with the notion of "improving" the village, so now a half–dozen largish *cottages ornee* stand on the east end of the green, dumpy thatched structures with crutch–like timbers propping toadstool roofs. They look appropriate dwellings for six of the Seven Dwarfs. In the middle of the village is a magnificent Jacobean market house, a lock–up shaped like a squat beehive (dated 1610 and reputed to be the villagers' concerted, if belated, response to the unfortunate Guy Fawkes affair) and The King's Leap, a meandering inn cobbled together from buildings that were once a glass factory and a brewery.

The King's Leap opened in 1898, although it pretends to be

Jacobean in origin, and its primitive sign shows a strange robed and crowned figure mounted on what seems to be a rocking horse, flying in the air above a stunted tree. It celebrates a specious legend that the sainted Charles I once found refuge at Ashpole Manor and when routed from this lair by rabid Roundheads fled on a Cavendar stallion of prodigious jumping ability. In the course of his escape, the horse was said to have carried him over a ravine in which grew a full-sized ash tree, the Ash of Ashpole House. A tiny ossified bit of this tree rests in a reliquary in the great hall of the house. Next to it is a battered copy of *Eikon Basilike* also reputedly given by the Good King to the eleventh earl (an odd notion, since the book appeared only after the Good King lost his Good Head).

The whole demesne might be an illustration to one of William Morris' late books or a sketch by Howard Pyle for a wildly romantic Merrie Englande tale, except for the intrusion of metalled roads and road-signs into the landscape. The heavy forest, the huddled village, the vast house, sited back in the meadows and woods, looming over the valley, are storybook stuff.

Imagination has always transformed the tranquil landscape of Ashpole Manor. The pragmatic imagination of a Capability Brown or a Humphrey Repton created lasting metamorphoses on the topography, indenting idyllic valleys and lees and watercourses, unsinister tarns inhabited by waterfowl and huge, mossy carp, surprising vistas with statuary groups guarding distant termini. Other forms of reality intruded into the place from generation to generation. A scaffold sardonically called "Ashpole Tree" by the locals stood for a half-century at the crossroads beyond Namur Gate, and a dozen or so malefactors were hanged there over the course of the years. A wily hermit lived in the deep woods beyond the Temple of the Four Winds for a decade in the middle of Victoria's reign, subsisting on herbs, vegetables and deftly poached game. The seventeenth earl's cadre of gamekeepers pursued him fruitlessly, until one very cold December morning he was found caught in one of the patent humane mantraps, quite frozen and coated with icicles. His ghost joined the battalion of shades said to haunt bits of the house and grounds.

In 1941, a Heinkel bomber was chased back from the Channel after a dawn raid on London, shot full of holes by three Hurricane pilots from the Polish fighter squadron and finally downed on the estate. It fell, trailing clouds of black smoke and futile Teutonic glory, into the Vale of Ida, barely clearing the obelisk dedicated to Lord Nelson there, and killing all four crew members on impact.

Village old-timers in Ashpole Norton still often date reminiscences as before or after the Heinie plane came down, and Arthur Hopcraft, village postmaster emeritus, still has a swatch of the aircraft's hide in his garden shed, a bit of wing fabric with an iron cross lacquered onto the camouflage motley. He sometimes inducts visitors into the mysteries of the past and lets them view the relic, telling horrific tales of the mutilated bodies of the Kraut airmen he saw. All for the price of a pint of best bitter at The King's Leap.

Past and present wars shaped Ashpole Manor. Bits of ancient armor and weaponry grace the walls of studies and corridors—a Spanish sword from the Peninsula, a French epee from Namur, three full suits of leather-and-iron armor from the Civil Wars, under a brace of crossed matchlock muskets. Several pikes, ending in unpleasant can opener-like blades designed to peel back a cavalier's armor. Swords so blade-heavy that big men could scarcely lift them, let alone wield them. A fine set of fifteenth-century Flemish armor, engraved like table silver all over, sporting a large, ragged hole through the cuirass, reportedly put there by a service-issue .45 pistol in 1944, when a contingent of U.S. Eighth Air Force bomber crews were briefly billeted on Ashpole Manor.

The twentieth earl had been as much a military enthusiast as every Cavendar, serving with the R.A.F. and piloting a Lancaster bomber in a dozen night raids on the Ruhr. After the war he had spent several years trying to acquire his former aircraft, named Miss Adventure, to have her mounted on a large steel pylon in the great meadow beyond the Vale of Ida. The small scale model he had commissioned from an architect still stands on the model of the estate in the grand foyer. The ugly little warplane seems toy–like in proportion to the rest of Ashpole Manor. The twentieth earl had walked out every morning in the great meadow, an excellent Purdy 12–bore tucked under one arm, to give his ramble an air of gentlemanly purpose. There he stood staring at the landscape where he hoped his beloved behemoth would one day hover, a dozen feet off the ground, as if lifting off for one last mission against the detestable Hun.

Death and taxes, irresistible twentieth–century nemeses, forestalled the scheme, although a large concrete pedestal stands in the midst of the winter rye planted in the great meadow. The twentieth earl's instructions to be buried under the slab were ignored, also, and he was interred in 1961 with the endless chain of his ancestors in the undercroft of the village church, surrounded by cold white statuary by Robilliacs and Grinling Gibbon and by swirling script carved on dozens of hatchments, preserving execrable funerary verse.

Ashpole Manor had also been marked by the long, guilty peace of the Victorians, by the revolution in the English countryside which had moved the nation from essentially medieval pastoral crafts and traditions into the rationalized, mechanized agriculture of the twentieth century. A contemporary of Piers Plowman had prophesied in semi–literate (but alliterative) rhyming prose that Ashpole Manor would stand until Ashpole sheep were no more in the high meadows. Now only an ornamental herd of dark–brown Highland sheep were kept, as a kind of petting zoo. Eighteenth–

century landscapers, lusting for proper naturalized vistas and glades, had obliterated the irregular old working fields and enclosed the meadows that had designated the manor as a productive farm. From 1750 onward, lords and ladies could play at pretty pastoral sports, but the vast acreage would no longer feed and clothe the county.

Hedges, fields and coverts still sheltered wildlife, and a pair of conservation–minded college–trained under–managers on the institute staff strolled the grounds to control the animal population, shooting an occasional fox or pheasant in a spirit remarkably different from that of the blood–sport–minded gentry. Scientific agriculture ruled, and the vast, distant fields under cultivation were tilled and tended and maintained by a suited–and–vested bureaucrat dependent on a personal computer. The main goal of the staff employed by the Cavendar Institute was to keep the place tidy as a very large, very whitewashed elephant, an immense stage set from the past, designed as a stately backdrop for purely contemporary dramas of group–process training.

It was a magnificent setting, a kingdom–within–the–kingdom, a little world made cunningly and set off by walls and hedges and fences and clumps of ancient plantations from the modern Britain that buzzed and bloomed and pulsed around it. A dozen miles to the east was a spaghettied nexus of major highways. A railroad line surveyed by Isambard Kingdom Brunel, still adorned with Greek Revival bridges and tunnelheads, nearly touched the northern boundary of the estate. Overhead, jets from Heathrow etched straight white lines in the blue sky, and occasionally small and nasty American fighter planes from a Midlands base pulsed over at lower altitudes, leaving ripples of small sonic booms to rattle the dozens of china services neatly displayed in the Palladian wing or to inflict hairline fractures in specimens from the eighteenth earl's lovingly preserved collection of 2743 blown bird eggs.

But nothing deflected or disturbed the deep calm of Ashpole

Manor. Peasant revolts, treason, threat of Spanish invasion, Civil Wars, Popish Plots, enclosure acts, industrialization, agricultural depressions, the catastrophic slaughter of young men in 1914 all left the look and feel of the place untouched. The depredations of architects and gardeners made only superficial changes. The whims and caprices of careless owners scarcely touched the solid soul of the place. Legends said a Roman villa once stood in the Vale of Ida, a minor east–country Saxon kinglet had camped where now grows a dense plantation of beeches and oaks decreed by Repton to keep the eye from wandering off a designated vista. A chest of plate is still buried, it is said, somewhere near the old kitchens' site, hidden from Cavaliers or Roundheads or other impromptu taxmen looking for war revenue in 1647.

The sun rose and set on Ashpole Manor as if nothing else existed, as if there were no worlds elsewhere, once the traveler set foot inside the boundless parkland. Poets had come to imbibe the placidity: George Herbert and Thomas Gray and William Collins and Lord Byron and Alfred Lord Tennyson and Ernest Dowson had indicted minor verse here. William Cobbett had ridden through and snorted at the bad farming he viewed. Robert Louis Stevenson had walked up to the Ramillies Gate, felt an incipient weakness in his chest and trudged on to Oxford. One of the Mitford sisters had described the house as "an awful pile in a wilderness," and Betjeman had been stumped for a rhyme in trying to describe the distant chiming of the parish church bells.

Into this setting Richard Poole walked, in early morning light, after a hasty breakfast in a nearly empty common room. His head buzzed with a mild headache, and he felt less like stout Cortez than Lemuel Gulliver, alone and afraid in Brohdingnag.

✧

Poole crossed the wide terrace behind Ashpole House and looked down at the dovecote with a little tickle of dread. No sign remained of the police squad of the night before. Mist coiled up

43

from distant meadows, and a few shadows moved in low rays of the rising sun, where a rearguard of the deer herd moved toward a line of forest across the meadow. It was a living echo of the small, bright painting by J.M.W. Turner, painted in 1844 at Ashpole, which hung in the main hallway and before which Poole had paused on his way to breakfast. Life continued to imitate art exactly at Ashpole.

Taking out a small notebook, Poole began tabulating chores to follow up with the police in the matter of the unknown dead man. He was interrupted by Amanda Evans, who came out a French door and hailed him. She carried two cups of coffee, and he took one with gratitude.

"You look a bit rested," she said, examining him closely, "but not a hundred percent yet."

"At my age you don't hope for one hundred percent," he said, sucking at the hot, bitter coffee. "It's a red–letter day when I can get to sixty–five percent without collapsing."

"You'd best try for more. The Cavendar Institute, even on an off day, will take a great deal out of you. And this complication of the… murder, accident, whatever…is already creating ripples."

"How So?"

"To begin, I had a call last night from Felix Schwann, in a state of more–than–usual moral outrage. And when I saw Jack Walker at breakfast, he was ready to issue a challenge and have it out with Felix. Squirts at fifty paces, or stale bathbuns while lashed together with a silk handkerchief."

"I was in the middle of that," Poole said. He tried to decide just how awful the Ashpole coffee was, and how it could be made so vile so consistently.

"Things don't normally explode so early," Amanda said. "The usual pattern is much repression, a bit of early acting–out then a series of little blowups leading to a really big bang. It worried me that everyone seems keyed up, including the staff, who can't have heard much about the…event of yesterday. When news carries, and believe me it will, it's going to be a hideous confabulation. And Sir Leicester's gone quite firmly into his guru mode, and nothing will flush him out."

"Hullo the terrace!" a voice cut through Amanda's.

They turned to see two young men hiking vigorously toward them. One was thin and blond, wearing an obnoxious-colored (pink and grey) blazer and grey flannel trousers, the other a head shorter and darker all around, in a blue sweater and brown corduroys. To Poole they looked like college students strolling between classes.

"The matchless Amanda," the blond said. "Out in first light to flush dragons and ensnare stray ogres, I presume."

The darker man caught at his companion's sleeve and said more quietly, "Let me tell her, Robin. You'll turn it into a s–s–soap opera."

They stopped and looked at Poole. Amanda said, "Our most junior staffers. This is Richard Poole, from the purveyor, TransAtlas. This is Robin Heyward and Donovan Stallings. They are both learners, but they think they have the Process down pat and should take over from Sir Leicester any day now."

Robin looked hurt then crafty and said in a Robert–Newton–as–Long–John–Silver voice, "Argh, Missie—you've taken our measure for fair, there. One of these foin days we'll come abilin up from the focsle and seize this leaky tub!"

Donovan Stallings glared at him and leaned politely to shake Poole's hand. Robin followed suit in a slightly parodic manner. "Welcome aboard, lubber," he said in the broad growl.

"Amanda," Stallings said, "we've just been d–down in the village, and there's a terrific h–h–hubbub going on. There are police…" He stopped and looked from Amanda to Poole.

"It's all right," Amanda said. "Mr. Poole is on liaison from TransAtlas. He'll find out whatever you have to say, anyway."

Robin interjected, in his normal, slightly fluty voice, "Donnie–

lad can't wait to blurt out the awfulness. As we came up past Long Water, I had to restrain him. He kept rushing toward hollow trees to yell into them, 'King Midas has ass's ears!' A little stately decorum, to go with our lofty surroundings, please."

"S–s–stop it," Stallings said. Poole felt worn down by their puppyish energies.

"There are a whole p–p–platoon of policemen in front of The King's Leap. We couldn't get a straight s–story, but someone said there's been a murder."

Amanda grasped Stallings" arm. "Now, listen, you two. There has been a crime or an accident, but I want you to keep it quiet, please. If wild tales fly about, the conference will fall to pieces. Just keep whatever you heard to yourselves, and I promise a staff meeting to explain it all."

"Aye, mum's the word," Heyward said. "They'll never screw it out of me. Or perhaps that's the wrong verb."

"You know I can't gag you," Amanda continued, "but you know how destructive rumors can be to the conference. Mr. Poole is working with the police to protect his clients' interests. We must insure that the learning processes carry on as usual."

The young men looked unconvinced. Stallings said, "All well enough for you to say, but all the locals will be babbling the news at the p–pub tonight. And we can't s–s–sequester the members and staff forever."

Amanda took their elbows and marched them toward the French doors. "You two hop it to your room assignments for the small–group sessions. I'll send a note for the staff meeting. Keep the panic button unpushed, please."

They left unwillingly, with mutterings. Poole caught up with Amanda, who shoved her hands into her cardigan pockets and stared at the ground. She walked with a long stride, almost matching his. "I don't think Inspector Whatsit would stir things up in the village, unless he connects it with our departed nonguest." she said.

"I'll go down there as soon as I can," Poole said. "But I need filling in about the conference and this mysterious Cavendar Theory. I promise you to read chapter and verse in Sir Alfred's book, but I'd rather listen to you."

Back in her small office, Amanda led him back in history: "The Cavendar Process was developed by Sir Alfred in the nineteen–thirties. He served as consultant for the War College and with sundry government offices after the General Strike—1926. He was fascinated with how groups function to accomplish tasks. He made notes about how impromptu groups work, in distinction to groups organized for specific, overt purposes. He had been an Army captain in 1914–18, and he compiled ideas about the ways people became functional and dysfunctional in groups."

Finding a small purse on her desk, she rummaged in it, found a small cigar, lit it and grimaced. "I'm starting up again, so I'll have something important to give up." She waved smoke away and continued.

"Sir Alfred shaped up his notions, and then about 1938, he ran into an odd genius, Thor Ibarrez, who had been cleared out of Spain by Franco. Ibarrez was the son of a brilliant Scandinavian expatriate and a Portuguese man, and he was a misfit. So he invented a bundle of theories about acceptance and rejection of individuals by groups. I believe Ibarrez was a bit loony, but his ideas sparked Sir Alfred to his major work, so I don't argue the point with Sir Leicester. Sir Alfred devised startling ideas on training groups, and when the Hitler War hotted up, the military and the government set him up at Ashpole to create instant officer cadres, ninety–day wonders.

"There's some depressing blood–and–guts stuff tangled in the Cavendar Process, but I've convinced myself it isn't basically a fascist idea. Sir Alfred found an interesting secret—that groups are formed by *doing*, by *being*, not by self–proclamation. He took Ibarrez's model of a social group, which said that people in a task–group behave in a manner that prevents the task from being accomplished. This is caused by covert forces, conscious or unconscious, multiplied by the number of people in the group. He also declared that the "here–and–now" is the time–frame in which behavior of a group should be evaluated."

Amanda watched Poole scribbling in his notebook. She shook her head sadly and stubbed out her cigar.

"Three things occur in groups, saith Sir Alfred: they begin with a stage of dependency, turn to an interlude of fight/flight behavior and then find ways of pairing. They finally reach a stage of apotheosis or false sense of completion. These are all negative behaviors when inappropriate. Sir Alfred devised the Cavendar Process as a way of observing groups in the here–and–now, and he found that this kind of self–study acts as a catalyst for these negative behaviors. In short, the process of self–examination by a group unleashes these processes. Sir Alfred laid down a dictum— that the goal of his process was not to *change* or *improve* the group's behavior but to heighten awareness in the individual of how groups behave. There is a notion of "group responsibility' which is thus learned. So endeth the lesson."

Poole shook his head and sighed. "Sounds esoteric."

"Anything but." Amanda said. "Sir Alfred accumulated ideas about leadership and followership and how groups operate covertly, as opposed to the way rules and descriptions say they work. He could take a squad in the army and show how the *real* leader was not the noncom prescribed in Queen's Regs but one of the Other Ranks who could inspire trust. The military became fascinated in discovering 'natural leaders.' Sir Alfred was something of a showman himself, so he set up the Institute to study group–process as it exists in the here–and–now. The question asked is "What is this group doing, right now? Why? How?' The staff acts within the groups, small or large, to facilitate answering of such questions. It is all intensely practical and pragmatic."

Poole tapped his pencil on his notebook. "What is it." he asked, "that your staff members actually *do* in the Process?"

"They act as observers and commentators. They attend groups, but not as moderators or directors. As Ibarrez described group development, all members are equal, in practical terms. So our staff serve as consultants for the group, and they participate by making comments which may illumine the processes that occur."

"You want me to attend a group. What's to prevent me from going to one and just sitting there, a nonparticipant?"

"You'll see. To be in a group and not active is still to affect the group. That's one usual flight reaction. You sit grumpily with arms folded and say, 'You bunch of twits can't touch me. I'll just think my own thoughts.' Yet that has a direct effect on the group. The mere presence of a passive–aggressive nonparticipant deflects the direction of the group process."

Poole pondered and said, "Look—I believe you, but I've never been a joiner. Harvey Lewis keeps me on with TransAtlas because I don't get taken in by all the corporate bullshit. He needs an outside eye."

"Ah–ha: 'Cast a cold eye on life, on death—horseman, pass by.' You Yanks are sold on rugged individualism and the I–me–my viewpoint. You ought to stitch another corner onto the good old stars–and–bars or whatever they are, with the motto 'Ego ergo sum.' I–am–who–I–am and therefore–I–am."

"Oy," Poole said, "I yam what I yam."

Amanda rose and straightened her skirt and sweater. "It's off to the first session. You're with Robin's group at nine hundred hours. I'll be interested to hear your reactions."

The big house rattled with sounds of life, dishes clattering in the refectory, footsteps on hard floors, conversational fragments echoing across vaulted ceilings. Poole felt better about the place in the daylight. It was only a very large house and the people normal hominids of the species *homo sapiens*.

Amanda deposited him on the second floor before a massive carved door open to reveal a small stateroom with a dozen gilt–and–plush chairs scattered about. Poole followed several people in, feeling he was back in Miss Abernathy's third–grade class. There was a homework assignment due, and he had no idea what it was. With this tardy–schoolboy feeling lodged solidly in his solar plexus, Poole crept to a chair and waited.

For the first twenty minutes, Poole simply catalogued the group members in his mind, while they drifted aimlessly through complaints and queries. He could read badges and link up forms with the names and data on his conference roster.

There was Helen Corbett, a small brassy blonde with casual–but–expensive clothing and a Seven Sisters accent. There was a large, shapeless man in a shaggy sports coat and rumpled wash pants, with huge lemur eyes behind thick glasses—Aaron Spellman. There was a short, stout woman with a carefully–coifed helmet of steel–grey hair and a kindly mellifluous voice—Louise Houston, who was (or had been) a nun. Next to her was a large, beefy man in a badly cut blue suit, with an Italian accent of impenetrable density, one Giorgio da Silva. Behind him, eclipsed by the Italian's bulk, sat a weedy redheaded man in a faded flannel shirt and tweed trousers. His nametag read Arthur Stanley, and his voice had a Scots burr. Beside him sat a stout redheaded woman, big–boned and slightly horse–faced, with a loud voice and laugh—Annette Drew. These six were dominating the directionless discourse. Robin Heyward sat on one edge of the group, his face expressionless, emanating attention but to no effect.

"I'm not the only one here who could get things organized and shipshape," Helen Corbett said in a brassy voice, "but I've run *hundreds* of meetings, and *some*one has to shape this up."

"And you, dear lady, are just the someone we need?" Aaron Spellman said. "We could have an election and impose democracy on the group."

Arthur Stanley said, "That's stupid. That's not what the Cavendar Process is about."

"Let's ask the resident guru." Spellman said. "Come, oh wisest one, and lead us to the light of reason."

Robin Heyward was slumped back in a relaxed, meditative pose. He did not respond.

Louise Houston looked up from a small tangle of knitting and said, "When the sisters got into a fix, I'd always invent jobs for them to do—little emergencies to take their minds off themselves."

"I wish I had knitting." Spellman said. "A really brilliant idea. I'd at least be doing something useful."

"The instructions we got this morning," Helen Corbett said, "were that we should make this group aware of its behavior. Damn it, I don't see what this has to do with anything."

Heyward shifted slightly and intoned, "This group thinks it is on the road to Canterbury, but it might be trapped in deepest Brixton." People sputtered or groaned. Giorgio da Silva raised a meaty hand and said, "I theenk...I theenk...this is a way to drive us...crazy." In his struggle with the language, da Silva emitted a shower of spittle on the final word, and someone in the back muttered, "Look out, George Saliva's at it again—break out the brollies."

Arthur Stanley said, "Hold on—it's a *clue*. Let's decipher it. I'm here because dear old TransAtlas plucked me out of the bowels of the engineering division at Rediflex and gave me two jolly weeks in the country. But I don't think of it as a religious experience."

"That's Sister Louise's province." Helen Corbett said. "She can be our spiritual counselor."

"Everyone isn't being heard from," said Louise, pointing at Poole and a slight, moonfaced young man next to him.

"Well?" Spellman said, turning to crane at Poole. "Hey, I saw you wandering around taking notes this morning. Are you some kind of stooge from TransAtlas HQ? That's about like their crypto-fascist policies."

"I've listened carefully, but I don't have anything insightful to add," Poole said, forcing a grin.

"Oh, boy, there's a terrific term—insightful." Stanley said. "I'll bet you put him up to it, Aaron. You probably asked him to vote for you too, if we hold elections."

In a moment of glum silence, Heyward shifted again and said, "This group wants to find Mine Host and leave the traveling to him."

Stanley gaped at Heyward and spluttered, "By God, I think old Giorgio's right—it's a plot to drive us all round the bend!"

Helen Corbett coughed and said, "Nearly everyone in the room has managed to say something idiotic. What a supreme waste of time! At least the food is good and the quaint old buildings are fun to stare at. If the damn sun would come out, I'd go out there and work on a tan."

Giorgio shifted his massive bulk and said, "What is it we... accomplish now? I want to make an...understanding."

Sister Louise leaned toward him and said, "We're seeing if anyone has something useful and intelligent to say."

"What is...Canbury?" Giorgio asked."

"Oh, for God's sake," Stanley said.

"This is stupid, pointless and childish," Helen Corbett said.

"We're all supposed to be at least acquainted with the theories of the Cavendar Process," Spellman said. "I wish our consultant would fill us in on what the staff expects us to do with these golden hours."

"If you'd read the materials carefully, old bean," Stanley said, "you wouldn't be so stubborn about involving Robin. He won't say a blind word until we pull ourselves together. Our task is to decide what this group can do as a group, and we've just wasted the hour talking in circles."

Annette Drew laughed boomingly and said, "You people aren't real. This is like a sorority rush—an hour of polite conversation, and we can decide who comes into dear old Tappa Kegga Beer. Aaron is just dying to be inducted, and Stanley wants to be rejected, so he can say 'Piss on you all.' And Mr. Poole wants to determine which of us is the biggest asshole, so he can make a note."

"You have us all neatly pigeon–holed, don't you, dear?" Helen Corbett said. "I'll bet you're in personnel. Right at the top of the class in industrial psychology or management relations."

Annette Drew smirked, and Poole thought she looked like a horse about to utter a horse–laugh.

"You women are easy to read, too," Spellman grumbled. "Louise wants to save our collective soul, and Helen wants us to find ourselves and then go clean our rooms, and Annette thinks she is the toughest super–mom in the joint."

A spindly man who looked like a worn–out accountant said, "Here, I don't think we have to get so personal about everything, do we? Can't we just be businesslike?"

Heyward spoke again in a flat, mechanical tone: "This group wants to get to Canterbury by motorway, and no one needs to tell stories to pass the time."

"Please," said Giorgio, "what is this Canbury?"

"What's the Italian for 'you big, dumb wop'?" Annette said to Louise.

The tempo of the cross–conversation had accelerated. Embarrassed or tentative pauses were gone, and members stared each other in the eye. Something was happening to bind members, if only in antagonism, Poole decided.

As Helen Corbbet began to speak, Robin Heyward consulted his watch, stood and walked quickly to the door, which he left ajar as he exited.

"I'll be damned." Helen said. "Was it something I was about to say?"

"It's gone eleven" Stanley said. "We're supposed to adjourn."

"I was just getting started." Spellman said. "Time flies when you're having fun."

The members argued thinly for a few minutes, but eventually the group dissolved. Poole watched as they filed from the room to see if they were forming what the literature called "affinity groups." Then he decided he was too hungry to care. He followed them toward the refectory.

As he drifted across the great hall, he saw Amanda Evans rushing up the grand staircase, looking grim–faced and taut. Before he could greet her, she caught his elbow and led him to an alcove. "Stop here a moment," she said. "The news is worse and worse."

While she spoke, Poole looked out at the rotunda and the masses of people hurrying in the monumental space. The marbled floor, the classical pillars, splashes of mural all made the crowds seem small and inconsequential.

"Are you listening, Richard?" Amanda asked.

"Yes—go on."

"The hubbub in the village is not about our…discovery last night. The police found *another* body this morning. That's all I could pry from Constable Davies when he called, but he wants someone from the Institute down at once. I'm the only one who can break away, but I wanted to tell you before I left."

"I'm coming with you." Poole said.

"If you're staying in this conference, you must stick with the schedule. You can't pop in and out of group sessions."

Poole examined his instruction sheet. "There are two hours before the next session. To hell with lunch—let's go to the village."

"Very well—but let's do slip away discreetly—by the back stairs."

She led him down a narrow, dark staircase designed to give servants access to the kitchen and stables and keep them invisible to their betters.

"Servants were drilled to be perfectly efficient and utterly self-effacing." Amanda explained. "They ran through these windy corridors to meet any whim of their masters and mistresses, all around the clock, without a whimper. When a housemaid met one of the nobility, she was trained to turn and stand absolutely still, facing the wall, till the personage passed by. It was a way to become invisible. They were trained up from very young—twelve or thirteen —never to look at the masters, never to speak directly to anyone of a higher class unless addressed first. They lived their lives in little rooms under the eaves and trotted these stairs a hundred times a day."

"In one form of Japanese drama," Poole said, "a puppet–theatre that uses stage hands, men in black suits that cover them from head to toe are on stage through the play, changing props and pushing the action along, but the audience agrees not to notice them—audience and actors all ignore them."

Amanda stopped at the foot of the stairs and said, "How on earth did you come up with *that*?"

Poole looked sheepish. "I almost married a woman who was an authority on Japanese culture. But that was in another country, and the wench is dead—to my memory."

Amanda shook her head and led him through a small back door into the broad inner court of Ashpole House. "Yon must escort me through your infinitely fascinating past when we have time to stop at a pub," she said.

She walked Poole to a rank of parked caps on the graveled yard and stopped next to a low–slung, glittery car the color of a manila envelope, where she began to unbutton its tonneau cover.

"A Morgan!" Poole said. "A real beauty." He ran a hand along the sweeping front fender and patted the leather strap that secured the hood.

"My only concession to egotism and luxury." Amanda said. "I told myself a year ago I'd act out at least one childish fantasy—and this is it."

After Poole lowered himself gingerly into the car, she said, "Seat belt, please—it's the law, you know, and I'll feel better knowing you won't fly out on a bad corner."

She started the engine, released the handbrake and shifted into gear. She backed the car from the wall, cut the wheels and went into first gear. The car shot ahead, bumping hard on the rough cobble blocks in the courtyard then smoothing out as she aimed them into the sweeping driveway. She upshifted briskly, and the car squirted through the majestic landscape with impertinent zeal.

Amanda drove fast but well, Poole decided. He watched her handle the big wooden steering wheel and sat back contentedly to watch the scenery unfold past them. He felt very cheery and lucky —riding in a sporty car with a beautiful young woman in a June landscape unmatchable in his knowledge. At the bottom of the long drive, they passed through a subtle S–curve, straightened and crossed the camel–backed Palladian bridge, passed a pair of classicized gatehouses, where once liveried servants had waited in all weathers to greet coachloads of visitors. Amanda braked at the highway, glanced up and down the road and then shot out onto the macadam.

They zipped along the twisty road, which paced the perimeter of Ashpole Manor, following red brick walls, losses, hedges at the end of the parkland. They flashed past another set of tall gates, and Amanda slowed. The village of Ashpole Norton opened ahead—a patch of low cottages and houses sheltering under tall oaks and chestnuts, facing a broad green, complete with duckpond and yellow stone market house. Amanda turned the Morgan sharply and slipped it between a pair of black–and–white police cars before the facade of a long, three–storied building.

Poole read the gaudy little sign, with its primitive picture, swinging in a light breeze:

THE KING'S LEAP * FREE HOUSE

Inspector Griffiths and Constable Davies detached themselves from the regiment of uniformed and suited men scattered on the road and across the green and escorted Poole and Amanda toward a police van.

"Thank you for responding so quickly." Griffiths said to Amanda. "I know it's hard to be disrupted in the midst of your conference, but I thought someone from the Manor ought to know of this immediately. When Davies called me, I was heading home. I turned and came back out. I had thought to catch a few hours" sleep, but…"

"The constable." Amanda said, "only mentioned that there was *another* body."

"Yes, Miss Evans." Davies said. He wore his uniform cap now and looked more official. He also looked as worn as Griffiths.

"There is a direct connection with Ashpole Manor, as you'll see." Griffith said.

Back of the police van stood a stone building Poole could not identify, a stump of grey ten feet tall, shaped like a pepper–grinder. It was pierced by two narrow slit windows, barred, and by a wide oak door bound with iron straps. To Poole it looked like a militaristic playhouse for medieval children. The structure stood in a graveled clearing on the verge of the green, before the main door of The King's Leap.

Poole spotted a small sign staked by it:

ASHPOLE NORTON LOCKUP, 1610

They walked to it, and Poole saw that the big door was slightly ajar, with a uniformed officer posted at the top of the three worn stone steps leading to it.

"Miss Evans, Mr. Poole," Griffiths said. "We want you to look at a crime scene and make a formal identification of a body. I warn you, it's a nasty sight. But I need verification before we proceed."

Poole put his hand on Amanda's arm, and Davies led them up the steps and swung back the heavy door. The uniformed officer touched his cap and moved aside.

The inside of the stone cylinder was lighted by an emergency lamp strung from the van and from feeble light entering the slit windows. There was nothing inside but scraps of paper on the flag floor and a coarse stone bench built into the wall.

Lying awkwardly across this bench, as if flung there, was the body of Felix Schwann. His arms were spread in a gesture of crucifixion, his dark raincoat thrown open. In the center of the vast expanse of white shirt on Felix's chest was a large dark blotch. His head was thrown back, rolling off the edge of the bench, and his mouth gaped, open to a huge O of a silent howl, and all around his lips, matted on his face, was dark brown blood.

Amanda cried out and stepped backward. Poole gripped her elbow. In the hard white light of the emergency lamp, Schwann's body looked false, a taxidermic exhibit arranged in a sideshow or at the end of a Jacobean drama. Schwann's brown eyes were open and glittering in the lamplight, but he was as dead as anyone could get.

"How...was he killed?" Amanda said.

Griffiths stepped past and pointed a yellow pencil at the torso.

"Shot to death, we believe. Instantaneous death, I'd guess, but we await the forensics people's word. I'd say one shot from a small-caliber weapon, right into the heart. Very precise work, that."

Poole stepped closer. The frozen violence of the corpse was repulsive, and he found it hard to breathe in the confined space. But something compelled him to look carefully.

"That's not all," Poole said. He stared back at Griffiths.

Griffiths gazed back impassively. Then he pointed the pencil at Felix's face, its rictus of surprise and agony. As flatly as a surgeon at an elementary anatomy lesson, he said, "The blood here—and there's much more on the stones down in back—comes from the mouth. Another...event."

The inspector slipped the pencil into his shirt pocket and adjusted his jacket. He glanced speculatively at Poole and then Amanda.

"After the shooting—or I sincerely hope and believe it was afterward—someone cut this man's tongue out."

ONE UNDONE HUN

THE CADRES OF police swarming in Ashpole Norton seemed in chaotic disarray, but Poole knew they worked efficiently through an agenda into which each was synchronized. One group walked the green, scrutinizing the neatly mowed, emerald–green grass. Two uniformed officers walked the High Street, moving from one small shop or cottage to the next. Another leaned into a police car, talking over the radio. Several men in mufti—dark raincoats, hats—conferred outside the lockup door. An ambulance pulled up next to the police van, and a man in a white orderly's jacket emerged, while his partner unloaded and leveled a gurney at the rear. The group of disparate men and women functioned silently, according to ingrained routine.

Inspector Robertson Griffiths moved from person to person, group to group, unobtrusively choreographing activity. Poole stood with Amanda. She looked unsettled, pale and fatigued. If she broke down, he feared he would be unanchored in Britain, would float away like an errant balloon.

Light flared inside the lockup, where a police photographer worked. Constable Davies rounded the police van with a cigarette pack emblazoned *Silk Cut* in his hand. His round, puppyish face was pulled into a basset hound's frown. "Neither of you dropped this, did you?" he asked.

When they denied it, he shook his head. "Three of these layabouts handed this around before it occurred to one that it might be a bloody clue. Now the lab will send down another rocket when they trace prints from a gang of Her Majesty's Finest, and I'll have another little tick in my file."

Inspector Griffiths detached himself from conference with two mac–clad men and hurried to Poole and Amanda. "Dreadfully sorry about the confusion and shock," he said. "We had Schwann's papers and he wore a nametag from the Institute, but I needed an immediate confirmation, and I minded what you said about involving your staff and visitors. It seems a nasty situation is underway. Do you see any connection between Schwann and the, er, anonymous fellow yesterday?"

Amanda shook her head. "I'm...absolutely appalled at Felix's death. I can't think of any...reason."

Griffiths shifted Poole and Amanda from the bustle on the green. People were on the streets, and glancing semi–covertly at the policemen, who discreetly herded them away from the scene. Poole heard one officer saying, "Police investigation, move along now." Griffiths led Poole and Amanda through the front door of The King's Leap into a small square room crammed with bits of furniture evidently designed for tiny people.

"The landlord has been kind enough to allow us use of his snug as a field office for the moment," Griffiths said.

Poole perched on the edge of a minuscule hassock, while Amanda and Griffiths selected wooden chairs. Poole glanced around at dark oak paneling, thick black beams studded in a low, whitewashed ceiling, bits of glittery metal—tools, utensils, little badges—tacked to the walls. An old tortoiseshell cat as big and fluffy as a bolster was curled into a soft chair by a gaping, smoke-blackened fireplace. The cat seemed to be warming by the ghost of a winter fire.

"Miss Evans," Griffiths said, "I need a complete statement about Mr. Schwann and what he might have been doing in the village last night."

Amanda folded her hands on the battered black oak tabletop and said, "Felix Schwann has been on Ashpole staff for a dozen years. I can check exact dates for you. He is—was—one of the old hands. He was a student of Sir Alfred's. When Sir Leicester took over, he sent for Felix."

Griffiths made rapid notes. He looked up when Amanda stopped, and scrutinized her. "I know this is a sudden shock and a strain. But the quicker we put a picture together, the easier the case. Why would Schwann have been in Ashpole Norton?"

"I don't know. Nothing prevented him from leaving the grounds if he wished, but I don't know that he had any…social life here."

"Perhaps just a little trip to the pub?"

"I don't think so," Poole said, almost reflexively. "Excuse me—I don't mean to horn in."

"Go on, Mr. Poole," Griffith said. "I'll want a statement from you, also."

"I saw Schwann at the house last night, and someone said it was past time for the pubs to close then. Past eleven."

Griffiths scribbled. "The pathologist will communicate reams of scientific twaddle," he said. "Our best guesser thought Schwann was only a few hours dead when we arrived. So he was down here in the small hours. Why?"

Amanda shook her head. "Felix was a very private person. He blustered and talked at meetings and to staff, but he had no close friends I know about. Once he told me he had a 'refugee syndrome.' had a theory that people who were uprooted and transplanted when they were children can't develop close social ties."

"Refugee?" Griffiths said.

"His parents sent him out of Germany during the war." Amanda said. "I think they were killed by the Nazis later. He was smuggled out into Denmark or Holland. I don't know much about that, because Felix wouldn't really talk about himself. I mean, he talked incessantly about himself, but it was all the Felix Schwann of the moment." Amanda shook her head and smiled bitterly. "He was a perfect Cavendar product, always in the here–and–now, always too well aware of needs and feelings. But he backed away like a crab if you asked about his past."

"A secretive man?" Griffiths asked.

"Hardly. I would call him selfish. He had a life he wanted to own and possess, and he wouldn't give away a bit to anyone."

"Did everyone at the Institute feel that way about him?"

"Felix wasn't…popular. He was basically unsociable and irritated many of the staff. They tolerated him, because he was a brilliant theoretician and practitioner of the Cavendar Process. He had been touched by the hand of the Master, and he never let you forget it. But he had been touched. The staff called him cruel names behind his back—Dr. Gerbils, the Panzer Division, Schweinhund or That Bloody Hun."

Amanda stopped and put a trembling hand to her face. Poole reviewed the scene in the little dungeon—the open mouth caked with blood, like an awful word made manifest. Poole remembered Lady Macbeth's outcry: *Who would have thought the old man had so much blood in him?*

Griffiths scribbled and regarded his notepad critically. "Would you say he had enemies at the Manor?"

"No—not enemies. A commandment of the Process is that you don't have to be friends to work with others. Felix pushed that to its limits. No one would have wanted to *harm* Felix. Not…that way. To do him down or play tricks on him, yes. But…not *that.*"

"I've found." Griffith said, "that when it becomes concrete and immediate, no one believes in the reality of murder. But there is, indisputably, a dead man out there, indisputably killed by person or persons unknown. No one could concoct a scenario for suicide or accident to account for the missing, er, bit of Mr. Schwann."

"That baffles me," Poole said. "It's not just a murder—it's a ritualistic mutilation. A warning?"

"Yes," Griffiths said. "Symbolic. Someone wants to leave a message. That worries me."

Amanda said, "It all fits with Schwann's work on communication theory. As if someone took his farfetched theories and practiced them on his...person."

The doorway to the small room darkened, and a tall man with brassy blond hair in rigid waves, a florid pompadour, stood pointing toward them like a figure from a mystery play. Then the man stepped aside, and Constable Davies entered, carrying a little plastic bag.

"One of the lads fished this from the pond." Davies said. "It must be the murder weapon." The bag contained a small pistol, wet and muddy, with strands of eelgrass wound around it.

He set the bag on the trestle table, and they bent over it. Amanda pulled herself back from it with a little shudder.

"Umm." Griffiths said. "Not a biggish weapon. Do you recognize the type?"

"Yes," Poole said. "A Colt Woodsman .22. I haven't seen one in years. A very nice little handgun."

"So, you're a firearms expert," Griffiths said.

"No." Poole grinned. "Hate the damn things. But I almost married a woman who was an ace pistol shooter, Olympic grade. She had a steamer trunk full of Hammerlis and handmade shooting irons. I had to lug the stuff around for her, and absorbed the ideas. She had a pair of those, with engraving and ivory grips."

"Most of Mr. Poole's education came through matrimonial trial–runs," Amanda said with a grimace.

Griffiths looked at the constable and said, "Take it away and hand it to whatever firearms dogsbody has arrived to clutter the scene."

Davies ambled off, and Griffiths said, "I believe Schwann was killed where we found him, odd as that seems. Some villain shoots him inside a medieval gaol with a bloody American gun in the thick of night, and no one hears it, and then the bugger gets out a carving knife and fillets his tongue. Astounding!"

"Who found him?" Poole asked.

"A local kid—on his way to school, as it happens. Little bugger stood there waiting for the bus, and he saw the door ajar on the lock–up, says he. So he looks in, says he, and—behold the man! Kids have fiddled about with the lock–up for years, but it's usually shut up tight. No trace of the padlock that's supposed to forestall vandalism and mopery."

As if on cue, Constable Davies reappeared with another plastic bag and another sodden object. "Padlock, sir." he said. "Same johnny fished it from the pond where the shooter came from. He's wrapping up a tire iron, now. Our felon must have pitched them in at the same spot, about the closest bank from the lock–up."

Griffiths scribbled on, nibbling at his mustache. "Thus we can cancel the notion of a mysterious professional killer highly schooled in the finer arts of mayhem. It's all dead easy now, if forensics can tell us anything to help trace this ironmongery. All we lack is a knife or scalpel or patent tongue–remover."

"I still don't know why anyone would kill Felix." Amanda erupted. "I just don't understand the idea of murder."

Poole shrugged and said, "Sir Alfred had some paragraphs about conflict–resolution. I only got that far before I fell asleep. But whoever did this is practicing the ultimate form of conflict–resolution. He—or she—left us a rebus spelling out 'Dead men tell no tales.'"

✧

The drive back to the Manor was quieter. Amanda concentrated on the road without exploring the full panache of her driving

65

technique. Poole no longer wanted to laugh with exhilaration.

In the big house, people still milled around the refectory. Amanda found the biographical files on conference members. "Here is the pertinent data on the staff, also," she said. Poole juggled a mass of paper unhappily. She sat behind her desk, and Poole realized she was only barely suppressing tears.

"Look." he said, "no one said you have to be in total control of this situation. That scene would get to anybody."

She took a wad of tissue from her jacket pocket and dabbed at her eyes. She looked up at him and said, "Thank you kindly for the thought, Richard, but in the end—fuck off. I'll have to learn to handle it, and you have a large–group meeting to attend."

Poole meandered through the house until he located a larger salon on the second floor. He slipped in and sat quietly among the twenty–odd people distributed in the ubiquitous folding chairs. Across the wide room a small man in a tidy brown suit spoke in a low, pleasant voice: "…feel we should assemble a petition or list of questions for the directors. We can hope to clarify this aimless rambling…"

Robin Heyward sat several yards away from Poole. He spoke in his rapid, authoritative consultant's voice: "This group's task is to discover means and methods to apply small–group experiences to larger ventures."

Sister Louise sat a few chairs left of Poole, her knitting coiled in her lap. She said cheerily, "We've all read the literature, Mr. Heyward, but I don't think it helped much. We need tutoring in the present tense."

A large man in expensive casual clothes leaned out from the arc of chairs and said, "I don't know about the other groups, but I think our small group really got somewhere this morning. I was confused when it started, but the discussion gave me a handle on myself. I did a couple of courses in TA, and EST was a real trip—"

A ferret–faced woman who might have been an Indian–from–India cut in from across the room: "We have no license to impose all this...mere autobiography on the group. Let us cleave to the here–and–now. What are we doing in this room, at this instant?"

The large man patiently resumed: "I was saying that I was familiar with TA, but this looks like a wholly new experiential dimension, and I can—"

Robin Heyward cut in with, "Miss Vehta asked a pertinent question. Will anyone respond?"

The large man mumbled, "That's damned rude."

Sister Louise said sweetly, "Perhaps it was rude to revert to what you were saying about your fascinating history and not respond to the question."

A little blond man in shabby sweater and Jeans raised his hand and said, "I'd like to respond to both Miss, er, and Mr., er, if I—"

"Damn it," Mr. TA–and–EST said, "I have a right to get my two cents' worth in. What's wrong with taking some cues from other group theories? They work, don't they?"

A silence hung, and then something rang and rolled on the polished parquet flooring. It was a 2p coin that stopped, face–up, near the large man's feet. Snorts of muted laughter followed the coin. Poole heard outside the same unidentifiable bird singing throatily beyond the tall windows. Then a counterpoint of voices in the room drowned out the madrigal. Large Study Session Alpha was in full cry.

Four o'clock was teatime, as carefully observed at Ashpole Manor as a liturgical rite. Seven o'clock (p.m.) was pub–opening, when the Ashpole Manor bar, a wheeled ark of covenant, appeared. Poole began to acquire a sense of the ritualistic regularity of time at Ashpole—a shaped matrix into which the chaos of existence was poured and cast.

Tea was served in the study where Poole had met Felix

Schwann, and the room filled with conference members, balancing teacups and plates surmounted by bits of pastry. Poole stared gloomily at a large, sticky object the woman at the serving table had called "A bath bun, love." It was as big as his fist. He also resented the milky tea.

The room, with its lofty barrel–vaulted ceiling, installed in 1727 by Colen Campbell, filled with echoing voices: "...bloody great waste of time..." "explained we had to discover our own agenda..." "rudest man I ever encountered..."

Poole felt he was drowning in an ocean of irrelevant knowledge, discrete bits of information that could be fitted into a coherent scheme only by a supercomputer or by St. Thomas Aquinas' hyper–gnostic God. The man next to him jostled Poole slightly and murmured "Sorry." Poole recognized him from the large–group session—a balding blond with a perpetual worried look.

He smiled at Poole and said, "Off to a roaring start, eh? Of course, I don't understand bugger–all what's afoot. You can call me Ev—" as Poole read his nametag (Everard Allison)—and you're, er, Richard—is it Dick? Rick?"

"Just Richard," Poole said. "Would you like this...bun?" The monstrosity was studded with odd multicolored objects that might be ossified fruit. Poole held it under Allison's nose.

"No, ta. I'm just marking time till the bar opens. Me for real food and a pint or two."

"What did you make of the meeting?" Poole asked.

"I've been a junior manager—Weston Traction—for three years, but I'm not sure where this game playing will put me back home. If I ran a meeting the way these blokes do, Weston would see me redundant inside the week."

Poole started to ask another question when he was jolted by a fat hand across his shoulder–blade. The round, self–ignited face of Mr. TA–and–EST from the meeting peered at Poole, and his wide mouth opened wider, while he boomed, "Another Yank abroad, I reckon!" His nametag read Robert M. Edwards.

"I'm Bob," he said to them, "all the way from the West Coast—Pasadena. That's JetComm. Helluva long jaunt to this place." The hand on Poole's shoulder was large and heavy, and one finger was bound by a Masonic ring as big as a royal seal. The wrist was contrastingly clad with a super–thin gold oyster watch. Edwards exuded tidy well–being. He shook their hands heartily, jouncing both. Then he plunged on in his address: "You know, this is just a sifting operation by the head honchos at TransAtlas. Throw us into a tiger pit and see who survives. Keep us going up the old corporate escalator. Or over the side, if you go too high on the wimp scale."

Allison said, "You must be privy to great secrets."

"It's like that old movie—*The Wizard of Oz*, you know? Follow the yellow brick road, and when you get to the Emerald City, there's this old geezer and a bunch of hokey machinery for stage effects."

"Your startling theory." Allison said, unclawing Edwards' hand from his sleeve, "is that we're trapped in an old Hollywood film?"

"It explains all the hocus–pocus, doesn't it? You can cast the whole thing from our little group—Judy Garland and the Tin Man and the Scaredy Lion…shit, you pick 'em out. I'm just trying to spot the Wizard."

"You're from…JetComm?" Allison said, backing a step from Edwards.

"Yeh—top of the TransAtlas heap—you know where it fits on the corporate chart. How about you?"

"I'm a production supervisor at Weston—agricultural technology, as the adverts say. Tractors, harvesters, plowing thingummies."

"Yeh—TA grabbed that up in '66. One of their first English buy–outs."

"Wales, actually."

"Whatever. You know where it all started with old man Dawson, don't you? Back at Atlas Powder and Explosives, in what? —about 1910? You can't go broke making stuff to blow people up."

"Are you making some mysterious point?" Allison asked.

"Christ—the basic bedrock of TransAtlas has always been in megabucks military hardware lines. The rest is tax magic and PR— right, Poole? You look like you must be in…what? House organs and flackery?"

"You think the conference is a…paramilitary exercise?" Poole asked.

"Shit, it's not that simple. But it's a helluva way for the black magic boys to sort the carp from the barracuda."

"I see." Allison said. "You're going to pass your O—levels in the here—and—now and collect a high mark from TransAtlas."

"I'm going to be numbered with the survivors, sonny, not carried off to the boneyard."

"Umm—survival…" Allison said.

"You know who I admire most back in history?" Edwards asked. "I'll tell you—"

"I rather thought you would." Allison muttered.

"—old George Armstrong Custer and Douglas A. MacArthur. Those boys had the guts, the plain old *cojones* to put themselves on the line, no questions asked."

Allison shook pastry crumbs from his fingers and said, "By co— honays, I take it you mean *balls*?"

"Sure—pure testosterone."

"Yes—I thought you were talking balls. And I must be off to check my own inestimable pair." Allison said, moving off through the crowd.

Edwards stared after him and muttered, "These fucking Brits are all about half a step away from pansies. All the big security flaps here are about a couple of guys playing house and deciding they'd rather live in the suburbs of Moscow."

"I don't understand your choice of models," Poole said. "Custer wasn't exactly a winner, and Dugout Doug just faded away."

"They both had the guts to do what they needed to do, and to hell with the rulebooks and the brass. Wait and see—that's what TransAtlas is looking for in us."

"It may be more complicated than—" Poole began, but he was interrupted by a turbulence in the crowd, followed by a thin shriek and the tinkle of breaking glass.

Poole moved toward the sound and maneuvered until he was near the French windows, where he saw Marcia Draper and Marion Halley both sitting on the oak floor, in a welter of minor debris. Several people bent over them—Poole recognized Aaron Spellman's broad backside.

Both women gained their feet, and Marion hissed, "I'll see that Sir Leicester hears every detail of your abominable behavior!"

Before Poole reached them, both women plunged off through the crowd, and kitchen staff had appeared to sweep up the glass, pastry fragments and shards of porcelain they had scattered. Poole caught Spellman's arm.

"What happened?" he asked.

Spellman glanced at him and said, "Ah, Mr.—er, Richard. I was only on the periphery, but the ladies staged a little wrestling match. They were arguing, and John Walker and Robin Heyward tried to intervene. The next thing I knew, *boom*!—their table went over and they were rolling on the floor. The women, I mean."

The room quieted, and people drifted toward the doors. Poole consulted his schedule and opted for seeing Amanda to the chance for supper.

✧

Poole found the room in which the staff was meeting, and slipped in. He found a chair along one of the mahogany–paneled walls, away from the long conference table around which the staff

71

members had gathered.

John Walker was speaking in a precise drone. Robin Heyward and Donovan Stallings sat near the head, where Sir Leicester presided in a kingly sprawl. Across from them were Amanda, fiddling with a sheaf of papers, Marion Halley and a stumpy man with bright blond hair shaped in a Dutchboy cut. Next to him was Marcia Draper, glaring sourly at the tabletop. By her side was a neat, middle–aged woman with faded reddish hair, blue–rimmed spectacles and a tidy business suit. At the lower end of the table was a small man in a light corduroy jacket, who leaned forward as if to concentrate his presence on Sir Leicester at the far end of the polished slab.

Poole thought they could be rearranged easily into a Last Supper tableau, with a few recruits. The only members he had not met were Elmore Dee (Dutchboy), Caroline Crewe (rust–hair) and Phillip Jenkins (corduroy–coat), he deduced from his conference schedule. Only Felix Schwann was absent from the roll.

Sir Leicester pulled himself more erect as Walker spoke, and Poole gazed at the Director. His image resolved in Poole's mind— he recalled an old photo he had once seen of Sir Thomas Beecham, when that conductor was in his heyday—a leonine and theatrical figure always on the edge of histrionic display.

Sir Leicester nodded gravely as Walker ended, and glanced around the table. "It is always painful," he said in a low but powerful voice, "to deal with the passing of a faithful, long–time colleague, especially under such distressing circumstances. The police will speak with each of you tonight, and I have pledged them your cooperation. However, John's points are not to be discounted—our first obligation is to the Institute and to conference members. I must ask each of you to be circumspect and professional. This includes our *ad hoc* member, Mr. Poole." He waved a hand graciously toward Poole, and every staff member turned as if in choreographed response to stare.

"It is a…peculiar breach of procedure." Sir Leicester continued, "for Mr. Poole to sit as an observer, and we must cope with this eccentricity until the situation is more normal. Circumstances alter cases, and the circumstance at hand is of a violent and criminal nature. Mr. Poole and our local police may distract us from our work, but I trust you to behave as professionals."

John Walker said, "We are all eager to cooperate with Mr. Poole and the police, insofar as we do not compromise the integrity of the conference. Sir Leicester has asked me to assume some of Felix's duties. The rest will be shared out…" he paused and looked down at the papers before him, and Poole thought he looked haggard. "…shared between Caroline Crewes and Elmore Dee. If they will see me after the meeting, we can minimize disruption in the schedule."

There was a dull pause, which seemed to Poole full of unarticulated tensions. Then the meeting flowed on to ordinary matters of facilities, schedules and logistics. Poole let his attention drift to the impossibly rich appointments of the room and the irony of their contrast with the mundane business of the meeting. In a room constructed at the height of the baroque era for the pursuit of leisure, a handful of earnest individuals pursued everyday care.

When the meeting broke up, Sir Leicester rose, paused and then moved ponderously over to Poole. He removed a large, fat cigar from a leather case and began a ritual of trimming it with a small silver tool.

"In private, Mr. Poole," he began, "I must convey my distaste for the…problems at hand. My old friend Harvey Lewis briefed me on your status with the sponsoring organization, and so I agreed to highly unusual conditions from TransAtlas."

Sir Leicester walked toward the salon's door, and Poole felt tugged by his undertow. "You're an old friend from the OSS days?" Poole asked.

Sir Leicester glanced at Poole with irritation. "That province of knowledge is best left unexplored. Suffice it to say that we were both members of what the penny press calls 'the intelligence community.' You must take up salad–days memories with Harvey. I'm only concerned with your presence here."

They stood by a tall, deep window that overlooked the deer park. In the remote distance, William Kent's strange gothic eyecatcher was etched by declining sunlight.

"I told Harvey we could not afford anything like a loose cannon." Sir Leicester continued. "We agreed that you would have the unusual status of observer–with–portfolio. You will be treated as a conference member, but you will have some access to staff matters. I have never permitted such a bizarre arrangement, and I hope my judgment is not mistaken."

Poole felt piqued—should he apologize for living?

"I have detailed Amanda to inform you of all matters you need to know. I trust Harvey's faith in your judgment. I hope you will not contribute to the chaos that seems to have descended on us." Poole looked away from the supremely peaceful landscape and said, "I promise I'll stay out from underfoot—but I must ask you some questions—you may have parts of the puzzle no one else has seen."

Sir Leicester looked down the barrel of the big cigar and nodded reluctantly.

"First—your assessment of motives for Felix Schwann's death?"

"Felix was a…gifted individual, which dictated most of his difficult personality. Like most people burdened by intuitive genius, he was supremely egoistic and compulsive. He was abrasive and without a sense of compromise. He exaggerated his differences to other people. His Teutonic mannerisms were wholly a guise. They irritated the British, so they became his effective theatrical persona."

"But he *was* a refugee."

"Yes, but he came to Britain as a young man and went to a

respected school. The Ur–Germanic Herr Doktor Schwann was an invention."

"You aren't saying someone would murder him because they resented his, er, Germanness?"

"No—but it is a symptom. Felix dealt with others by setting them at odds with him, alienating them. If he found himself with Germans, he would exaggerate every English trait he could summon."

"You're saying we can't track down Felix's enemies, because he made *everyone* his enemy?"

"I am saying, Mr. Poole, that you will discover as many Felix Schwanns as persons you interrogate. He was slovenly to the fastidious, mendacious to the truthful, arrogant to the humble, and so on. Look very carefully at the descriptions of Felix you discover. Like mirror images, they may show reality reversed."

"Who would have felt so strongly about Felix as to murder and mutilate him?"

"I find it unthinkable that anyone could do such a thing to Felix —or to anyone else. I served in a brutal war—as you guessed—a nasty little war that existed under the big war of set–piece battles and Sandhurst strategies. So I'm no innocent. But there are limits to brutality."

Poole tugged at an ear. Are you saying that Felix's murder reminds you of…what? Resistance fighting? An undercover execution?"

"You Yanks have coined such strange euphemisms recently for it all. What is the current jargon?—'termination with extreme prejudice'? A silly way to create camouflage from language. Yet people who do such things invent shadow–phrases and looking–glass language to cope with the reality. Macbeth says 'If it is to be done, 'twere better it be done quickly.' And even his hired murderer says only 'Let it come down.' They could thus do acts beyond the thinking and talking of ordinary people."

"Could anyone on the staff be a…professional killer?"

"I *know* the people on my staff. It is impossible to believe we have here a…'mole,' a 'sleeper.' Ah, how I hate that melodramatic shop–talk! All contaminated schoolboy dramatics, as silly as Yank comic books." He led Poole to the salon door. "I will cooperate with you, Mr. Poole, but I will continue as Director without hindrance. If you must speak to me, use discretion. Treat the staff carefully and respectfully. For the moment, I can only believe Felix's death is a bizarre anomaly. You must convince me it has any real bearing on Ashpole Manor and the Institute. I hope to God you are unable to do so."

Sir Leicester left Poole and walked quickly down the great hall toward the refectory. He did not look back.

Poole ate supper hastily, sitting with a group of members mostly unknown to him. They exhibited various symptoms of anxiety, fretting about the pack and the individual, the One and the Many, how to become incasts not outcasts. He thought of Thomas Hobbes' description of society and humans in the state of nature, where the isolate found every man's hand raised against every other man, and life was "solitary, poor, nasty, brutish and short." He thought of Felix Schwann, cast into the outer darkness of death by a brutal stroke.

As he left the refectory, Poole saw Marcia Draper down a long corridor to the east wing. He turned and followed her, his soft soles squeegeeing on the marble floor. For the first time, Poole understood the term "gumshoe."

At the end of the hall, he saw a half–open French window and stepped out into the softly slanting light of late evening. He saw Marcia disappearing into an avenue of enormous hedge, a greeny corridor sculpted by generations of gardeners into a long, twisty tunnel. He followed.

The hedged avenue was empty, and Poole trotted to an

intersection of the hedges, which were at least fifteen feet tall and very dense. Where the rows crossed was a small cleared lawn, and in the center of this clearing reposed an oval, stone–rimmed pool. In its center was a delicate statue, a cupidon standing on tiptoe on a blunt Ionic column, one hand upraised. It was William Blake's "Glad Day" in stone. The pool over which the smiling cherub presided was shallow, dotted with lily pads now in open bloom. Marcia Draper sat on an edge of the pool looking into it, and Poole recalled an ancient advertising picture—the Flat Rock Girl. But instead of the faerie look of that creature, Marcia Draper looked droopy and forlorn. The tip of her nose was red.

As he stepped out of the hedged shadows, she started and said, "It's…Mr. Rivers, isn't it?"

"Close, but not a good enough association. Poole, as in this fishpond, but with an E."

Marcia smiled weakly and scrubbed at her nose with a tissue.

"May I sit?"

He lowered himself to the cold stone and stared around: tall, wavy hedges ran in all directions, and they were held in the cusp of a green world. Water trickled from a pipe under the cupidon and made little glassy sounds. Poole began to understand the minds that had reshaped Nature here to create a profound peace.

"I noticed the…fracas at teatime," Poole said quietly.

"I'm sure the whole world took it in," she said loudly. "That bitch has a million ways to humiliate me."

"Well, I don't think it really upset people. I thought perhaps it was over…Felix."

Marcia looked up sharply. "Not the way you think. It was over Marion's attempts to make herself the center of the universe. She always thought of herself as Felix's first leftenant and rightful successor. It got under my skin today, that's all."

"She started a fight?"

"Truth to tell, I damn well started it. But she finished it. She has a positive genius for wrong–footing me, and she made it appear poor old Marcia having another fit of hysteria. She tipped that table over herself, that conniving…"

She dabbed again at her wren's–beak nose. Tugging her sweater around her, she stared into the obsidian water.

"Do you think Marion had anything to do with Felix's death?"

"No, that's silly. I couldn't blame her for…that. Is it true the… body was mutilated?"

Poole nodded. She turned away and shook herself all over like a cat wetted by cold rain.

"Oh. I just can't accept it, the fact of his death. We're supposed to be so *tough*, such *realists*."

"Who would want to hurt Felix—do him physical harm?" Poole asked.

"I can't imagine such a thing. He was a hard person to know, and many people here despised him for his methods. But he was successful with the groups. He was always at odds with Sir Leicester. He began, you know—Felix—as Sir Alfred's pupil. I think Felix felt the son would never measure up to the father. Others said Felix was wildly unorthodox—they ridiculed him. But Felix was proving them wrong. If he had finished his book, he would have had the last word."

"He was writing a book?"

"It was an edition—all of Sir Alfred's fugitive pieces, things never gathered up when he died. Felix was writing an analytical preface that would vindicate him and Sir Alfred's methods. The police must have the manuscript, if they investigated Felix's quarters. He lived out at the Gothick Temple, you know."

She stood and made a circuit of the oval pond. "This is supposed to be the largest crinkle–crankle hedge in the world."

"Crinkle–crankle." Poole said. More looking–glass language.

"Oh." Marcia said, and Poole looked up. "A hedgehog. Isn't he the clever one?"

A small creature shaped like a badly worn shoe brush waddled steadily from one hedgerow to another. Marcia watched it.

"They're said to be infested with all sorts of parasites, but they keep a garden free of vermin. Rather like tutelary spirits, I suppose. If we had to have a new animal for the flag, now that lions and unicorns are *passé*, I'd plump for Mr. Hedgehog."

Poole saw beady little eyes under the shag of spines on the animal. It shuffled into the hedge, burrowing into the roots and grass at its base, and disappeared.

"I feel better," Marcia said, "and it's time for the small–group session."

Poole walked her to the deeper shadows around the house, and then he realized he had never really gotten Marcia to talk about Marion Halley. It would have to wait. Marcia turned to Poole and held up one hand. "I *know* Felix cared for me. He gave me this beautiful bracelet only a week ago." Poole looked at a silver–and–enameled bangle—pretty but not exotic or costly. She stroked it with one finger and said, "At least I have a memento."

Then she straightened and tugged her sweater taut. She strode into the house, while he found his schedule and trudged reluctantly toward his next appointment with the Cavendar Process. He felt like a hedgehog lurching toward a tiny bit of shelter, a private bower that might cover him.

By half past nine, Poole was even more a hedgehog—bruised, shrunken but covered with raised hackles, little spikes to ward off the world.

The session had drifted, but for long moments the members had focused on Poole. He had been threatened, cajoled, wooed and attacked, sometimes simultaneously. His head ached. He had been bullied into recounting disastrous romances, which Everard Allison dismissed as "ancient history," exhorting Poole to pull up his sox and inhabit the here–and–now. Poole struggled to say something less than cretinous about the group's present state, and Sister Louise had muttered "Stupid!" in a hollow voice. She was regarding the mutating wad of knitting in her lap, but Poole had shut up, nevertheless.

The session ranged from the surrealistic to the mundane. Giorgio had advocated the group's constructing a constitution to follow, the blessed memory of Garibaldi haunting him. He had been howled down in a small furious debate replete with outsprays of saliva and Italian vowels.

Robin Heyward spoke oracularly only a few times. Once he said, "This group has boarded a bus, but it believes it is flying in the Concorde and being served champagne and caviar."

Spellman had leapt from his chair and said, "Let's throw this pompous twit out the fucking window."

The group discussed Spellman's misdirected anger for ten minutes. Then Robin Heyward ostentatiously consulted his watch, rose and left. Everard Allison tried to form a rump movement to continue sans consultant, but the members drifted away.

Poole was exhausted when he wound through the corridors to his room. He fitted the big brass key to the lock and realized that the door was unlocked. For a moment he stood very still, then he twisted the handle and pushed the door open.

His room was lighted, and Chief Inspector Griffiths sat in the lumpy armchair at the foot of the bed, facing Poole. He was smoking a cigarette, which he waved toward Poole, saying, "Please forgive the liberty. Close the door. I wanted to be sure we'd have a private chat." Poole sat on the edge of the bed. Griffith said, "I had Fred let me in with his passkey. I couldn't hang about in the hallways. I assume it is best if as few people as possible know we're conferring." He produced from inside his jacket a manila envelope.

"I brought the ME's reports on both Mr. Drus and Mr. Schwann. You ought to look at them and ponder their implications."

Poole spread the loose photocopied sheets on the bedspread and began to read the blunt, greyish type and its precise, scientific exposition of the obscenities of death.

THE KING'S LEAP

AFTER THE MORNING and the evening of the third day, Richard Poole was pleasantly tired by his labors. He looked around him at Ashpole Management Training Institute and saw that—in some ineluctable way—it was good. And so he rested.

He rode in a silence more comfortable than his last drive as Amanda Evans drove him in her shiny little Morgan again, making a wide tour of the estate on the way to Ashpole Norton. Poole was surprised at the simultaneous solitude and density of population in the countryside. Small villages seemed to pop up abruptly from the empty, tufted woods and rolling fields. The names of places and the variety of old buildings fascinated him—this was a landscape unlike anything he recalled from his travels.

Amanda drove swiftly and skillfully down narrow lanes heavily bowered by hedges and ancient trees. They circled through villages named Steeple Amsted, Cobden, Little Arrit, Masefield. Every village had its stone church looming up from a graveyard grove. Houses were thatched, half–timbered, old, crooked, of stone and stucco, built right up to the verge of the road or set into postage–stamp–sized yards ("gardens" Amanda called them).

One village centered on a classical–temple–like building squatting in the middle of the cobbled town square. In another village, men in white clothing flashed across a broad lawn in lowering light.

"Cricket." Amanda said.

Poole was slowly acclimating to sitting on the wrong side of the car. He stifled his urge to reach for a nonexistent steering wheel and watched the road. Strange intersections appeared before them, not the two– or four–way stops of rural America but wheels of paving preceded by diagrammatic signs.

"Roundabouts." Amanda explained. They appeared chaos come again to Poole, but she navigated them unhesitatingly, and traffic seemed to flow in order. He resolved to ask her how they worked.

Twisting down another little lane, they burst suddenly into Ashpole Norton, and Amanda slipped the little car into a slot before the long, low profile of The King's Leap. As they climbed from the Morgan, Poole glanced at the little turret of the lock–up. It was tied with a rope cordon, the door flagged with a black–lettered sign.

Poole followed Amanda toward the front portico of the inn, where orange light blazed through mullioned windows. They entered, and Poole instinctively hunched—the place was low. They walked down a hallway, and Amanda led him into a side room, like the one Griffiths had brought him into earlier. Across the hall was a larger room, noisy with many people. The building seemed a maze of turning corridors and discrete rooms.

This room contained several dark trestle tables, pew–like benches with high backs, a clutter of small hassocks and wingback chairs. A very broad stone fireplace took up one wall, opposite a small bar. The rough black ceiling beams were festooned with handmade implements held in place with horseshoe nails.

A young woman in a plum–colored sweater and white half–apron was behind the bar, tugging a belaying–pin–shaped tap handle. She smiled and said, "Good evening."

Amanda took a bench with a table about the size of a checkerboard before it, and Poole maneuvered around a tribe of stools to a captain's chair. Amanda stretched and said, "Good God,

I'm absolutely knackered. Thank the Lord for the infinite wisdom of the planning committee and their allocation of free evenings."

She lit a small cigar and stared into a dark corner of the room. The pub was quiet, only a murmur of voices from the other room, no crash of voices and background music, as in an American bar. Poole sat comfortably, until Amanda said, "Don't you want a drink?"

"Sure—I'll fetch the waitress."

"For heaven's sake," Amanda said, "let me teach you pub etiquette. First—she's not a waitress. That's our landlord's fancy lady, but for the moment she's our landlord. You walk up to the bar and order, and she will produce what you wish. Then you pay her and carry back our drinks. Be sure to say 'please" and "thank you.' She's here to serve us, but she's not a robot."

Poole said, "What should I order?"

"What do you want—some sort of hideous Yank cocktail?"

"I thought I'd try your warm, flat beer."

"Right." She fished glasses from her purse, donned them and peered toward the bar. "Sorry. Bit of a blur in here. They have at least three bitters on tap and I suppose more in the bottle. They also have cider on tap. That's what I'll have. Here—I'll coach you. You approach the bar, and when the nice lady speaks to you, ask her for a half of cider and a pint of…well, read the signs, or ask her, or just say 'A pint of your best bitter, please.'"

Poole crossed the room to the tall oak bar. He stared at the tap handles, each with a badge: one read Ruddles County, the next Everards Tiger, the third a handmade sign lettered Old King's Headache XXX. Other taps wore logos for ciders, and one was marked Guinness. He knew that one and that Guinness Is Good for You.

The woman was busy at an opposite bar that backed up to the room, but she turned from serving a man, dumped a palm-full of odd-sized coins into a cash register and turned to Poole. "What's your pleasure tonight?"

Poole smiled and recited, "I'd like a half–pint of cider, the stuff there—" he indicated a tap—"and…" But she had dived under the counter and emerged with a small glass into which she drew the drink. When she set it on the rubber mat before him, Poole continued, "And a glass of…a pint of…what's this?" He pointed to the third tap. Maybe XXX meant moonshine, as in *Snuffy Smith*.

"Our house beer, love—brewed on the premises in the old way. Guaranteed strong enough to make you forget yourself. The locals call it 'brain–damage.'"

Challenged, Poole said, "Fine. That is, a pint, please."

"Right." she said. "Handle or straight?"

"Umm," said, pretending to ponder. "Straight," he hazarded.

"Here we go, then," she said, producing a big glass Poole associated with milkshakes. She pumped strenuously on the wooden handle, and Poole watched dense foam and dark amber liquid flow down the glass.

"That's fifty–three pee and eighty–six pee, a pound and thirty–nine," she said, lining up the glasses. Poole held out a horde of coins in his palm. He found one of the pseudo–gold pieces he recognized as a pound and laboriously sorted 10p pieces, 5p pieces, copper pennies too large for their own good. He felt like a stooge in a silent comedy, the rube from Podunk trying to cope with big–city currency.

When he had it sorted and dropped into her palm, she smiled broadly, and he saw she was gap–toothed like the Wife of Bath, a trait in women he found infinitely fetching.

"Right as rain," she said. "Cheers."

He thanked her and carried the glasses to their table. When he sipped the beer, Poole found it not warm but cool, slightly sweet, pleasant. He had never been one for beer since the puking Olympics of college days, but this was good stuff.

"Did I pass?"

"Perhaps. She gave you a handle mug, which might be a bit rude."

"Rude?"

"Ladies should have dainty glasses. Perhaps she thought the cider was for you."

"So?"

"Men generally don't drink cider. Men are supposed to drink gallons of beer and be the better for it."

"She said this was very strong."

"And you'll find out."

They talked and drank, and the pub filled, the noise level shifting upward. The place still seemed more like a living room than a bar, a small private party in someone's quaint home. There was, however, the ubiquitous beeping cry of video game from a distant room.

"My round." Amanda said, and expertly elbowed–and–hipped her way through a small crowd to the bar. She re–emerged in a moment with the same glasses, refilled. She set them down and said, "I worked several years as a barmaid when I was at University. I learned all the tricks of handling a raucous crowd." She sat, raised her glass and said, "Say 'cheers.'"

He hoisted the big tumbler and said, "Cheers!"

"There—you'll do for a short evening at the local."

They segued subtly from social chat into the events at Ashpole Manor. Amanda was obviously disturbed by the deaths so near her.

"*Why* would someone kill Felix?" she asked. "I understand people in the heat of passion saying 'I could kill you.' But I'd never *seen* a murder victim before, until…"

"Someone did it. We have to begin there to find out who and why."

"It's madness—what the newspapers always call 'mindless

violence.' How else explain it?"

"There were *two* murders—maybe. That seems like a pattern—premeditation, a plan."

"You Yanks are used to all those crimes—muggings, robberies, random killings. It just doesn't happen here."

"And yet it did."

They drifted into an odd cross–cultural argument, with Amanda defending the British way of life and Poole being stubbornly pragmatic. She ended by saying, "I'm not trying to shift the blame, but I can't imagine that a Briton did this. The Manor is packed with people from everywhere in the world—the answer must lie there."

Poole pondered: two non–British people—people thought of or labeled as non–British—were dead, on British soil. Perhaps it was irrelevant, but they had died in ancient monuments.

"I'm going to the loo," Amanda announced, standing and plunging into the crowd.

"Going to the loo," Poole mouthed, as if trying out a phrase in Urdu. "I'm going to the bloody bar."

He stood and discovered a glitch in his navigational system, his knees trembling and the room itself going out of square. He tiptoed to the bar, lurching slightly into patrons.

"Sorry, sorry," they murmured, as they parted. Why were they saying "Sorry"? What should he say?

He tried "Excuse me." in a *mezzo–forte* growl, which caused the group to part like the Red Sea. They stared enquiringly at him. He thrust the glasses at the barmaid, who said, "Again, love?" Nodding, he began the intellectual feat of separating out the coins in his hand.

A man standing at the bar said, "You're not from here, are you squire?"

"Nope—U.S."

"Ah, then—that's it."

He carried the glasses with mind–blowing concentration back to the table, where Amanda took the cider and said, "Oh, right—you're trying to make me pissed as well."

Poole sighed. "Let me get this straight—you say 'loo' for bathroom and 'pissed' for drunk. You're all prissy one second and then going on about toilets and peeing and what–all the next. If I'm about to be pissed, what is it I do in the loo?"

He giggled at the impromptu rhyme then sternly repressed the laugh. He couldn't remember giggling since third grade.

Amanda smirked, "That stuff *is* alcoholic, you know. People here can belt it down because they've spent forty years building up a tolerance. I advise caution."

He plunged on, "Your cars have "wings' and 'boots' and the hood is a 'bonnet' and the top is a 'hood.' Don't get me wrong—it's your damn language, but I have a hell of a time seeing how you use it to communicate."

"You're beginning to see the light. People with a language so circumspect and quaint don't go around…slashing one another. Hamlet tells Gertrude that he speaks daggers but uses none. It takes him about four hours of blank verse to use his sword—he'd much rather talk and think about it all than do anything."

"Yeh," Poole said, "but when he gets started, the stage is littered with bodies. Let's see—he stabs old whatsisname through the curtain, arranges to have a couple of messengers executed, beats up Ophelia's brother, gets his mom poisoned, and ends up stabbing *and* poisoning his uncle. Jesus, that's typical of the quiet English character? Makes American TV and movies seem tame!"

"All right—bad example. However, Hamlet doesn't *want* to do those things. Circumstances drive him to it."

Poole swigged at the remainder of his beer and said, "Let's say you're right. You say, One, it's unlikely to be a Brit—staff or member. Or Two, if it *is*, then it's somebody really desperate, acting out of character. That leaves a long list of non–Brits to check."

"You're the investigator—how would you sort it out?"

"I've read the coroner's reports," Poole said. "I can't tell you all the details, but it's a weird situation. Nothing fits right. We have a guy who arrives here somehow from Hungary. Interpol says this *is* Jan Drus, by the way. A smalltime import agent and government courier, evidently going to meet someone at Ashpole, for reasons unknown. The ME's report says he was strangled—death by asphyxiation. His necktie didn't break the cervical bone—an ugly death. But nothing indicates he didn't do it himself. Or that it wasn't a freak accident. The medical team is going over the tie, pictures of the body, the way the knot was wedged into the rung. They can't say it didn't happen by him losing his balance and toppling. That spiral ladder could have swung out from under him. Griffiths is up there with a couple of police and an expert from your army intelligence, trying to re–enact it. Christ, I hope they don't end up strangling a cop."

Poole felt his head slightly clearer, but he regarded the empty beer glass sullenly—that stuff *was* dangerous.

He continued, "We don't know if Drus had a connection with Schwann. If he did, was he meeting Schwann at the dovecote? Why? Did Schwann kill him? Why? And if he did kill him, who killed Schwann? The ME says Drus died at about nine o'clock. I got there within fifteen minutes. Schwann died about four a.m. Does that mean someone did them both in? If so, who, why—and is that *all*? Or did someone see Schwann kill Drus and then kill Schwann to even things up? It doesn't make any damn sense from outside. I don't share your belief that *anyone* is too rational to commit murder. If you can envision the right circumstances around a person, you can envision that person committing murder."

As Amanda started to reply, a man stepped through the press of drinkers at the bar and leaned over their table. It was the brassy-haired man Poole had seen ushering Constable Davies into the snug. He smiled whitely and asked, "All's well with the fare, I trust, Miss Evans?"

"Of course," she said. "We're just in for a brief drink–up. Let me introduce. Eliot, this is Richard Poole, who's at a conference. Eliot More is our host and landlord, Richard."

Poole rose to share the man's square hand. He was a large man, muscular and ruddy, his hair's metallic sheen complemented by his bright complexion.

"We've glimpsed each other." More said. "You were here the other morning on…business, I presume?"

"Yes," Poole said. He made no offer to explain, despite Amanda's glance of curiosity.

More went on, "We've had our spot of high drama in the sleepy village this week." He glanced at Amanda and said, "The unfortunate…event on the green."

Amanda looked away. Poole let his greeting smile slacken. More watched him with one eyebrow raised. Poole took in the casual flamboyance of More's dress—sweater and slacks of dusty purple, a massive wristwatch with a gold chain like a manacle, a silvery kerchief knotted at his neck, all expensive goods.

Poole said, grudgingly, "I'm attending the conference and, er, responsible for security matters."

"Ah, "helping the police with their enquiries," and so on?

"Exactly." Poole said.

"I can't say I was totally amazed when I heard it was Felix they found in the lock–up. At first, I assumed he was pissed and sleeping it off. That awful urchin who discovered him was running up and down the street howling. Then everyone offered to tell me the gruesome details, and I certainly didn't want to hear that. Felix wasn't precisely a friend, hut he'd been in and out of here nightly for a goodly number of years."

"Had he been in that night?" Poole asked.

"The copper grilled me about all that. I think he stopped in a bit before closing time, but I can't swear to it. I was busy with the books and conducting my weekly argument with the fool cook. Everyone assumes a landlord keeps a running tally on every customer every night. But I'd be astonished if Felix hadn't stopped in. The fuel he consumed was pink gins, and he was partial to our Marie's prescription. Now, *she* told the police he stopped for at least one gin that night. I'll take her word on it."

Amanda said, "Eliot, you seem to be equivocating genteelly."

"Everything I do has its little spark of the genteel, love. It's a landlord's stock–in–trade. But Little Miss Priss behind the bar has a genius for spearing out of both sides of her lovely mouth at once."

"Why would she lie about Schwann?" Poole asked.

"Lord, I don't think she needs a *reason* for anything she does. She may need attention. If she doesn't have it from me, she goes all sulky." More brushed a hand through his hair, and Poole guessed how conscious he was of the glittery crest. "I must move on now, or some customer will corner me and insist on buying me an awful drink or telling me an even more awful story. Enjoy yourselves. Glad to make your acquaintance, Mr. Poole."

More pushed away through the crowd, smiling around with patently artificial joviality. Poole shook his bead to clear it further, warding off a second attack of mild drunkenness.

Amanda muttered, "Atrocious man!"

Poole raised a brow but lowered it as he remembered More's expression.

"He's a tiresome font of gossip and innuendo." Amanda said. "It's impossible to tell when he's not playing some silly game. That nattering about Marie was to impress you and put me in my place."

"How?"

"Do you know how Oscar Wilde ended up in court? That bloke,

the boxing fellow, er, Queensbury. He sent Wilde a note accusing him of posing as a poofter, and Wilde took him to law. That led to poor old Oscar's downfall, the *Ballad of Reading Gaol* and so on. I think most of Eliot's games are about whether he is homosexual or just playing at making you think so, so he can laugh at you behind your back for laughing at him behind his."

"Well—he seemed effeminate, but not—what?—*flaming*."

"Exactly—it's a diabolical charade. Here's Eliot posing as a man posing as a perfectly straight man posing as a poofter, if you can follow that. This damn cider is tangling me."

"Are you saying that More and Schwann may have been… involved? Schwann was gay?"

"I didn't say that—it's not so simple. I don't think—*know* — anything about Felix's sex life. But I think Eliot is insinuating things. He'd love to capitalize on a scandal. He thinks it's good for trade at ye olde King's Leap."

"And what about Marie?"

"Great heavens!—I can't explain the man. He goes on to make you think he's at least a promising bisexual, doesn't he? But he's so oily and crawling—that's what puts me straight off him."

In a rush of voices and mild confusion, Marie raised her voice, saying, "Last orders, gentlemen. Time!"

Poole stared balefully at the empty glass before him. Amanda laughed and said, "It's not compulsory, Richard."

The pub began slowly to empty out. Amanda traveled looward again, and Poole found the Gents, down a narrow stone corridor at the back. The urinal therein was a sheet of porcelain against a wall, footed with a little trough. Poole interpreted it as further evidence of stubborn British conservatism and utilitarianism. After untold centuries of pissing against walls at the back of inns, they had simply moved the pissing–walls halfway indoors and glazed them to satisfy twentieth century sensibilities. A curiously elegant solution.

Amanda waited by the front door, talking with the barmaid. As Poole approached, he heard Marie saying, "…another bloody great lie. Our Eliot knows full well Felix was here, and after closing time, too. He wasn't legless, but he was working at becoming incapable. Belting away at gins."

Amanda introduced Poole to the barmaid, Marie Winter. He noticed that she wore a quieter manner when out from behind the beer engines. She also looked younger and more innocent, in a worn windbreaker and a loose scarf on her head, like a young housewife dodging out to the shops for a second.

"Marie thinks she was the last to see Felix leave the pub," Amanda said, "But Eliot was talking to him after closing."

"Too right," Marie said. "They usually ended up wrangling when Felix hung about—but that night Eliot brushed him off."

"What did they argue about?" Poole asked.

"They didn't need an excuse, I've only been here since fall, but I gathered they had lots of rare old times to chew over. And money."

"Money?" Poole said.

Marie looked uncomfortable. "I don't really know about it. I think Felix loaned Eliot money for the pub. He's always nattering on about big investments and improvements, and he tries to touch half the regular customers. He drives around in that bloody big Daimler and pushes those flash clothes in your face, but…"

She glanced back and forth at Poole and Amanda and said, "There—I've gone and shot off my face. I told the police everything official I could think of. I don't want to find myself made redundant in the morning, and Eliot would put me out for the dustman if he even guessed what I said."

She pushed past them into the dark. A slightly flattened moon drifted over spear–point tips of poplars across the green. Before she was out of earshot, Marie turned and hissed, "And if that old queen told you he's had me in bed, you can write that off as wishful thinking, right around." Then she was gone down the lane, head down, hands in her jacket pockets.

It was chill for a summer's night, Poole thought, but Amanda made no move to raise the Morgan's top. Poole gritted his teeth and decided it was manly to resist the blast of cold air. It would wear off his residuum of drunkenness. Probably a very *English* experience, like cold showers, wool next to the skin and sticky grey porridge.

✧

Sobered, but with a drumming in his head recalling the ghosts of barley and hops, Poole sat in Amanda's shadowed office. On a notepad, he listed everything he could recall about the case, with Amanda prompting. In pauses, he doodled with the purple Biro, indicting little sketches of daggers, ropes and pistols.

"We have a handful of nothing," he finally sighed. "A dead Hungarian who may or may not have been at Ashpole on legitimate business, who may or may not have been murdered, killed himself or died in a freak accident. The associate director of the Institute was clearly murdered and hacked by someone. Schwann had a series of minor enemies and irritated acquaintances. No method, motive or opportunity that makes sense in either case."

"What did Inspector Griffiths suggest?"

"The usual police PR guff—it could be this, that or the other, and they have the situation in hand. Forensics may help. The gun— that's what intrigues me."

"Why?"

"A little weapon for a murderer—a target or plinking pistol. An old *American* pistol. And I know it's hard to lay hands on a pistol here."

"Why didn't someone hear the shot?"

"If the murderer had Felix in the lock–up and shoved the muzzle against his chest, you wouldn't hear the report from a. 22 pistol a dozen yards away, even in the still of night."

"Can't the police trace it?"

"They're working on it—all computers running. They know it's forty–odd years old from the serial number. It doesn't seem to have been registered here, and Griffiths awaits U.S. data. Also, there's the oddity of the missing cartridge."

"What?"

"This pistol is an automatic, which means it ejects a spent casing when it's fired. No casing found in the lock–up. His men combed every niche and crack. Why would someone bother to pick up a casing and then toss the pistol into a pond a hundred yards away? That's like being smart and dumb at the same time."

"Do the police need the casing to prove it was this gun?"

"No—they've matched the pistol through the slug. It's just another damned annoying detail, another contradiction." Poole shifted and said, "Maybe it's off somewhere in limbo with Felix's tongue." Amanda winced and said, "Ugh—I keep trying to put that out of my mind. I think you're only going to unravel this through the *people* involved. It revolves around *who* the people are and how they were connected. It has something to do with the Cavendar Process. I'm sure that."

"It's coming out of the past," Poole said only half–aloud.

"The past?"

"Your process puts all its marbles on the here–and–now, people working and talking in the present. But these murders…deaths… have to do with who or what people once were. I'll bet on it—and it's receding into the past through every minute we don't know the answers. We can hardly subject Jan Drus or Felix Schwann to intensive group–process analysis, can we?"

Amanda stared at him. "You said something about it meaning 'Dead men tell no tales.' Do you think someone was trying to… *silence* them?"

"It's the ultimate solution to an argument, isn't it? You and Felix and Sir Leicester and the others live in a realm of words—mostly *spoken* words—the way birds live in an aviary. You're free inside the confines of the cage—but in the wider world outside there are hawks and owls and other predators who don't use words as weapons. They use *weapons* as weapons."

Amanda said, "I'll ignore the hostility, Richard—a common response to the Cavendar Process is a reaction like yours—it's airy-fairy nonsense, mere talk, fantastic theory an no practice. But it springs from practice. What we *do* in groups constitutes the groups."

"Do you mean the deaths may be aimed at someone else—or to make a point to the world in general?"

"Perhaps. It's a terrible thought, but Felix could be a victim not because of what he did but because of what he thought or represented."

"Then we can't know if it's over," Poole said. "Whoever killed them may have more points to make, more messages to deliver. Maybe this is a whole god damned telegram to the world from some loony. Right?"

Amanda nodded. She brushed her hair from her eyes and said, "I think that's entirely possible, Richard. But I don't know what to do or think—I'm completely knackered, and we're up again in a few hours."

✧

Poole left Amanda in the staff wing and walked back across the sleeping house. He stopped by the French windows in the east wing and stared out into the solid black. The moon had gone down, and no lights showed across the endless fields of the estate. Poole stepped out and walked along the broad terrace. A fine mist blew in the air.

Before turning back to the house, Poole looked down at the garden and dovecote. He saw something move, a mere hint of motion. Quietly, he walked to the broad stone steps and descended. He was almost sure he had seen someone crossing the path from the tall yew hedges to the rose garden. He felt anxious but unfrightened, as he moved down the broad graveled path.

At the edge of the rose garden, another path swept the perimeter of the garden and flowed under a clump of great cedars and oaks. Standing very still, he strained to hear: a tiny scuff, like a single footfall in the coarse gravel. He moved toward it.

Wind soughed in the cedars' foliage. He heard the trace of sound again, ahead of him, and moved around the thick bower of cedar limbs. The night was utterly black, and he moved with his hands out at chest level. Over the small sounds of his own movement—breath, a crinkle of clothing, his shoes in the gravel— he heard another footstep. Poole moved on until he felt heavy shapes looming thickly on either side. He had entered something like a structure, a room of night.

He stood, twisting his head like a dog testing the wind, when there was a louder sound, a rush of motion or displaced air, and a human body struck him, a cross–body block, shoulder and elbow striking him low and obliquely. In a millisecond, Poole reverted to second–string left guard of Gower College's football team, rolling atop the rush, shifting his weight ahead and down, so his own momentum would keep him from being hurled backward.

Rolling, Poole grabbed at his attacker with his right hand, his left out to break his fall. He hit the gravel with a handful of clothing in his grasp, pulling it toward him. He rolled to his knees, pulling at the attacker. Noise crashed in his ears—churning gravel, wheezing breath, grunting. Surely it was audible clear to the house?

Up in a crouch, Poole whirled toward a bundle of invisible force he sensed. It was second–string football again as he took a charge— head, shoulder and a hand—in his chest. He was loosely planted on the gravel, and the rush carried his hundred–and–seventy pounds backward. His feet left the gravel, skittered on wet grass, and his back struck something flat and firm but yielding, like a basket or

97

net. Then a hard, round head drove into his solar plexus and he jackknifed, the wind driven out of him.

He lay on his back, tangled in twigs and branches, fighting through the pain and paralysis. He started breathing again, choked, wheezed, rolled into a sitting position. Slowly, he tottered to his feet. He could hear nothing. Staggering a few feet, he felt a flat, rough wall ahead, the face of a hedge. He believed he would live, but for the moment it was not a salubrious idea. He rubbed his belly.

"God damn!" he whispered. Then he realized there was no ban of silence. "Hey!" he shouted. "I see you! I know who you are!"

Not even a mocking answer. He ran his hand along the cropped surface of the hedge. Evidently he had been knocked right through it, carried by the violent assault. He felt raked all over, as if he had been shot out of a cannon through a screen of fish hooks.

The phantom tackler had fled. Poole walked slowly, his left hand on the hedge. Soon he would find a break in the hedge, get back on the path and retrace his way to the house. He assessed his body: nothing seemed broken, though his right knee was weak and wobbly. He remembered the morning–after mementoes of football that made him drop the sport in his junior year, convinced the ratio of gain to pain was unfavorable.

Poole trudged on, aches and twinges in his body counterpointing a chorus of taunting cheerleaders exhorting him to give his all for Alma Mater. His hands and one elbow had been shredded by the sharp gravel, one kidney pinged, he felt covered by a network of bruises.

Soon—a break in the hedge, then home to bed. He felt personally oppressed by the night. It was his motto that it was better to light a single candle and to curse the darkness, thus covering all bets. He shuffled on, swearing in *sotto voce* to a locomotive rhythm his own stupidity, the unreasonableness of this time and place and the unknown assailant in the garden.

✧

Mist and fog joined the blackness, and Poole knew he had traced the hedge for an impossibly long time. He found corners and joints, even small breaks in the hedge, into which he plunged, to find—more hedge. After only ten minutes or so, he had realized he was inside a maze. Amanda had told him, "Ashpole is famous for two mazes."

Poole stopped occasionally to shout "Hey!" and "Hello?" He felt a complete idiot, as the wet, dark air absorbed his voice like blotting paper squelching a puny inkblot.

He felt slightly unnerved, alone in limitless silence and darkness. Poole had read somewhere that you could solve a maze by always turning through it in the same direction. He shambled on, opting for right–hand turns. He stopped occasionally and tested the hedge, but it was dense, tough and prickly, and his torn hands curled back.

The lanes in the hedge seemed about ten feet wide, too wide to span, so he assumed that creeping along the right–hand wall kept him moving through an alley. He envisioned the maze in his mind as something from a behavioral psychology lab or a video game. And he was the rat or the blob of light tracking through it. He continued gyring through the maze, wet and miserable, his clothes and shoes cold with damp. Finding a box of matches in his pocket, he stopped and lit one. The seconds of light only revealed a wall of leaf and destroyed his weak night vision.

Eventually, Poole realized he could see better. There were wisps of white around him, blurred outlines of leafy shapes. He could make out textured shapes. In a few more minutes, he could plod faster along his leafy wall. And then he worked his way to a gap in the hedge and saw a dully gleaming path beyond it. He stepped from the maze as if released from a real prison of stone walls and iron bars. Dawn was coming up, an aubade or orison of birdsong in attendance. He saw the jagged roofline of Ashpole Manor above the ground mist like an illustration from a fairytale book—crenellations, turrets and gables hanging in a cloudbank.

He hurried up toward the house, hammered by stiffness and fatigue. He hoped for just one second in his lumpy servant's bed.

His watch, however, was implacable. He cleaned himself and his minor abrasions, changed jacket and trousers. His mirror showed him a face imprinted with fatigue. Poole limped down the long corridors to the refectory, hearing echoes of the breakfast gong. He carried a tray to the table nearest the door to watch those entering —someone else might carry battle scars.

Poole ate quickly, surprised at his appetite, and members entering glanced incuriously toward him. He decided that anyone over the age of twenty looks battered and exhausted at seven o'clock in the morning.

Working on a second cup of coffee, Poole saw Everard Allison and Aaron Spellman enter, bracketing Marian Halley. The men were arguing vociferously, while she looked abstracted.

Poole tried to summon memories of the attack he had suffered. A big form, wool under his fingers, muscled shoulders, a whiff of— what? Cologne? Deodorant? Shoe polish? A masculine scent, a masculine bulk that had cannoned into him. He did not want to think he might have been so effectively pummeled by a woman.

The three moved down the serving line, and Marion Halley glanced at Poole. Her lips moved, and she turned away. Spellman glanced at her and then at Poole. He bent to ask her a question, and she shook her head.

Poole then saw Marcia Draper entering the line. She paused dramatically on the threshold of the room then saw Marion in the line. She took an involuntary step backward. Then she saw Poole watching her and moved ahead. She was stylishly dressed in a manila silk blouse and a carefully fitted dark blue skirt–suit. Without consciously deciding, Poole waved at Marcia. She flinched

100

but continued down the line. Poole pointed to his table in wide pantomime gestures, and she nodded slightly.

He fetched another cup of the acidic coffee from the giant urn, and when he returned, Marcia was at his table, setting out an array of breakfast dishes.

"Good morning," he said. "I'm surprised how many people are up and functioning so early."

She smiled wanly and said, "I suppose everyone's eager to dive into the meetings."

"You don't sound eager."

"Don't I? I've never been one for early rising and hearty breakfasts."

She picked at the food, and Poole watched her. "You feeling bad?"

"I had a bad night. I'm not all the way awake yet. I haven't slept well since…poor Felix. I can't stop myself thinking about it. I Iim."

Her eyes were watery, her nose reddened again. Marcia always looked to be leaning into a winter headwind. She seemed trembly and disoriented. Poole smiled and said, "You look fine—very nicely dressed."

"Mother always told me to be smartly turned out if you are quite upset. Something to take my mind off…everything."

She pushed her plate aside and said, "Ugh—these sausages. It all looks…disgusting to me." She rubbed at her eyes with the paper napkin and looked directly at him for the first time. "Richard—I'm very frightened."

As he started to speak, she caught his hand across the table, glancing quickly around. A square of paper was in her palm, which Poole took. "Don't let anyone see I've given it to you."

He unfolded the paper, a fragment of the Institute's goldenrod yellow schedule paper twisted into a billet-doux. On one side were a few words in mimeographed typing. He turned it over. There was on the blank side a scrawl of blunt penciled printing: YOU'RE NEXT.

HOW THE WHITE KNIGHT MOVES

CHIEF INSPECTOR GRIFFITHS, C.I.D., had spread across his desk a sheaf of notes, several dozen large photographic prints, a stack of photocopied materials from Cavendar Institute and typed pages of transcribed notes from Constable Davies. Folders contained medical examiners' reports and forensics findings. This hecatomb of words constituted Griffiths' knowledge of the two cases revolving around Ashpole Manor. Much data had been processed electronically, and a computer terminal behind his swivel chair crawled with glowing green letters and numbers. Griffiths was old fashioned and preferred his evidence in palpable form, distrusting the perpetual dance of electrons inside the plastic cube.

Richard Poole sat across the desk. They had rummaged through the evidence for an hour, and Poole felt as perplexed as Griffiths looked.

"There's not a damned thing," Poole said, "to link the murders. Deaths. Aside from the fact that they occurred within a couple of miles of each other and a half–dozen hours apart."

"We're overlooking something obvious," Griffiths said. "There's a key, but we don't see it, and a lock that doesn't look like a lock. I hate cases like this. The usual run of prole–bashing or mugging is only a matter of hunting down the obvious villain out of two or three choices. Here there's no starting point, no connections to make."

Fidgeting, Poole flipped over grisly photos of the late Felix

Schwann as last discovered. The black–and–white photos accentuated the gruesomeness of the corpse, eyes glittering in the glare, face contorted and blackened with gore. The body was as artfully arranged as an exhibit. Whoever had done this wanted him to be found and viewed, wanted a horrific effect.

Griffiths poked a bundle of typescript with his Biro and said, "'The White knight is sliding down the poker. He balances very badly.'"

"What?"

"A favorite passage from Lewis Carroll. I think of it at about this point in every sticky investigation. Alice writes it in the King's memorandum–book. She's guiding the King's pencil, you see. Then she finds a book all written backward—Jabberwocky. That's what we've assembled."

Griffiths' telephone whined in its strange British way. While he answered it, Poole leafed through forensics reports. The last item was Marcia Draper's note, which yielded no clues. It was only a bit of mimeo paper from the previous day's schedule, available to all members of the Institute. Poole imagined searching every wastebasket and desk in the Manor, demanding everyone to produce page 12B of the schedule for inspection, grilling all non-compliers with rubber hoses. It was indeed a mad, backward world they had fallen into.

Griffith cradled the two–tone phone (*Why two shades of green?* Poole wondered) and nibbled at his mustache. "I take this case seriously, but I'm damned if I know what to do. Miss Evans called to remind me to stay out of the way of the conference, so we can't easily post a person with Miss Draper. We can only watch her room or escort her when she's off the grounds. Very unsatisfactory."

"It may be a smokescreen. It may relate to something else," Poole said. "She's scared all right, but it may be a malicious prank, somebody just trying to scare her."

Griffiths asked Poole to stop at a pub with him for lunch, but Poole realized he was running late to reach his one o'clock meeting and declined. Griffiths gave him a lift and deposited him before Ashpole's massive portico. As he slid from the car, Poole said, "Why did you quote that thing from Alice? What does it mean?"

"It's about chess, I think. The pieces in chess move in different but characteristic ways. Each can only follow a certain pattern. They're...limited. Circumscribed. But that's only visible from the outside. The chessmen keep trying to move as they wish, but they can't get away from their boundaries. That's the way the White Knight moves. He keeps falling off his horse. But he goes on ahead, anyhow. So I tell myself when I'm really strapped for ideas—'keep moving, even if you topple a great deal.'"

Poole nodded, trying to envision the way a knight moves on a chessboard: sideways and forward. The chessboard in his mind's eye was like the Ashpole maze. You could not escape in a straight line, only by indirection. Invisible barriers, though, in chess only indicated by red and black squares. You must watch your feet carefully if you are a chess knight.

The large-group meeting mutated explosively, as members offered innumerable suggestions for ordering the Process. Aaron Spellman and Everard Allison argued ferociously about relationships between their small group and this session. The group was trying to create communications between the large and small groups, with Spellman advocating envoys and Allison insisting on written memos.

A bulky black man spoke slowly but fluently: "I agree with old Ev. We need to keep track of what we're doing. But there's no way to build a paper system that's any good in a couple of days. On the other hand, we can't remember everything we say and do. On the other hand..." He paused abruptly, realizing he had conjured an improbable number of hands. In the laughter, Poole envisioned

105

Dewey Reger as Shiva, many–armed but short, very black and balding, in a neat blue suit.

"On the *third* hand," Allison purred. "It's a mystical concept, like the third eye that opens upon total enlightenment."

Dewey Reger was from TransAtlas's Atlanta office, and he had been an Olympic–caliber track–and–field athlete, briefly in pro football twenty years before. Reger grinned at Allison and pointed a finger pistol–fashion at her.

Marion Halley, sitting as consultant, drawled, "This group of drones thinks words are work, and if they simply buzz loudly enough, the hive will fill with honey."

The Cavendar members were inured to consultant comments by now. Aaron Spellman plowed on, "We must pull ourselves together and vote on the proposals."

Robert Edwards, a quarter of the way around the circle from Spellman, erupted in a drill–sergeant's voice, "Shit—this isn't some hick–town council meeting, buddy. We need an executive committee to handle all communications—a security measure."

"Security?" Allison said. "Are you afraid we'll be taken over by the Russians?"

"Hey, I know how to organize operations like this. First you get an executive board in place, and they make decisions about the database you use and how information flows. Otherwise, we blow smoke out our asses till it's goddam teatime."

"Ooh, I love it when he's so masterful," Allison said, *sotto voce*.

Giorgio, next to Poole, sweated to follow the argument. He waved a hand in a loose circle, like a referee regulating an esoteric athletic contest. "No good…to break up…break down people," he said. "Too many votes. You get all bits of peoples in little groups want to run things. It make…" He stopped, eyes rolling, searching for English for a concept running in lyrical Italian through his mind.

Diane Hamilton, a trim, businesslike woman, said, "He means we could fragment this group into even less than the two small groups. We might Balkanize ourselves."

"Vulcanize?" someone said.

"This group has a collective fantasy," Marcia Draper said. "It believes it is one mind—but it remains many wills."

In the brief pause, Allison interjected, "However, on the *third* hand..."

Shuffling, groaning, muted whispers. Sister Louise knitted placidly. She peered over her glasses and said, "I know a training exercise which might help us. It's called Big Fish. We appoint a small group as our cabinet, seat them in the center and let them solve problems. The rest act as congress. We can only speak by permission of a delegate, but we monitor their discussion. So, we have parliamentary democracy. Big fish make decisions, but little fish must agree and ratify."

Wrangling erupted but eventually a number allied themselves with Sister Louise, and a junta was formed of ambitious volunteers. Five of the nearly thirty members sat in the center of the large circle: Spellman, Edwards, Diane Hamilton, Reger and Allison.

The novelty focused the group, but as the council of five pursued ideas animatedly, those in the larger circle became restive. After several people blurted questions, Sister Louise said, "Remember— you must ask permission from a big fish to speak."

The makeshift system buckled after a few minutes. Two separate discussions fulminated among the big fish, and the little fish swam in all verbal directions. Giorgio mopped himself and muttered, "This is the devil come."

Poole saw Marcia Draper blanch and flinch at something shouted in the small circle. Then Marion Halley rose, and Marcia scrambled after her. As the consultants departed, members ran down like unsprung gramophones.

"Come on," Edwards pleaded, "we're going to get somewhere with this. We don't have to knock off because *they* left, dammit…"

The groups dissolved. People rose and shuffled like old convicts toward the door. Poole moved quickly and tried to spot Marcia, but she was gone. He would look for her after teatime, when she returned from the staff meeting. He felt worried: events were accelerating and assuming a strange, cryptic pattern. He, like all the frustrated group members, longed for order in this chaos.

✧

"I've got to go into London, make a call and wait for a Telex."

Poole stood with Amanda under the portico, watching a sullen rain. The dinner gong was due to sound, but Poole had pulled Amanda aside from the influx of members at the refectory. He had to brief her on his plans before he left Ashpole.

"You have a free afternoon Friday," she said. "After three o'clock. Do you want me to drive you?"

"No—I want to be as unobtrusive as possible. I'll catch the train. I don't know how long I'll have to wait. I should catch Harvey Lewis at…midday in the States. He can put data on transmission right away. But you should stay here to keep an eye on Marcia…and anyone else you might notice."

"Why do you need such detailed information? We have fairly exhaustive files on the members."

"Yeh—files *they* submitted. I want to backtrack everything TransAtlas shows in their files."

"You think some prior connection will explain all this?"

"It's all I can think of. Eliminate the impossible, and so on. We see these people in meetings, but there's got to be some hidden connections we can't understand."

"It just sounds so…conspiratorial."

"I know members were screened and selected by different branches, and we thought we had a pure mix of administrators and executives without direct working relationships. But we don't know who these people *used to be*."

"Perhaps…perhaps it's not linked to TransAtlas at all, but only to the Institute? Neither Schwann nor Drus were linked with TransAtlas, and it's happening…here."

They went to dinner, separating in the refectory. Poole listened to members espouse paranoid theories about John Walker, Sir Leicester, Marcia and Marion and the whole infernal concept of the Cavendar Process. They looked, Poole thought, like extras in an old Warner Brothers prison movie, damning the warden and plotting a break–out through the laundry.

After the meal, Poole found an old sweater and strolled out of the house and around the massive stable block, marveling at its intricate architecture—a large polygon of stalls around a central courtyard, with two wide gateways, crested with towers and heraldic reliefs.

Poole strolled aimlessly, peering into the stalls for the huge Shire horses that once worked Ashpole land. He admired old carriages and wagons restored to museum condition and relentlessly polished. One stall held a Dalmatian bitch with three half–grown puppies who stared enquiringly at Poole.

The stable was carefully finished, of yellow stone with massive oak doors and trim, and above the stalls ran a story with small gabled windows. Poole guessed the outdoors servants must have been quartered with the horses. As he stood in the middle of the cobbled yard, he felt a prickle of discomfort, a sense of being watched. He saw a slight movement in one dark window. He watched. Nothing.

He crossed the yard and went through a wide gateway. Each segment of the polygon was, on the outside, like a small stone cottage, with a green–painted and numbered door, a pair of windows up, a pair of windows down. It was designed as trimly as a child's building–block village by William Kent so the fourteenth earl could gaze on a quiet pastoral scene and remain ignorant of the workaday functions of his estate.

Poole walked along, regarding the brass door numbers. He paused before Number 3. He peered into a mullioned window: in the dimness, he could make out little—an empty, dusty room, with an old grate in one wall and narrow stairs leading up from the parlor. The heavy door seemed firmly locked.

Dismissing the nagging discomfort, Poole walked away from the stable and the house toward the quiet river coursing sinuously through the estate. Lancelot Brown and Humphrey Repton had reordered the old river into canal–like passages, sensuous curves of beauty and little weirs and waterfalls, connecting the three little lakes.

He strolled on the riverbank, watching a flotilla of swans drifting downstream. One held her wings half–erected like sails on an exotic ship, and between them rode several cygnets as passengers. He passed the Palladian bridge, which displayed the Five Orders of Architecture, along with caryatids, gods and goddesses in niches and a beautifully carved balustrade. Despite its wedding–cake top–heaviness, it arched the stream gracefully. Poole noticed several conference members strolling in the distance but elected solitude and continued upstream, following a narrow path toward the Vale of Ida.

A small pink–and–yellow building, a tiny round temple, stood nearly swallowed by rhododendrons, the broad green leaves anarchic against the white Doric columns that marched around the little structure.

Poole walked from the shadow of the trees toward the temple, when he saw a figure move through the barred pattern of the columns. It turned away quickly, and he increased his stride. In twenty seconds he had crossed the lawn and strode up three shallow steps into the temple. It was empty. Out the back of this little tea–

or summer–house, Poole saw a slight figure moving, several hundred yards away. He strode down the back steps of the Temple of Ida in pursuit.

He was sure it was a woman, but the figure faded into dense latticed shade under a triad of gigantic cedars. He started to run, then he recalled how rubbery his legs could be and how scant his breath. He was twenty years past an all–out footrace. He angled toward the grove, guessing which way his quarry would move. Wrong. Little Ms. Whoever had exited on the other side and was well out into the broad meadow that led past the gothick eyecatcher and up a steep hill to the Gothick Temple.

Poole lurched onward. He straightened his course to a deflection interception in about five hundred yards, if he didn't die first. He aimed by the little silhouette of the Aegyptian Pyramid centered in the meadow (a mausoleum for the favorite rat terrier of the sixteenth earl), a squat obelisk on stumpy Carthagenian pillars. As Poole made his course–correction, he moved from smooth lawn to stubbly meadow grass, and he saw—with a bolt of horror—a small stone ledge under his next stride. Then Richard B. Poole, investigator–with–portfolio and trusted administrative assistant in the middle echelons of the world's most diversified multinational corporation, ran right off the edge of the earth.

"It's called a ha–ha," Amanda said. "Actually, they said it was an 'ah–ha,' originally. You were supposed to exclaim with surprise when you finally saw it. Of course, you weren't supposed to see it—most of the time."

"I was surprised when I saw it," Poole said. "I was going about five miles an hour faster than I should."

He sat propped in a leather chair, contemplating the fat bandage around his left foot, which lay on a hassock like a first–aid exhibit at a county fair.

"Do you know what they invariably find on those airline voice recorders after a crash? The last transmission, always, is "Oh, shit—we're going in." That's what I wanted to say, but I just opened my mouth and ate dirt."

"I can't work up much sympathy. You had no business bulling about on your own." Poole was inured by now to this instant frigid schoolmarmishness that every British woman kept on tap.

He had experienced the hideous sensation of running off solid ground into thin air, and a spectator might have recalled Wile E. Coyote bushwhacked for the billionth time by the Roadrunner. But it had been exquisite terror for Poole as he toppled, legs and arms churning in marathon–runner form, into the loam at the bottom of the fosse. When he could sit up, he found the ankle bad, a sore wrist and bruises distributed among ribs, elbows and thighs.

"You know, I didn't do it on purpose," he said. "I wasn't out for a big chase scene—it just *happened*." He still felt, as always around Brits, subtly in the wrong. It was *naughty* to hurt yourself, you big, silly Yank oaf.

"You're a grown man, with some sense. People have been murdered, you've been assaulted—so you rush off to fling yourself in a ditch!"

"All right, but my stupidity aside, what does this mean? I think it was a smallish woman, and I'm sure she saw and heard me. And she was definitely running *away*. Damn fast, too."

"You don't know this was connected with what you saw—or didn't see—at the stables."

"No, but something seems to be going on that someone wants to hide. We've got to assume it's connected with the murders."

Poole had hobbled, propped by a twisted oak branch, back to the Manor. No one responded to his angry shouts of "Hello?" and "Help!" But he found John Walker as he limped across the lawn, and Walker had driven Poole to the village. The doctor there, a young man with a ginger beard and dense bifocals, was routed from

The King's Leap to treat Poole in his surgery. He applied a small brace he described as "one of your space–age polymers" and wrapped a stout bandage. He opined it was a bad sprain but recommended X–rays. He gave Poole mild sedatives and a rent–a–crutch. The story would circulate in pub legend as "Dim Yank drops in ditch—Doc diagnoses dislocation."

"You're still set on going to London?" Amanda asked.

"Yeh—but this is a complication. I'd like to scout the grounds tonight, but I'm not up for it."

It was black dark outside, anyhow, so Poole sat back to listen as Amanda summarized the plenary session he had missed.

"No one missing, no one unusually agitated or odd?"

Amanda snorted, "No more than the Process makes everyone by this stage. Of course, I wasn't looking for evidence of wild chases cross–country."

"She could have circled back. And I didn't see anyone close enough to be a witness. Damn it—I know this all connects, and it's creepy being right in the middle."

Amanda flounced on Poole's bed. He was wedged into the room's one chair and he felt claustrophobic and shriveled. Another effect of the class system, to make you feel small and humbled—keep in your proper place, you tiny shit, you.

As Amanda started to speak, there was a soft knock at the door, then Robin Heyward opened it and thrust in his head.

"Hullo, people. Thought I'd find kindred spirits interested in bashing a drop of the old single–malt." He waved a bottle and a tumbler.

He sat cross–legged on the floor and carefully decanted a large drink. Poole accepted the bottle and poured dainty measures for himself and Amanda. He wondered how Scotch would meet the doctor's painkiller.

Robin raised his glass and chirped, "Cheers!—and confusion to your enemies." Poole decided Heyward was slightly drunk and pretending to be more drunk than he was.

"I was in search of uncluttered companionship," Heyward said. "Everyone I found was deep in the mysteries of the conference, plumbing psyches, unraveling relationships. Gawd!"

"Where's Donovan?" Amanda asked. "I thought you two always went pub–crawling at moments of deep disillusionment."

"Ah—our young Mr. Stallings has found fresh fields and pastures new. He's hard at work revising the Cavendar Bible, at the express direction of Sir Leicester himself."

"Bible?" Poole said.

Heyward slumped. "Sir Leicester sent out a decree into the land of Babel that Sir Alfred's sacred writ is to be scrutinized and edited, to bring his light more clearly to the Gentiles."

Amanda said, "Sir Leicester has been trying to revise and update the text for years. That was one of Felix's main chores, but he spent more time arguing with Sir Leicester than in writing. So— Donovan inherited the job?"

"So you might think. I believe the little toad crawled right into the presence chamber and appropriated the holy book unto himself."

"A touch of envy, dear Robin?" Amanda asked.

"No fear! I wouldn't touch the thing with tongs. But I have dark reservations of the basic competency of little Donovan. He's so full of himself and his precious theories that he's absented himself from all felicity. Oops—a little touch of Felix in the night, too— Felicitous Felix. Not a chance! As felicitous as a boot up the arse from Heinrich Himmler."

"You always had a knife out for Felix. I thought he ignored your silliness with much patience."

"Ah, but you've distanced yourself from the civil warfare in the conferences. And our Felix had a soft spot for women of your neat and trim variety. He regarded me and Donovan and even donnish John Walker as his fags, to fetch and carry for him."

"Nonsense," Amanda snapped. "I hold no brief for Felix and his behavior, and I squabbled with him as much as anyone. But you could be fair about his contributions to the Institute."

"Nae, lassie, you dinna ken the *darrrker* side of our Felix. He had, after all, mastered the essence of leadership. A mastery of mastery, you might say. But for us lesser mortals, it was—" Heyward lurched to his feet, spilling the dregs from his tumbler and singing —"Lift dat barge, tote dat bale, getta liddle drunk an you lands in jail!"

He collapsed again and said, in a normal voice, "Sorry—I was dragged to a Paul Robeson concert as a toddler, and I've never recovered from the trauma."

Poole fastened on the notion of getting drunk and landing in jail. Did that apply to Schwann? His mind percolated, as the whiskey collided with the doctor's nostrum. He invented word–puzzles: Schwannsong, Schwann's last flight, swans on the river, cygnets in tow. Mixed with the last was a vision of Edwards' signet ring. The legend of the swan dying on a song. Felix Schwann shut up in jail, shut up permanently with a gun and a knife. No tongue his tale to tell. *You always had a knife out for Felix.*

"Has Donovan cleaned out Felix's files?" Amanda asked.

"He's moved himself, liver and lights, into Felix's digs. That's another hop up the Cavendar ladder. He'd been hankering to move from the east wing, and now he's got that poncey suite to rattle around in. Next, he'll be dressing up in a monk's habit or bloody armor or dragging around old chains."

Amanda sat up, the bed swaying and twanging under her. "He's staying out at the Gothick Temple? Now?"

"Yes, indeed. He grumbled about the distance and terrible inconvenience, but he was perfectly chuffed with the notion of dwelling like an eremite in splendid solitude, beavering away at his text, like some blithering monk illuminating a manuscript."

"Richard," Amanda said anxiously, "Donovan's out in the Gothick Temple…you see?"

She sent him a meaningful look, but his brain ran slowly, as if filled with viscous jam, not whiskey. She clucked her tongue. "You were out there tonight."

"Oh—right, the Gothick Temple."

"I should go see him. No—I'll phone him," she said.

"Hold on, what's up, love?" Heyward said. "Bit late to go knocking him up. And I don't believe his phone works. He was going on about getting it repaired or replaced."

Amanda was up and out of the room. Heyward stood, peered confusedly around and fixed on Poole's bandaged foot.

"Sorry—I didn't even notice. You bunged up a trotter. What happened?"

"Oh, an accident, but I want to stop Amanda—it's black as Ned's hat out there." He managed to stand and tuck the aluminum crutch under his arm. Heyward leaned against the wall. He now looked genuinely sloshed to Poole. When he put weight on the ankle, a bolt of lightning found Poole's brain. "God damn son of a bitch!" he bawled.

Heyward started to reach out toward him then toppled slowly sideways and landed face–down on the foot of the bed. He flopped like a beached fish and went inert. Poole negotiated around Heyward's legs and, using the wall and the crutch, managed an ungainly hop to the door.

The corridor was dim and empty. He shut the door and lurched down the corridor.

In a hoarse whisper he called out, "Amanda! Amanda!" The rhythm matched his stumbling gait. He caromed off the rough plaster wall and forward, experiencing the way the White Knight moves.

✦

He found Amanda about to exit through the old kitchens, and she reluctantly agreed to help him along. Poole was wedged even tighter in the Morgan with his ballooned foot, and his ankle reported every bump on the dirt track. He watched trees and brush swell in their headlights and once saw a spangle of bright eyes as several deer froze off to the left. Then the fantasy–baroque silhouette of the Gothick Temple sprang up in the glare. No lights showed in the narrow windows that pierced the stone walls. Amanda slewed the Morgan to a stop before the peaked portico and tooted the horn.

Then she walked up and knocked on the front door, while Poole dragged after her. She raised a big iron knocker wrought in the shape of an owl, and echoes rumbled inside. Then silence.

"Damn, damn, damn—Robin was right," she muttered. "The phone doesn't seem to work. And now…nothing."

She peered into a small arched window. "I can't see a thing." Poole twisted the iron door handle, but it was firmly shut. He nudged with his shoulder but there was no give. It might be fake–medieval, but the folly was solidly built.

"Isn't there another door?" Poole fell into Amanda's stage–whisper by contagion.

"I think so. Stay right here."

She vanished around a clump of yew shrubbery, while Poole cursed her and the darkness with equal venom. He heard her pushing through brush, then it was dead silent on the hilltop. Time slowed down and stretched into a thin membrane of quiet. Poole stepped back and squinted up to survey the building.

It looked like three gothic steeples fused in a peculiar wedge shape, about three stories tall. Poole decided each steeple must contain small rooms or niches opening into a central hall. There were no signs of light, life or occupancy.

Laboriously, Poole limped around the structure, his crutch slithering on grass or digging into soft turf. Poole picked his way on the steep hill, thinking, *My kingdom for a flashlight!* No sign of Amanda.

His anxiety stepped up a notch, and he felt futile. The building was a dead-eyed Chapel Perilous, and his only weapon was an aluminum stick. Then he rounded the building again and saw a faint light in an oriel window over the portico. Amanda's voice floated down from the blackness: "I'm inside. But I can't find light. The mains may be out. I'll come down and open."

The oak door creaked and scraped open. Amanda peered out, saying, "I always mean to carry a torch in the glove box, but I never do. First thing tomorrow."

He groped into the place behind her. It smelled of must and wax, like a place carefully cleaned but rarely aired. Amanda struck another match, and its feeble sputter made the darkness move closer. Poole glimpsed stone walls, an oversized hearth and a ribbed, arched ceiling.

She moved away in the ensuing darkness and said, "Aha—stand still. I've found light." A match struck again, then a stronger but still minuscule light flickered. She knelt on the hearth with a small oil lamp. She adjusted it, and it seemed she emanated a divine aura, as shadows leapt back to the corners.

Poole looked around the small stone chamber, the center of the trefoliated building. In the room were a large oak table and two heavy wooden chairs, a stack of boxes and sacks and a coat-rack dangling several garments.

Amanda lifted the lamp and said, "This will serve—but I'd like to know why the mains are out."

She walked to one of the three small doorways in the room's corners and shouted, "Hello! Donovan?" peering up. She repeated the procedure at the next door.

"Damn!" she said. "You stay here—these stairs are too bloody narrow and steep. I don't want you breaking more bits on my account."

Poole listened to Amanda clatter up the steps in the left tower, then traced her footsteps overhead. Her light proceeded her back down the stairs.

"Nothing much. Those two rooms haven't been used in donkey's years. Try again."

She ascended the right tower. Her footsteps stopped and Poole stood motionless in black silence. He called, "Well? Anything there?" He heard her muffled voice. "What?" he said.

Then her steps descended. She stepped out in a spangle of brilliance and chiaroscuro. In her left hand she held the lamp, and gingerly she extended her right hand, from which a small pistol dangled. She held it like a loathsome prize won in a contest.

"Well," Poole said, "I've met your twin brother." He slipped a finger through the trigger guard and examined the handsome pistol, a blued .22 Colt Woodsman semi–automatic.

"It was on the floor by the bed. But there's no trace of Donovan. His things are scattered about, and there are heaps of books and papers that must have been Felix's."

"Somebody tossed the place?"

"Tossed?"

"Uh, searched, ransacked."

"I don't know—and remind me to explain why you shouldn't use that word. Perhaps Donovan is moving his things in and Felix's out. It's a mess, but it didn't look...violent."

"How did you get in here?"

"I prised a window open in back. It was quite easy."

"So anyone could have done the same," Poole said. "But it doesn't look as if Donovan were dragged away."

"I saw him at the staff meeting this afternoon, but I can't swear to supper. He must have been at the plenary session tonight. I didn't see him, but he may have come in after I left."

"*You* didn't see him, though?"

"No, but John or Sir Leicester would have mentioned if he had gone missing, I suppose."

"You saw them after the meeting?"

"Oh, no—damn it, that's when you turned up with your bad leg. The last time I actually saw Donovan was when the staff broke for tea—four o'clock. Do you think anything's seriously wrong?"

"I don't think people leave loaded pistols lying around on the floor, even if they're confirmed slobs. Especially in this country. Something's wrong here, but I don't know what it means yet."

"It's loaded? Has it been...fired?"

"I can't tell. It just smells like gun oil. But it's not only loaded, it's cocked and the safety was off when you handed it to me. Not a safe gewgaw to leave on your bedroom floor."

Griffiths looked as imperturbable as ever when he arrived, but Davies was distinctly frayed. A bit of gaudy pajama sleeve showed at his cuff. Griffiths looked as if he never changed in or out of his matte grey suit but stood like a manikin in a corner at night, waiting for duty the next day. Amanda had driven to the Manor, phoned Griffiths and escorted the policemen up to the folly. They had explored the towers with powerful flashlights, asking a series of questions about Stallings.

"That weapon wasn't here when we inventoried Mr. Schwann's effects," Davies said.

"So Stallings brought it," Griffiths said. "Or someone left it here. I hope you two haven't mucked things about too much. It will be light in—oh, an hour—and the squad will be in for a thorough search. But I don't see much to arouse excitement except for the pistol. And that's an innocent object thus far."

"You must admit it's weird to find a gun identical to the one used on Schwann," Poole said.

"My old supervisor would call it 'a grand coincidence,' and I don't believe much in coincidences," Griffiths said. "But we have no evidence of criminal activity, setting aside possession of the weapon."

Poole had explored the temple as far as he could while Amanda was gone. The spookiness of the place was more effective than the eighteenth–century builders could have anticipated. He kept an eye out for ghostly monks or headless knights. Their jokey little edifice might be a real house of horrors, even without traces of blood, murder or inflicted terror. He felt better when Amanda and the two policemen showed up—after all, this was just a heap of stone and timber pretending to be a storage depot for ghosts and revenants.

"You two ought to return to the Manor and get some sleep. I'll keep the squad out of sight, if at all possible, Miss Evans. But I'll have to check with you before we pack it in. If anything…vital turns up, we may have to pitch a major investigation here. Please let me know if Mr. Stallings shows up at breakfast."

They bumped across the landscape in the Morgan as rosy–fingered dawn plucked at the horizon. Poole was astounded at the number of times he had seen sunrise in England, since he firmly avoided such insane activity in the U.S. He thought of bed and remembered that Robin Heyward was sprawled oblivious across it. He groaned and shook his head as Amanda steered the car into the courtyard and parked it.

Poole reached his quarters after a marathon–like staggering session through the immense house. He was relieved to see that Heyward was gone, his only reminder the empty whiskey bottle, which Poole kicked as he entered. It rolled under the bed, Poole cursed tiredly, stripped off his sweater, loosened his shirt and collapsed on the bed to catch a few minutes' rest.

Broad, cheery day streamed through the small window and

flung itself like a flag over him. Poole sat up abruptly, felt jagged warning pains from his ankle as he shifted and scrabbled for his watch. It was after one o'clock. He had slept the morning out.

He forced his tired body to stand and navigate him cautiously around the room. His ankle telegraphed mutinous objections. He changed his clothes, noting that he had hit bottom in his wardrobe. He recycled a grayish white shirt and dabbed at scuffs on one shoe. Hoisting his crutch, he left to seek coffee and Amanda, in that order.

Finishing a lumpy bath bun, Poole said, "Griffiths had no sleuth–like insights to share?"

"No," Amanda said. "I've enquired discreetly of the staff. No one recalls seeing Donovan after the staff meeting. He shifted himself to the Gothick Temple over the weekend, and no one noticed anything odd in his behavior since. I didn't locate Robin to talk with him. Did you put him to bed when we came back?"

"Gone. He must have come to and dragged away while we played spook–chasers up on the hill."

"Oh. I wonder. You don't suppose he's gone missing, too? Bloody hell and double–damn! He's scheduled down in the old kitchen now with his group. I'll tippy–toe down and check."

"Hold on. He'd killed that bottle of whiskey. I don't think he'd be up with the birds. He's probably crashed in his quarters with a head like a balloon."

Amanda tried the phone. "No answer. I must start tracking him."

Poole caught her wrist before she could go. "Hold on a second. I'm into this over my head, and I need to share some ideas with you. You can help me untangle this knot."

"Does that mean you've stopped regarding me as a choice suspect?"

"Aw, come on. I wasn't sure how much you wanted to know—or

should know. People here seem to get into trouble when they possess information."

"And I've proved myself? My intrepid Girl–Guide–cure–Raffles performance last night? Or does your gammy leg allow you to recruit me as a tweeny investigator? You and John Walker! Only with him, it's an ultra–convenient dicky heart that twinges when navvy work's to be done."

"Whoa!—don't get so steamed. Jesus—I wasn't trying to insult you or demean you. I thought I was treating you as an equal."

"Great God!—that's the ticket, isn't it? *You* get to confer bloody equality on me. How superbly condescending! Should I be eternally grateful that you've put my name in for the great male club? I can be an honorary man, even if I'm not qualified."

He tightened his grip on her wrist. "Just settle down. I'm truly sorry for what I said and did. I'm clumsy and myopic—but I've got a good heart."

She turned away from the most winsome smile Poole could muster, but she sat still and semi–civilly extracted her wrist from his grasp. Poole sat frozen. Words bumped and caromed around in his head, and he felt like a computer game unfolding displays and tripping circuits.

"Now you've gone deaf on me," Amanda said. "I don't know damn–all what goes on in your head."

"Yeh—that's it. I don't know either, Amanda. Back up. You said a bunch of things. Uh, tweeny and navvy.."

"You want a language lesson now?"

"You said something about John Walker's heart. What was it?" She frowned. "I said he had a bad heart. Or he says he has a bad heart when he spies heavy work on the horizon."

"That's not the words you used."

"Oh, very well…I said he had a dicky heart. Just silly jargon…"

"Damn it!" Poole said. "The language barrier again. Somebody said the British and Americans were two nations separated by a common language. I heard that word down at the pub, when that insidious beer was getting me in a hammerlock. I thought—for God's sake—it was a name!"

"A *name?*"

Poole scribbled on a notepad on her desk: DICKIE HART. She stared and burst into laughter. "That's the silliest idea!"

"Listen—after old whosis, the pub owner, talked with us, he was at the bar with Marie. I thought he was just putting moves on her. I stood there waiting for the beer and heard him say something about Walker and Schwann, so I eavesdropped. He said something about dicky heart, and I assumed he was a local character."

"You think this is a…clue?"

"Everything's a clue. Does Walker use that word?"

"I think so—it's the kind of affectation he picks up."

"So someone might repeat it emphatically, in quotation marks. That's what it sounded like. A little sarcasm."

Amanda stared. "Do you know, Richard, that I believe about half the time you're trying to take the mickey. But I just *can't tell*. It's dreadfully unsettling."

"Do the which? Oh, no—don't explain. I've got enough data for now. Listen: there's one, er, clues I haven't mentioned. But it's not because you're a woman, so don't blow up when you hear."

"Stop blathering and get on with it."

"Okay—king's X, olley–olley–oxen–free, truce. I read the complete reports on our hanged friend. His name was Drus or Dros —there seems some doubt, or he used aliases or he was a bad speller —or maybe Hungarian works any way you want. Anyhow, he was a registered foreign national, in and out of the U.K. on courier business. All legit, as far as the police can tell, but I'm asking TransAtlas to double–check. But…here's the thing—they found damn little on the guy, as you know. Wallet, business cards, odd papers. But they also found in an inside jacket pocket something we missed. He was carrying a bit of jewelry—a silver bracelet."

Poole paused and wiped his forehead. "Can you go to Griffiths and look at the thing? The forensics report includes a jeweler's assessment. He says it's a cheap Moroccan or Algerian piece, worth maybe fifty pounds. If you look at it, you may have some idea why he was carrying it. Don't get whizzed off—I don't mean apply your 'feminine intuition' or whatever. But maybe it will ring some bells. It really seems to be a clue, whatever that means."

Amanda replied calmly, "All right. I think I accept that as a kind of apology. Will the police let me see it?"

"I called Griffiths yesterday."

"So you knew I'd agree to run your errand?"

"Don't get on your high horse again. I told him 'maybe.'"

"Jolly decent of you. Oh, all right—I'll leave the topic." She started to rise then sat abruptly. "Wait a tick—the sound of silvery bells. Do you really think this might revolve around stolen jewelry?"

"No, but it's a loose thread to pull on."

"But if it *did*...I just remembered something. There's a case I hadn't thought of. We lost something from the Cavendar Collection —that jumble on the third floor. About a month ago, the housekeeper reported the George snuffbox missing."

"George snuffbox?"

"Part of the family collection—a bauble George the Second gave the umpteenth earl back in the forever. There's a whole cabinet full of snuffboxes and pill cases and tiny flasks. And this was the only one gone. Very odd."

"Was it valuable—studded with gems and such?"

"That's hard to say. It's a plain silver box with fancy engraving. That's what jogged my memory, when you mentioned that bracelet. I suppose to certain collectors it would be very pricey, but it would be hard to sell, and the silver alone is only worth half a hundred pounds."

"Like the bracelet."

"Yes. Do those two things fit together?"

"Damned if I know. We'll have to put it on our list of impossibly disconnected coincidences."

Poole sat still, feeling he was sliding down the poker and that he balanced very badly indeed. One miscalculation and he would tip and crash. Leaning his weight fractionally on his ankle, he felt a bolt of pain up his leg. A reminder of his fragility, mortality and fallibility.

As if he needed that particular reminder.

BODY–LINE BOWLING

ANOTHER SUMPTUOUS DINNER, with enough courses to founder Henry VII and his entire court. Poole shuffled through the bowels of the great house to another meeting. He was scheduled for what the agenda labeled an "Application Group." He recalled that this meant a session based on a hypothetical model, a way to use developing experiences.

They met in one of the old kitchens, a dungeon–like chamber with intricately fan–vaulted ceilings, monster fireplaces, stone floors and small high windows now dusty and barred. Poole clumped to a chair, noting that members were assembling in happy chatter. Marion Halley was silent, and members joined her.

Robert Edwards caught Dewey Reger's sleeve and towed him to a fireplace, where they stared up into the cavernous opening. Edwards bubbled heartily, "You could barbecue a herd of longhorns in there, couldn't you? And look up there. What's that mystery story where people get stuffed up the chimney? You could shove the whole damn conference up here, and nobody'd miss 'em."

Reger tried to disentangle himself, but Edwards boomed on: "We oughta show the Brits a U.S.–style cookout before we get out of here. Boy, we could put on a real spread, roast us a piece of prime beef. I'll bet you Dewey here has a fantastic recipe for barbecue tucked in his head."

Wrenching himself loose of Edwards, Reger bellowed, "You ham–handed cracker! You callin' me 'boy'? You think I've got a gang of soul–food secrets tucked away in this–here woolly old head, Marse?" He flung away from Edwards, who said, "Hey, just a damn minute! I didn't mean it that way…"

"Let's get down to our task," Sister Louise interjected. "We've never tried these exercises, and we have only an hour."

Reger sat muttering, while Edwards found a chair across the circle. As he passed Poole, Edwards said, "I swear, these black people are sure still touchy as hell, even when they get shoved way up the corporate ladder."

Marion Halley and Marcia Draper sat as consultants, rigid as manikins, observing but not interacting. He tried to fathom their relationship but gave up—they were as mute as statuary. The group seemed to ignore the outburst between Reger and Edwards. Members busied themselves with raspberry–colored instruction sheets. They were told to establish a specific achievable goal and discover means to accomplish this task. Individuals bubbled with suggestions.

Everard Allison suggested they become a contract–writing team to draw up a document defining the group and creating principles for the remaining week of the conference. Aaron Spellman outlined a table of organization to transform the group into a theatre company, who would then stage skits for the staff and members, acting out group–process concepts. Diane Hamilton wanted the group to define itself by categories of Cavendar theory and allocate specific topics to members for formal reports.

Proposals were engulfed in an ocean of comments, queries, barbs of ridicule and general tumult. Marion Halley intoned, "This group is cozy before the fireplace and imagines roaring fires that spell out magic words for them."

After the usual stunned silence, Diane Hamilton turned to Poole and said, "You just sit there. I want to hear what you think we should do. I haven't heard a dozen words from you this week. You're just judging us. You stare at us like monkeys at the zoo."

Poole thought of evading the challenge, but he cleared his throat and said, "I've listened carefully. I don't have any special answers, any more than you. I guess the task at hand is to test us on how well we work together. Maybe we can draw up a list of questions we need to explore."

Allison said, "Mr. Poole is a great question–asker, no? I think you're sitting in ambush for us. I agree with Diane—you're not contributing to the group. Aren't we good enough for you?"

"Are we back to that tail–chasing psychiatric bullshit?" Edwards said. "You folks are all supposed to have executive talents, or TransAtlas wouldn't have sent you. Let's set ourselves up as an operations board, with a table of organization, an outline of procedures…"

"And you'll sit at the head of your table," Reger cut in. "Us field niggers will fan you and bring you mint juleps, while you hand out croker sacks and send us to the old cotton patch, huh?"

Marcia Draper said, in her thin but penetrating voice, "A way to avoid the task is to pretend you alone know the task. The task of the group is to discover the task."

Allison waved his right hand, and when people turned to stare said, "Oh, that's the sound of one hand clapping."

Poole wanted to summarize the meeting for Amanda, but she grabbed his hand and dragged him to her office. She opened a large manila envelope. "Inspector Griffiths was most forthcoming. He showed me the Drus file and let me bring this back."

She offered several photos of the bracelet. Poole looked at the glossies: a simple bangle set against a ruler for scale, plain silver with a sinuous enameled design and arabesques of engraving. It looked like something he might find in Woolworth's.

"The jewelry expert said there was no way to date it, but it's probably only a few years old. It's not an antique, and it has no extrinsic value we know about. His term, 'extrinsic.' A bit of junk jewelry Jan Drus carried wrapped up in his pocket. Why?"

"Wrapped up?"

She pointed to another photo. "In that fancy paper, as if it were a present. The paper is common and untraceable, too. From any stationer's."

"Well, damn—another non–clue."

"I felt the same way. At the least I expected a giant emerald plucked from the forehead of a heathen idol."

"It must mean *something*. I've got to get to the London office. I'm going to ask for every shred of data on everyone here."

"In the meantime, let's think a bit. This man—whoever he may have been—carried that trinket. Had someone given it to *him*? Not likely. Had he *stolen* it? Why bother? Was he going to give it to someone? *That's* my deduction."

"*Induction*," Poole said abstractedly. "So—if that's it, we assume he was bringing it to…a woman."

"We can assume. But would he be murdered *because* of it? Or is this another incidental tiddle in a grand design? It may not connect with…anything."

"Did you mention the whatsis snuffbox to Griffiths?"

"Yes, and he searched out a thin file from the Robbery people. Notes and a description. I don't see how to connect *it*, do you? I mean, the wrapping–up business makes this different to what I thought."

"Yeh. But…I hoped for a real simple idea like robbery we could tie it all to."

"How does it connect to Felix?"

"I don't know. Could Felix have taken the snuffbox? Maybe he was going to give the snuffbox to Drus, and Drus was going to give him the bracelet. *Why?* I'm stumped."

Amanda frowned. "Of course, Felix had access to the collection, but so did the whole staff and the housekeepers. Why filch an antique snuffbox? And would someone *kill* him for it?"

"What does Griffiths say about it?"

"He assumed a dour and professional mien. He wouldn't commit himself to an amateur like me, but he said the only clear fingerprint on the bracelet was Drus's."

"Maybe this is all irrelevant. Griffiths may be right—we ought to butt out."

Amanda led Poole up to the third story, with its long gloomy galleries, and showed him the Cavendar Collection, a vast room lined with cases and shelves. One cabinet housed knickknacks and bibelots. A small card and a depression in velvet backcloth marked the site of the missing snuffbox. The card read

SILVER SNUFFBOX, CA. 1720

PRESENTED BY HIS MAJESTY GEORGE II

TO HENRY, TWELFTH EARL OF CAVENDAR, 1733

Poole stared at the ranks of glittering nonsense in the case and felt further depressed at the slim prospect of understanding events at Ashpole Manor. A weight of tangible but inscrutable history pressed on him.

Amanda tried again to locate Robin Heyward. She hung up the house phone in the long gallery and stared at Poole. "He doesn't answer. Fred hasn't seen him today, and neither has anyone else I can find."

In the morning, Poole realized he had been at Ashpole a week and a day. Jet–lag had passed, and now he felt like a character trapped in an under–cranked motion picture, everything accelerating and zipping past in unbearably frantic movement.

Leaving the refectory after an early breakfast, Poole saw the bulky form of Sir Leicester bearing down. The baronet waved a hand casually, which Poole interpreted as a peremptory summons.

"Miss Evans tells me more mystification has developed," Sir Leicester said after ushering Poole into an empty salon. They sat side by side on a long brocaded couch, and Sir Leicester fiddled nervously with one of his howitzer–sized cigars.

Poole, after an instant of hesitation, summarized the situation. Sir Leicester, when the involuted narrative was finished, leaned back and blew a small snort, reminding Poole of a walrus surfacing after a record under–ice dive.

"Mr., er, Poole. I am extremely anxious that this affair damage neither the operation of this conference nor the ongoing work of the Institute. This is nasty business, and I must take you into my confidence. You must report to TransAtlas to evaluate the Institute, but I hope you have a sense of...tact, when you select information to report."

He stared at Poole, who remembered his officer's training, the moment when a commanding officer thought *I'll have to accept this silly little shit, because he's the best we can do, God help us!*

"I'll be, er, judicious."

"Very well. I know Lewis and the TransAtlas directors will eventually supply you this information, but it may help you now. I must repeat that *extreme* discretion is necessary. I am bound by provisions of the Official Secrets Act—which don't impinge on you."

The old man looked away toward the three tall windows at the end of the room, which opened onto the front drive, a towering yew hedge and a row of elms flanking the drive like attenuated guardsmen on parade. Then he said, "Does the name Bletchley Park mean anything to you?"

"Cryptography," Poole said after a second.

Sir Leicester looked at him for the first time with genuine

interest. "Very good! It was operations center for cryptography, encoding and decoding—and other processes. You may have heard of it in context of the history and pseudo–history that publicized the so–called 'Enigma' operation. What has not emerged—and God willing, will not emerge—is that Ashpole Manor was an adjunct site. Actually, it was an alternative operation, working on different lines to Bletchley."

He paused, and Poole prodded: "And you were involved here then?"

"Very much involved. Not in command—in coordination. I was chief information officer, a dicey spot, as you might appreciate. When the unit was shut down, just as Operation Overlord was underway, my last duties were to bury it all. Not literally, you know, though we probably could have done that, with all this acreage. But to see records were destroyed, personnel debriefed, and so, down to the last jot and tittle."

"So—forty years ago, you closed out a cloak–and–dagger academy here, and you're saying this links with everything happening now?"

"Softly, now—it's not so simple a case. I assume, Mr. Poole, that like most Americans you know bugger–all about cricket?"

Poole started—another blindsiding *non sequitur* from a Brit. He felt listening to a Briton was like living on a Moebius strip.

"Right—that is, I haven't a clue about the game, although I've seen people doing it."

"The *game*," Sir Leicester said drily. "To certain kinds of Englishmen it's far more than a game, although that's what it always and exactly is. Let that pass. Without giving you a lesson in cricket, let me draw a metaphor: cricket is a process of finely tuned strategy and tactics. Bowling is an infinitely tricky art, not mere technique. Two generations ago, some players discovered that it is possible to pass over the invisible but inviolable line between *done* and *not–done* in the sport. A famous—or notorious—captain urged his bowlers to aim in such a way as to threaten the batsman. To throw off the batsman by making him anxious and physically afraid. In sum—a method of intimidation."

Poole thought. "Like pitching a beanball in baseball?"

Sir Leicester looked blank. Baseball, Poole realized, was no good as a Rosetta Stone. Sir Leicester must be at least as ignorant of the National Pastime as Poole was of Britain's older sport.

"If you will—I wouldn't know. In fact, I detest cricket, but I think the metaphor is just. This process—known as 'body–line bowling'—created wild controversy. You see, it was not exactly a foul. It was simply something a gentleman cricketer *would not do*. It was unthinkable. But someone thought of it. It was an unfair advantage which cancelled the skills of batsmen and equalized them before the bowler.

"I regard this as a kind of *memento mori*—a way to bring skilled, capable people back to a sense of their human limitations. Anyone struck by a cricket ball hurled by a fast bowler is abruptly put into a purely physical context, a context of pain and injury. In cricket, as in any intense sport or exercise, the athlete strives to use his physical abilities to their limits, by imposing transcendent mental control— *will*, to name the idea. The batsman wills himself to focus one-hundred percent on the oncoming ball and to coordinate his muscles and reflexes, honed through repetitive practice, to meet that ball a certain way at an exact instant.

"But if you make his concentration split radically, so he is also thinking about being struck, possible pain, you cancel a large percentage of his attention. So, body–line bowling was like circuit-jamming. And *that* is what Ashpole specialized in. Now, people have created all sorts of jargon—'disinformation,' 'black propaganda' and so on—for what we were busily inventing."

"Ah–ha—dirty tricks."

"Yes. You Americans always produce the, er, succinct phrase. We were charged with finding means to jam German circuits—and I don't mean only electronic ones. We were asked to create fear and tension and uncertainty in the flow of information itself, to invent a technique of body–line bowling for the data–games we played, With a small, select staff of resident brains–trusters, we tried to describe and invent processes to link with Bletchley's code-breaking. It was vitally important to create illusions, smokescreens, so the Germans would not know that we knew that they knew that we knew that they knew their codes were compromised. Something on that order, at any rate."

Sir Leicester shifted himself and frowned. He was clearly making a powerful effort in telling this to Poole.

"The point I come to, after these divigations, is this: on the small staff, which I knew well, was Karl Dros. Or Drus. He spelt it several ways, for reasons known only to the Magyar mind. He was a bolter —he'd come to Britain during the Spanish Civil War, from a tangled background of Hungarian, Danish and Serbian backgrounds. He was vetted through several branches of intelligence before he reached Ashpole, and like many of the types assembled for the operation, he loved to cloak himself in several layers of mystery. So, aside from the heavy official dossier on Karl, little clouds of strangeness floated around him. I hadn't consciously recalled him in twenty years before last week. When you and the Inspector sketched the death in the dovecote, it came back vividly."

"Karl Drus was Jan Drus's—father?"

"I am guessing he was—or an uncle. The files are, of course, long ago ashes. I have no memory of children or connections, but as I say, he loved to keep secrets about himself."

"So—why would Jan Drus come back here?"

"That I cannot explain. I wouldn't credit nostalgia or desire to trace his...father or uncle, would you? I only know that Karl disappeared on the continent working with another agency—long after he left Ashpole. He was thought killed in the divided Germany after the war. Several agencies made tentative matches later between Drus and Soviet agents. But that kind of paranoid identification is endemic in the work, and no one established an exact identity. Enquiries ceased in the mid–fifties, as far as I know. I have, however, been long out of the field."

"You're suggesting I ask British Intelligence for a check on Drus? Or on all Druses?"

Sir Leicester grimaced. "I suggest nothing. This is information to aid you in clearing up the present…situation. Nothing more. And now, I have a staff meeting to oversee. I've told you everything I can, Mr. Poole, and I urge you again to be discreet and cautious."

As Sir Leicester rose, Poole asked, "What does the body–line bowling business have to do with this? What was Karl Drus's niche in the organization?"

"Karl Drus," Sir Leicester recited in a neutral tone, "was a commando organizer. The staff called him the Grey Angel. He was our most ingenious lecturer and trainer on the theory and practice of assassination."

Poole decided his ankle was mending. It no longer throbbed and twinged through the night, and he was expert in tripodal locomotion, at least enough to keep his mind off his disability. The train journey to London tested his stoicism. He staggered up and down stairs, lurched across platforms, through lengthy tunnels. Fred drove him to the rural station behind Ashpole Norton, a kind of Tudor gatehouse tucked back of a hill, where the sixteenth earl had located it out of range of his planned landscape. The train wound through a concealed cut, like a giant's ha–ha, below sight lines from the Manor.

At Marylebone Station, Poole descended into the underground, down a dizzyingly steep escalator, where old intimations of acrophobia visited him. The tube was not packed, but he was jostled, and someone trod heavily on his bad foot. Poole remembered to bellow "Sorry!"

Poole puzzled over the underground map and rode to Oxford Circus. He stumped up the stairs and emerged into a dazzling swirl of humanity which made him flinch. The week in rural isolation had nearly erased urban congestion as a fact of memory. He stumped cautiously through the mob. An extended Indian family held an impromptu conference before the front doors of Liberty's, amidst a wholly cosmopolitan crowd. Poole made several turns into Soho, down an alley–like street, past a row of Chinese restaurants, redolent of airborne MSG. He paused several times to check the tattered copy of what Amanda had called her "London A–to–Zed."

He found his address—a small, plain building wedged between an oriental bakery and an abandoned Greek restaurant. Merely a doorway up to what Brits called the first floor. A brass plaque on the door read WIDE WORLD TRADING ENTERPRISES LTD. In this district that could mean anything from junk toys to pornography to a discreet bordello. Poole wondered how they handled walk–in enquiries for any of the above.

At the top of the stairs was a frosted–glass door with the same uninformative sign. Behind it was an anteroom containing several battered side chairs, a table strewn with old magazines and a secretary's desk. Possibly the waiting room for a failing chiropodist. The desk held a complex phone center and a largish CRT.

Behind this palisade sat a slender woman with slashes of faint purple run through a white–bleached, teased cockatoo–crest pompadour. Her blouse was silk, expensive, of broad green–and–puce stripes. She chewed gum steadily and assessed Poole as he navigated toward her. His line of vision was partially blocked by the phone and computer module, but he was fairly sure her right hand rested in the top desk drawer.

Poole stopped about five feet from her, transferred his crutch and slowly drew his wallet and passport from his jacket. His eyes were locked on Ms. Cockatoo's, which he noticed were slightly mismatched hazel. He smiled cherubically.

"Good morning—you'll want to see this to verify. I'm Richard Poole, and Mr. Kennington is expecting me."

She took the documents left–handed and smiled a narrow *pro forma* greeting, with one crack of her gum. She glanced at the papers and said, "Have a seat, love, and I'll announce you."

Her accent, Poole assumed, was broadest East End. He lowered into one of the decrepit chairs. She turned to the CRT and rippled its keyboard, referring to his ID. Then she spoke briefly into her phone, keeping Poole in her line of sight.

Behind her desk was a battered old solid door. Poole took it for wood until he identified rivets and seams in it. Someone had carefully stained a steel security door as ancient fumed oak. Poole regarded the magazines on the table: *Punch, The Illustrated London News, Country Life, Private Eye*. None more recent than the previous year. The room was nondescript and dingy, although Poole knew this office had been open less than a year. The decorator for TransAtlas' overseas security was evidently an old theatre hand.

On the wall opposite him was a dim, low–quality reproduction of Gainsborough's *Blue Boy*. The place was an environmental artwork, a statement in *kitsch*, a sardonic comment on failure–bound business taste. Poole half–expected a shabby, desperate character from Graham Greene to emerge from the riveted door—an alcoholic dentist or anomic vacuum–cleaner salesman.

Instead, the woman rose from her battery of high–tech implements and smiled more genuinely. She was short and slight, and he filed her as the Twiggy Type—but that covered much of the female population of London under thirty in his imagination. And who remembered Twiggy, anyhow?

She extended his passport and wallet and said, "Welcome to the U.K., Mr. Poole. I'll show you to our Mr. Kennington." Her speech had slowed by a factor of four and assumed a lilt and smoothness Poole assumed to be University or upper–class or BBC or whatever variant Brits used in polite conversation out of earshot of Bow Bells.

As she turned, the door clicked open—evidently a foot–operated electric bolt. She bowed Poole ahead. Down a narrow corridor were three doors in frosted half–glass, and she opened the end door for Poole. He stepped into a small, modern office with a desk, a table laden with two CRTs and a bank of machinery recessed into a cabinet on the end wall. Behind the desk sat a dapper man—in his late fifties, Poole guessed. He wore a neat pinstripe suit in black and grey worth the price of Poole's whole wardrobe. He rose and offered a small hand.

"Hugh Kennington," he said. "Sit and be comfortable—take the weight off your good trotter."

Poole shook the hand and sat at a plain desk chair. Kennington waved loosely. "Care for a drink? It's just opening time, and an ancient conditioned reflex drives me to think and ask."

Poole declined, and Kennington seemed mildly disappointed.

"You go ahead—I've learned damned little in a week here, but I know not to come between a Brit and his drink."

"No, no. I only indulge when it's on a sanctioned agenda or in company. I thought you might fancy a taste of painkiller."

Kennington sat back and smiled, more at ease with Poole than most of the English men he had met. He picked up a manila folder and riffled it loosely.

"I took the liberty of swotting up on you this morning. Like to know outlines on visitors. I don't see much of you main–office types. Ah, by the bye, Harvey Lewis sends regards and good wishes and keen interest your way. He called for one of his infamous midnight chats, and you figured prominently."

Poole grinned, conscious that he produced his notorious lopsided look, one a colleague had suggested he reserve for frightening small children.

"I'll bet Harvey was in a swivet. But he's always jabbering about autonomy–in–the–field and independent–decision–capabilities and so on."

"Indeed, you've captured the essence. But he gave me file–one priority on your enquiries, so our Miss Jupiter whom you just met came in with the lark and began search procedures. We've been banging out hard copy for hours. And more is on the way. Our Telex man is sorting and collating like the hammers of hell."

Kennington led Poole to the next office, empty except for a long conference table on which was heaped sheaves of paper. He pulled out a chair for Poole and left him with the data as Miss Jupiter appeared with a tea tray. Poole saw that she carried a small purse tucked under her arm even as she struggled to balance and shift the tea things. He calculated the purse would contain a small pistol and a couple of clips. Ah, well, he thought, she could hardly be required to find a Carnaby Street shoulder holster. She set the tray down, fussed with cups and pots and stood back with a dazzling smile for Poole.

"You just give me a buzz if you have the merest demand, love." She pointed to a small button on the wall.

"At least they don't make you wear a bearskin hat and stand in a sentry box at attention," Poole said.

"No, more's the pity. I'm a bit kinky about uniforms and boots and buckles. But they saw straight away I wasn't built for the Guards." She exited on a brooklet of suggestive laughter. Poole grinned to himself and resolved to…what did the Brits say?—chat her up."

Poole gazed at the mountain of paper before him with less–

than–Hillary–like enthusiasm. He poured a cup of pungent tea, already deciding against testing the coffee flask. He peeled a giant green–and–white sheet from the accordion of data. It would be a long day.

✧

And day had shaded off slyly into night, the misty midsummer night of England Poole was beginning to appreciate, when Poole reversed his course to reach Ashpole Manor. Miss Jupiter—who confessed that her first name was Judy—drove him to Marylebone Station in a genteel black Rover. She now wore a fuzzy–textured black jacket with giant shoulders, and Poole decided she did wear a shoulder holster under this. Yet she still managed to look one of the Soho irregulars, perhaps a fashion model *manqué*.

"Judy Jupiter," Poole mumbled as she drove quickly and expertly through the narrow streets.

"Sod you, you wally—get your finger out," she said, braking sharply. She glanced at Poole and said, "Sorry—not you. I've acquired a loathsome habit of cursing London traffic. Yet another solitary vice."

She accelerated out of the Soho streets into a broader thoroughfare, merging fluidly with traffic. Poole still felt disoriented by wrong–side–to traffic flow.

"I tried going by Judith when I was at University," she said, "but they soon saw through that. And my other name is Winifred, God help me. My mother's family was in the music halls years ago, and I suppose they decided the name was a winner. I still feel I ought to be pulling rabbits from hats or stripping off in a club whenever someone pronounces the whole bloody name."

"Sorry—I didn't mean to sound—"

"Forget it. Did you absorb all that flaming bumf you were served up by Hugh?"

"Yes. I still don't know how to put it all together, but I've caught the drift of the hidden agenda or subtext or whatever it is that

141

Harvey Lewis is manipulating now. Have you worked for the, er, organization long?"

She laughed. "I was recruited straight out of University—that's about five years now. I spent years thinking about a glamorous foreign service career, and when Hugh dazzled me into this place, I thought I'd grabbed the prize jug. So I spend a sentence in that bloody tiny room—or others exactly like it. Still, it's a living and a life, as Mum says."

Judy accelerated the Rover into a dense swirl of traffic at a huge roundabout, cut toward an outside lane and shot up another wide street. Then Poole saw the rococo silhouette of the railroad station ahead. She zigged past slow–moving taxis and up to the entrance. Leaning forward, Judy peered into the rearview mirror and then checked the outside mirror, too.

"Persistent buggers," she said. "Been with us the whole route."

Poole glanced back. A small silver car nosed into the lane before the station.

"Do you know of any villains that might be breathing down your neck?"

Poole shook his head. She said, "Can you go on from here? I'll sit and keep an eye on them. You're not carrying anything worth stealing, I take it?"

"Nope. I made notes, but I wasn't about to carry any sensitive data out. I was afraid you'd strip–search me right there in the waiting room. "

He left the car and limped toward the station, carefully looking only ahead. In the cavernous station, he located the train schedule and the proper track for the Ashpole Norton local. He shuffled toward the outbound gates, checking his shirt pocket for his return ticket. The call board said his train departed in fifteen minutes. A short string of blue–and–yellow cars stood at the platform.

Poole had difficulty staying alert. The long day had drained him, and visions of computer sheets danced in his head. The ambience of the railroad also swayed him. He had forgotten about trains, stations, the symphony of feelings evoked by a train journey, no matter how ordinary. He had spent years flying over odd corners of the world, in everything from jumbo jets to patched–up bush planes. A recurrent travel nightmare that afflicted him placed him in an ancient DC–3, wondering if one of the unsynchronised engines would quit, then landing at a bit of arid airstrip hacked from brush, climbing down into a tropical heat haze and discovering nothing but a few rusty Quonset huts and a crumbly cement block control tower.

The world he had grown up in said the glamor of travel, the infinite possibility of adventure, began with trains. He read Richard Halliburton's books, and for Poole the royal road to romance would begin with the Pennsy line or the B & O. Twice a day, big Pennsylvania R.R. passenger trains howled like wraiths through his hometown—the Jeffersonian eastbound, the Spirit of St. Louis west. He would leave a penny on the rail and search next day to find it squeezed into a little elongated lozenge, like a St. Christopher's medal.

Soberly, Poole knew the BritRail trains were penny–ante commuter specials, little diesel–electric containers for clerks and shoppers. But he was still uplifted by the sight of the vast shed and the waiting cars.

As he shuffled toward the train, something bumped him, and he almost pivoted over the fulcrum of his crutch. Dewey Reger pressed against him, one large hand grasping Poole's bicep, while he smiled broadly.

"Richard Poole—imagine meeting you here!" He clasped Poole and patted him clumsily. When Poole pulled back, Reger leaned in.

"I understand you played college football," Reger said.

"Yeh. But I saw you play with the Steelers. You're way out of my league—in several senses."

"Ah—the point I wanted to establish. Nice of you to save me the trouble of a lecture, or a demonstration." Reger steered Poole away from the platform, toward a side exit. He kept enough pressure on Poole's arm to lift him slightly off his bad foot.

"I could tell you my life story as we stroll. You know, I was nominated for a Rhodes Scholarship in college. Went to Princeton, on one of those damn programs with a stupid acronym—G.R.A.B. or P.U.S.H. or something. They thought they'd caught a half-bright black boy who could play a little Ivy League fullback and maybe squeak by in Poli Sci, but damned if I didn't surprise them. I *grabbed* all right—honors program, *summa cum laude*, the whole string." Reger snickered softly. "Then I went and reverted. When an agent came along and said I could play with the Steelers if I just signed a little bit of paper—*whoosh*! And after two seasons I discovered my knees were just as vulnerable as anybody's. You think that's a sad story? I could have been over here studying with all the little lords at dear old Oxford, and there I was, another disadvantaged youth from the get—toe, entertaining over—weight executives on Sunday afternoons. Don't you think that's a sad story?"

Poole let himself sag against Reger's thick grasp. "Can we slow down?"

"You pooping out on me, Poole? You had a long day there at the listening post, but you haven't lost your legs, have you? I've been out of training for ten years, but you, old man, are down to one good leg. Don't think you can whip me around the head with that dandy walking stick, either. I'd hate to have to tie it around your neck. Here—sit."

Reger lowered Poole onto a bench and shifted his grip to Poole's jacket collar, leaning over him and scanning the waiting room.

"Sit still and don't do anything cute, and I'll let you hear another installment of my fascinating biography. I know you're fascinated—you've been digging away at the files all day."

"What's the game, Reger? Are you running some free–lance thing?"

"No indeed. Ours is a fully legitimized, authorized and carefully crafted operation, sport. You'll know all soon, or at least what we choose to tell you."

"We?"

Reger turned himself partially around the bench, still gripping Poole's collar. Standing behind Poole, he leaned over and grinned. "Just keep on keeping on. We're making chitchat, and these good citizens are not going to think too much about a big old Nee–grow talking to a handicapped Yank. Right?"

Two policemen crossed the end of the station, a hundred feet away, walking in a relaxed lope, one speaking into a handset. They glanced toward Poole and Reger and continued onward. Poole wished he had a reason to wear a blue helmet shaped like a topi and emblazoned with a big brass badge.

"'Oh, but they *don't* go,'" Reger hummed. He shook Poole. "Dear old Gilbert and Sullivan. I tried out for every damn production in college, and I always got the exotic parts. The Mikado, pirate number three, that stuff. I wanted to do the patter songs. Maybe that gave me a trauma. Subtle discrimination, jive like that. What you think?"

The policemen disappeared out the station doors, and Reger leaned back. "Up an at 'em. We're going to continue our stroll, right back out the way you came in. Then we'll provide private transport for a little cross–town drive."

Poole stood, realizing he had Reger at full stretch, with the bench between them, but he could not figure out what to do if he broke loose. The big ex–fullback looked capable of picking up the bench and dumping it on him. Reger held Poole, then stepped around the end of the bench and regripped Poole's arm.

"You feeling old football pains? I used my expensive education about the time the Steelers dropped me and made myself a motto: *ad astra per aspirin*."

Reger chuckled, then sucked the sound in. A light voice breathed between Poole and Reger: "The pressure on the back of your neck is a small but efficient pistol, Mr. Reger. You Yanks are contemptuous of itsy–bitsy firearms, but a seven–millimeter slug will give you a headache into eternity."

Judy Jupiter slid between Poole and Reger, tucking the Beretta pistol into Reger's shoulder, its blue muzzle below his ear.

"Now—ever–so–gently release Mr. Poole, and we'll continue our pleasant stroll, as you directed, Mr. Reger."

Poole glanced at her, and Judy winked pertly.

"I'm glad you waited for the bobbies to clear off," she said. "We don't want to run afoul of the metropolitan coppers. Ever so much paperwork and phoning–up involved. Mr. Reger, please move slowly and clasp your hands behind your back, as if you walked deep in thought and conversation. I don't want to—what?—'frisk' you as your telly police say, and I don't even want to *see* the preposterous giant pistol you carry—or your collection of readable documents. We'll have a nice sorting–out session in a moment."

They traversed the station, and Poole heard a train hum alive and rumble away from the platform—another missed train in his life.

Reger said, "Where's—" and stopped.

"Your Mr. Edwards is entangled with a pair of Smith and Wesson handcuffs and the steering wheel of your abominable hire–car. And the revolver he carried is locked in the boot. Don't forget it when you return the car, or you'll be buried in paperwork."

Poole muttered, "I'm damn tired of being hauled around like a sack of potatoes."

"Relax, love—Hugh Kennington will make it all well for the lot of you. It's a pity I can't demand overtime wages. We'll just march out and clarify this whole situation. Steady the buffs."

Outside the station, a needlelike rain blew, the streets were obsidian streams and nothing seemed awake or alive. Judy Jupiter, as they reached the Rover, made a quick pass at Reger, removing a .38 S&W revolver from his jacket and handing it to Poole.

"My friend Richard Poole is a crack marksman with a preference for killing his prisoners. I'm going to fetch Edwards back to our party, and you must stand very still or Deadeye Dick will drill you."

She bustled past a row of inert black taxis, hips and shoulders swaying—a career woman completing a cheerful task. Poole smiled weakly at Reger and regarded the pistol in his own hand.

Back at Wide World Enterprises, Judy Jupiter transferred her prisoners efficiently from the Rover to a back door in the building. She had Reger and Edwards cuffed together, and neither had spoken on the ride back. Judy drove even more briskly on the midnight streets, while Poole sat half–turned in the front seat, revolver in hand. The pair looked more like shamed schoolboys than desperadoes.

Judy, Poole and the cuffed men entered a conference room upstairs, where Hugh Kennington waited with a tall young man with closely cropped blond hair. Kennington introduced him to Poole as "Geoffrey St. John—your opposite number for the U.K." Poole heard the name as "Sinjun" and for a moment pegged it as exotic. The man said, "Very pleased—your legend precedes you," in a strangled University accent.

Judy lowered Reger and Edwards into chairs, recuffing them through the sides of the chairs. She enjoyed a minor genius for snaffling prisoners. Hugh Kennington glared at the bedraggled pair from across the long table.

"We're about to have an intense discussion, gents," he said quietly. "Your responses, their clarity and degree of forthcomingness will settle your futures with TransAtlas. As my old dad would say, 'Think on.'"

Reger glared from Kennington to Poole, while Edwards stared at the floor.

The others took seats along the table, with Judy next to the door, her jacket and purse across her lap. She looked tidy, prim and alert.

Kennington began, "Richard—can you decipher these events, given your research today?"

Poole dug out his little notebook and summarized some of his intensive scribbling: "Dewey Reger—joined Gearham Industries in 1963. Seven years with the F.B.I., last as assistant field director for six southeastern states. Currently ticketed as Gearham's Customer Services Coordinator. Sent as an alternate to the Institute. Damn it —I forget the name of the person he replaced. Robert Edwards— with MagnaCorp, Inc., for eleven years. Listed as Personnel Development Manager. Six years Army, four in Southeast Asia. Impeccable record at MagnaCorp, regular promotions. You want addresses and family data?"

"No, thanks," Kennington said. "We could cite reams of further data, gentlemen. Richard has your fascinating careers in memory. Now for Q and A time—and I repeat that your best course is to open your hearts freely."

In an hour, both men had been prodded into laconic replies and agreements with posed questions. Edwards pushed the easiest.

"Look," he said, "we weren't trying to screw up the works. We weren't going to hurt anyone. I ran into Dewey at the Institute, and we...went a ways back. We compared notes and started gassing about the murders. Dewey said he knew a little about the guy you found in the garden—Drus."

Reger looked both bored and furious. He muttered, "Shee–it.

You going to bust us down with the home office?" He glared at Kennington.

Twirling a silver fountain pen between his fingers, Kennington regarded Reger blankly and said, "I really have no idea. It depends on how much further than this room the, er, affair must go."

Reger said, "I met Drus in 1983, in Budapest. It was right after I got the Gearham job, and I went as part of liaison team. We met with purveyors to set up a parts–distribution deal. I was along as a watcher, to learn the ropes. Drus was handling the deal as a host and tour–guide. In other words, he was steering us clear of government problems. He knew who to romance, who to fix, who to avoid. I couldn't get a reading on him. We met a couple of times at a little café—he gave me some jive about business transcending politics. He was doing a routine by the numbers, trying to get a handle on me as a future contact. He got into 'the plight of black people in America' and that shit. But that's all the further it went."

"So—he turns up at Cavendar Institute unannounced, and you coincidentally arrive as a deputy." Kennington looked massively skeptical.

"Yeh—that's the goddamn weird situation. I found out Drus was here and somebody snuffed him. I figured my ass would be in the fire if anybody found out about that Budapest trip."

Geoffrey St. John stood, stretched and paced the length of the table. Stopping behind Reger and Edwards, he said, "The situation is clear–cut: Drus was a minor operative with the Eastern Bloc and a career opportunist. He often worked as a courier and drop–man. You two thought it was a fine opportunity to make a drop with him, arrived at the conference and met him. Now—tell us exactly what went wrong. A bit of extramural extortion? Drus put you in the wrong? Or was he already squeezing you, and this was a pay–off?"

Reger shook his head. "I know this looks like some kind of heavy duty shit, but it's not. I never laid eyes on him."

Edwards shifted, rattling the handcuff chain. "We weren't going to hurt Poole here. Dewey just said we'd get some answers about Drus."

Kennington said, "The tale you're spinning is that this was merely a little lark, that you two grown men decided to indulge in amateur sleuthing?"

"I conned old Fred into telling me he took Poole to the train. I've got this address, so it wasn't a big deal to figure out where he'd go in London. I thought…look, damn it, it was important to find out where I stood. I don't want some kind of flag on my record because of this Drus shit." With his free hand, Reger swiped at his brow.

"Why the phony fight you two staged yesterday?" Poole asked.

"It was Robert's idea—a little theatre to make folks think we weren't connected, or—you know—we couldn't work together."

During a heavy silence, St. John paced back down the room and leaned against the wall. Kennington twiddled his pen and sucked at his teeth. Judy looked alert.

Kennington glanced at Poole and said, "Do you buy any of this, Richard, or is it all fairy–story time?"

"I hate coincidences. I have a hell of a time believing you *just happened* to show up here and Drus *just happened* to turn up out in the countryside at the same time and he *just happened* to be killed. "

Reger shook his head: "Yeh—it's a bitch. But…"

Judy rose abruptly and left the room. St. John reiterated questions about Reger and Edwards and their positions in the TransAtlas subsidiaries. It felt like an all–night session. Then Judy peered around the door and said, "Richard—telephone for you."

In the next office, he picked up the phone, anticipating Harvey Lewis' irate grizzly bear growl. Instead, it was Amanda Evans, saying, "Richard? Hallo? Are you all right?"

He had left the number with Amanda and told her he would be

back on the last train. He felt guilty that she was up and calling in the middle of the night.

"Yeh—I'm fine. What are you doing up? Doesn't anyone in the U.K. believe in eight hours' sleep? I get over—"

She cut him off, her voice crackly and unsteady: "Richard—it's Robin. He's been found—but he may be dead!"

ON THE MADNESS OF CROWDS

AMANDA'S STORY WAS disjointed, but Poole absorbed pertinent facts. When he returned to the interrogation room, Kennington and St. John were ending a sotto voce conference. Edwards and Reger sat muted and bedraggled.

Kennington nodded toward them and addressed Poole: "We'll have to accept the tale these two spun. Provisionally. Geoffrey will pursue discreet enquiries with TransAtlas and with officers of Gearham and MagnaCorp." He turned to Reger and Edwards.

"Consider yourselves dangling by a single thread. I hold the golden shears with which to snip it, so be on parade at the Institute. If Richard sees a misstep, I'll hear of it."

Poole said, "You're not contacting the police?"

"We'll assume responsibility. They know they face a whole string of felony charges, and I don't think either of these Boy Scouts wants to stand at the Old Bailey."

"Two more questions," Poole said. "First—which of you jumped me in the garden two nights ago?"

Reger and Edwards shifted. Finally, Reger said, "I didn't mean to hurt you. I didn't even know it was you at first."

"What were you doing there?"

Edwards said, "We'd been checking that tower–thing—where they found Drus. I was in there, and Dewey stood watch. I think we may have…found something."

Poole decided Edwards was too whipped to lie.

"Second—where did you get the guns?"

Reger shook his head wearily. "You ain't gonna believe this—we found them at the Manor."

Kennington stared at them and said, "Perhaps I was wrong. We're getting a pack of bloody lies. The police would be much more patient in teaching them veracity."

Edwards struggled against the looped handcuffs and said, "Jesus, Mr. Kennington, it's the truth. There's a collection. I turned it up, and yesterday I went back and...borrowed a couple."

The weapons lay in the center of the polished conference table: a snub–nosed S&W .38 revolver and a nickel–plated Browning .32 automatic.

"Tell me about this...collection," Poole said.

Edwards said, "I was trying to find stuff in the files at the Manor. We thought we could find something about...you." He looked toward Poole. "The locks on those office rooms were jokes, no big deal to pick. But the files didn't have much—probably all on computers now. I found a big wooden cabinet with a bunch of shotguns, a couple of .22 rifles and a drawer in the bottom, with a shitload of handguns. I was knocked over. Then when Dewey and I thought we'd need them, I took those two. I was going to put them back tonight."

Edwards looked like an outsized schoolboy called into the principal's office over a prank. Reger looked sullenly angry.

"Which office?" Poole asked.

"It doesn't have a number. I can show you. I went through three different ones—it looks like different staff people share them. What the hell is a small armory doing at the Manor?"

Kennington and St. John continued with questions. Poole left the office to find Judy in the anteroom, curled into a decaying armchair. She had tugged her jacket around her like a shawl and fallen asleep. Her right hand was inserted into her purse as into a muff. She looked about twelve years old, Poole thought, feeling a twinge at waking her. But when he touched her shoulder, she was not only awake but upright in the chair, with the Beretta leveled at the bridge of his nose.

"Jesus!" she gasped.

"Amen," Poole breathed as she made the pistol disappear. "Can you drive me back to Ashpole? I hate to ask this, but I have to get back, pronto."

"Surely—with an okay from the boss–man."

In a few minutes they were rolling in the Rover through streets already greying with dawn. The massy buildings of central London intensified the contrast between night and faint intimations of sunrise. The rain had stopped and the air was fresh. Judy drove the empty streets and roundabouts with zeal.

"Did I ever tell you about the woman I almost married who drove formula–one cars?" he asked.

"You haven't known me long enough to tell me wonderful lies."

Poole saw a curious little milk truck waddling along the curb, and a few cars with headlights fading in the dawn. Otherwise, it was their city. Once, Judy cursed a looming tank trunk, which she called an "articulated lorry." Then they had passed the torso of the city and rolled through villages surrounded by trees and fields. The placid landscape contrasted with Poole's feeling of being caught in a rushed, out–of–control drama.

He sat up suddenly and slapped his forehead, muttering, "Damn it to hell—I shouldn't be let out without a keeper!" When Judy peered in amazement at him, he said, "Is there someplace we can stop for breakfast? You must need sustenance, and I've got some leads for you to check out when you go back."

"It's very early, but keep an eye out. Some pubs have started breakfast serving for the lorry drivers and commuter jockeys."

When they curved into a village from an open stretch of

country, she said, "Tally–ho!" They crossed an open public square, and she slewed the car on the cobbles before a small stone pub. A colorful heraldic sign read THE CROOKED BILLET, over a painting wrought by a prentice hand depicting a bit of wood or perhaps a dog turd or a half–melted chocolate bar. By the oak front door stood a sandwich sign reading MORNING COFFEE & ENGLISH BREAKFAST.

They left the car, Poole feeling every joint protesting, Judy with a cat–like stretch. The rows of stone and brick cottages, bathed in roseate light, were stunningly picturesque. In his present mood, Poole damned them to hell.

"'And now the morning sun doth shine / Through the briar and twisted eglantine,'" Judy said. "Or words to that effect. I think I just hashed up the resident genius's language." She nodded off to the left. "John Milton lived there."

As they approached, the publican, a large hirsute man reminding Poole of the ubiquitous villain of Charlie Chaplin's comedies was opening the hefty door. He said softly, "Good day— step in. The cook is firing up, so we can serve you in a moment."

They sat at a tiny table in the nook of an immense hearth. Tacked to every wall were dozens of what Poole assumed to be agricultural implements—they looked like Jack's giant's collection of impractical can openers.

Judy announced loudly she was visiting the loo, and Poole found his pipe. It was broken neatly in half at the joint of stem and bowl. Judy saw it as she returned and said, "Oh, a pity!—was it a good one?"

"I think I only carried it as a fetish. A rabbit's foot would have been better. But I've got to sort all the rubbish in my head. When we were grilling Reger and Edwards, Edwards said they found something at the dovecote. Can you or Kennington follow that up? I forgot to ask him what he meant."

Judy produced a notepad and a purple–tipped pen (*Why* purple? Poole's mind shrieked). Poole continued: "And—Edwards is with MagnaCorp, right? Last week he told Everard Allison he was with Jet…Jet–something. In California. Can you check that out? Is that another TransAtlas holding? Why the hell lie to Allison? Maybe you'd better run a deeper check on *him*, too. There was nothing out of the ordinary on him that I saw."

Breakfast arrived, and Poole found the coffee not only drinkable but borderline excellent. The meal included flabby sausages, fried tomatoes, cardboard toast, potatoes, and fragments of mystery food. Judy attacked the food with single-minded savagery, and Poole decided Brits were small only because of a genetic anomaly of metabolism, that they burnt up calories through sheer nervous tension.

When they left the Crooked Billet, the sun stood high and brilliant. Judy drove more circumspectly out of Chalfont St. Giles, facing a stream of commuter traffic bucking toward the city. Poole was absorbed with ideas and barely noticed the scenery as they rolled over the spine of the Chilterns and across the Vale of Aylesbury. He woke from reverie when Judy swung the Rover into the shadow of Ramillies Gate and they sped up the long ride toward Ashpole Manor.

Poole levered cautiously from the car. Judy leaned over and looked out the door: "Be careful, love," she said. "You need to watch your back. Put in a call if we can help."

"Thanks for everything—you've saved my life in several ways."

"Nonsense." She gave him a mock salute. "It's all in the line of duty with dear old Wide World. We aim to please—and you aim, too, please. Oh—and ta for breakfast."

"I'll see you again."

She flashed a dazzling gamin's smile, rolled up the window and gunned the sedan out from the shadow of the portico. Poole limped toward the steps, culling through ideas in his mind. He looked up to see Amanda Evans standing before the broad oaken doors, arms folded, staring down at him like a schoolmistress waiting for the last forlorn hope of tardy students.

"Good morning, Richard. You look like the morning after a night on the tiles."

Poole gritted his teeth, ignored thoughts of rest and quizzed Amanda on the Heyward situation. He was, she told Poole, in the intensive–care unit of a trauma center near Bedford. A groundskeeper had discovered him unconscious and trussed in the Chinese Dairy (an outrageously fanciful summerhouse built by William Kent in 1732 far beyond the Vale of Ida, over a mile from the Manor). He had been wedged under a stone bench in the little building, and only by sheer chance did the groundskeeper enter it in search of mislaid hedge clippers.

Poole called Griffiths for more details. Preliminary examinations at Bedford indicated a severe concussion, some hemorrhaging, shock and exposure. Griffiths said, "It's as good as murder at the moment. I have plainclothes patrols around the grounds, despite objections from Miss Evans and Sir Leicester. I reckon the situation is an emergency now. We also have a policewoman at the hospital to watch Heyward's condition."

Poole sat in the old kitchen after lunch and watched members of the large group filter in. He ticked off mental notes as he waited: Donovan Stallings was still missing. Griffiths and Davies had no useful leads to his whereabouts. He pondered his research through TransAtlas's code–one files. He wondered if he could leech more from Sir Leicester about ancient spook history and the halcyon days of the OSS and MI–5.

When the group achieved some order, Sister Louise bustled about with brightly colored round tokens Poole thought were poker chips. As she counted a dozen into Poole's hand, she said, "It's good to see you again, Mr. Poole—I hope your injury is healing. We were all distressed to hear of the accident. It must be dispiriting to miss any of the process."

He smiled and inclined his head. Some story was satisfying curiosity among the members. He assumed a stoic mien.

Sister Louise and Diane Hamilton, in duet, explained they were about to do an exercise called "Star Power." The purpose was murky. Each member was to decide on the value of the chips he or she held and to devise ways to use them for currency. The hour would be devoted to the task.

Discussion and cross–talk erupted. Someone said, "Do different colors denote different values?" Everard Allison said, "I was given seventeen, and you have twenty, love," to a small tidy woman next to him. A large bearded man Poole only recalled as Arnold (but who reminded him forcibly of Charles Laughton impersonating Henry VIII) whined peevishly, "I hate red. I'll swap my reds for blues."

Immediately the room echoed with a cacophony like the New York Stock Exchange at a peak of crisis. People fell into diads and triads, examining chips, handing them back and forth, arguing over symbolic values. Allison had assembled five members who listened to a rapid lecture.

"A proposal," Allison shouted, jumping lightly up onto a folding chair. "We have a complete economy. We'll collect all chips and divide them equally by color and number. Bring them here."

"Bullshit," Arnold said. "That's some kind of cockeyed communism. I want to know what these things are worth before I hand them over."

Aaron Spellman intervened, leading his own small cohort. "I'm sure Allison has charitable motives, but we have a better proposal. Why dissipate the wealth by fragmenting it? Let's invest in a total fund, figure out rates of interest and accept schemes for development. Then we'll see who's worth what."

Giorgio, awash in sweat, waved his handkerchief frantically: "Listen, I think we must...we may use the powers as ways of... giving values to peoples." His lips moved, but he seemed to have crashed headlong into the language barrier. He shrugged and sat heavily.

John Walker sat unruffled in a neat Bond Street suit, hermetic in his consultant's role. He intoned loudly, "This group thinks it is the Bank of England, but it may only be the crew of the Titanic."

As usual, the comment froze the members. Then Aaron Spellman whirled, howling, "I've fucking had it! These news flashes from the Oracle of Delphi totally fuck up the works."

He bolted across the room, bent and lifted Walker—chair and all—and staggered with his burden to the door, reeling like a super-heavyweight lifter going for the world's title in people–jerking.

"Bravo!" Giorgio cried. He and Allison followed. They returned, slamming the heavy door and bolting it.

"Now back to business," Spellman wheezed.

"But we need direction," Sister Louise said. Diane Hamilton rushed to her support: "That's right—how will we know if the exercise is working?"

"The purpose of this whole lunatic program," Spellman shouted, "is to foster independence and judgment, right? I just followed an old American custom—a declaration of independence. No goddamn taxation without representation. *We're* the representatives now. To hell with the King's governor!"

The discussion resumed, escalating in volume and ferocity.

Poole turned to Diane Hamilton, holding out his fourteen white chips.

"Here—you want some of these? Take what you want."

"You want to trade?"

"No. If you want them, just take them."

"It's not fair just to opt out."

"Who said I'm opting out?" Poole asked. "I've made a choice, and to choose is to act, isn't it?"

The transaction had drawn attention. Allison and Spellman peered at him.

"Oh, no—Richard has been reading the Sermon on the Mount," Allison said.

Spellman said, "That's the craziest damn thing I ever heard of. What if everyone did that? Who're you trying to impress, Poole?"

Falteringly, Diane took Poole's chips and added them to her stock of blues. She stared at him as if he had developed a tremendous zit on the end of his nose.

Sister Louise said, "I really don't think we as a group decided to eject Mr. Walker. We must decide whether he should—"

"That's over and done," Spellman said. "I'm so frigging tired of this namby–pamby bunch. Can't we make one decision and stick with it, for Christ's sake?"

Anarchy bloomed. Fiscal policies were invented and rejected with dizzying rapidity. Members accumulated stacks of red, white and blue chips in operations ranging from labor–credit values (a la Henry George) to small–scale Ponzi schemes. Allison declared himself economic oligarch of Ashpole kitchen, and Spellman fulminated on currency history in a vein reminiscent of Ezra Pound at his wackiest. At the stroke of the hour, as members moved to leave, Spellman rushed to the barred door.

"Oh, no—today we're ditching their artificial schedule," he said.

Arnold stepped before Spellman, looked him up and down and then took him in a massive bear hug, spinning him from the door and bowling over a gaggle of folding chairs.

Spellman sat stunned on the flagstones while Arnold muttered, "One stupid dictator is enough. I ain't about to give up King Log for King Stork. Ladies—if you need an escort, we can move along."

Sister Louise and Diane Hamilton remained in one corner,

counting a mountain of chips into discrete heaps. A birdlike woman whose name Poole forgot begged a short man in a golf outfit for his handful of blue chips.

"I'm just sure blue is the color of value," she said.

A skinny young man in a three–piece suit had unrolled a long scroll of computer paper, on which he indicted numbers in pencil. He was, he had said, a systems analyst specializing in number theory.

Slowly, the room emptied, but Poole still detected barely suppressed violence and egoism. The merest whiff of money had triggered all the atavistic impulses of the group: a little self–interest makes the world go round. He found a solitary white chip in a corner and flipped it backhand across the room. It skipped off the cold stone floor, twinkling like promise.

Members gathered for tea, and Poole tried to describe the large-group meeting to Amanda, who was impatient for news of his data-chase at Wide World. He found his notes and extracted choice bits.

"Oh—your little playmate, Judy Whosis, called," Amanda said, handing Poole a sheet from a Cavendar notepad. The penciled message read :

Edwards unconnected California JetComm. MagnaCorp only TA connection—11 years. Security clearance code one. No red tabs in file.

E. & R. found traces on dovecote wall—silver or other metal. Police not acknowledge. Can you check?

Handguns checked C.I.D.—registered legit. to Sir L. Insp. Griffiths confirms—also checked on murder gun. Suggest you check further on E. More, publican, Ashpole Norton. Files show connection w/Cavendar staff.

Wotcher backside.

Luv/Jay–Jay

"Jay–Jay?" Amanda said mockingly. "She sounds like a panto walk–on in a Winnie–the–Pooh story. About the right size, too—Christopher Robin in drag."

Poole grinned crookedly. "Not jealous, are we?"

She jumped from her desk chair and took a few steps. "Jealous? What presumption! If I were jealous, it would make you fantastically conceited, wouldn't it now?"

"Okay, okay. Let it pass. You wanted a scoop from the TransAtlas computers. Here's what I gleaned."

He riffled pages in the notebook: "Karl Drus was a Hungarian Connection for the OSS in World War II. Sir Leicester ran him as a courier to Czech partisans—maybe the Balkans generally. At some point, Drus got his son and the son of a friend out of Germany, probably through Denmark and then Sweden. The son of the friend was Felix Schwann. During the deepest freeze of the cold war, Jan Drus left Britain and went back East. He kept some contacts with Felix, and he was presumably back to see him when the conference began."

"You *know* all this—or is it educated guessing?"

"Enough to guess right, I hope. See if you can shoot holes in the story. Drus comes back for a reunion with Schwann. He's also on a business trip for his masters. Two birds with one stone. He's arranged to meet someone at Ashpole—*not* Felix—on business. The meeting is fouled up, and whoever–it–is cancels Drus's ticket. Why —I don't know."

"That accounts for *one* incident."

"It's the end of a string we can pull. See if you can make sense of these connections: We turn up two Colt Woodsman pistols, about nineteen–forty vintage. Sir Leicester, we find, has a cabinet stuffed with old guns. I'll bet my cache of poker chips there were a pair of Colt Woodsmans in that batch. I'll call Judy at Wide World and confirm that. Social connections: I'll bet Marie Winter worked at Ashpole Manor in the recent past. She said she grew up in the village and just started working for More. Query: did she work on the housekeeping staff here? I'll also bet we find a connection between Marie, More and either Stallings or Heyward."

"Why these wild surmises?"

"I think there are connections between the village and the big house that we're missing, going right back to the war. Edwards and Reger, I think, are beside the point—they've just stumbled onto the scene and made a mess. But we've got to locate Stallings and talk with Heyward, if and when he can talk. We've also got to sort out the Bobbsy Twins—Marcia and Marion. One is Tweedle–Dee and one is Tweedle–Dum. I'm about convinced one of them was the specter I chased across the damned meadows. But why was she running? Can you dig further into Cavendar files on them? Also on Marie Winter and Eliot More."

"The house files aren't totally transferred from paper to computer, but I'll trace what I can. I'll have the most complete printout on staff, managers and consultants I can run by tomorrow. We'll have to comb the records for real connections between people here."

"Bravo," Poole said. He paused to look at Amanda in the soft light filtered through the high window in her office. *A beautiful, self–contained lady*, he thought. The light turned her hair russet and made her fair skin glow.

He flipped his notebook around, saying, "Here's a little I gleaned about members who might be even remotely connected with this mare's nest."

His penciled notes read:

Everard Allison, age 37. Educated Tyne and Wear Polytechnic. Engineering Director, Weston AgriCo, Llareggub, Wales. Hired 1977.

Helen Corbett, age 32. Educated Radcliffe Hall and UCLA. Filmmaker and advertising director, Pasadena JetComm. Hired 1979.

Giorgio da Silva, age 51. Purveyor–import agent for Italia Traction, Milan. Not payrolled TransAtlas but working under license.

Diane Hamilton, age 38. Educated Northwestern U. and Pratt Institute. Sales manager and ad writer, California Caterers. On board 1979, transferred from Monterey to Baltimore, 1983.

Louise Houston, age 39. Supervising nun, Little Sisters of the Poor (Atlanta), joined TA as manager of Barnegat Foundation 1977, based in Syracuse, N.Y., on extended leave from order.

Aaron Spellman, age 41. German immigrant to U.S., 1949. Educated Stanford and M.I.T. Personnel director, Intercontinental Paper, Seattle, since 1978. On board TA, 1973.

Arthur Stanley, age 30. Educated Brunel Institute. Assistant works manager, Tallifiero Harvester, Manchester. On board TA, 1979.

"I don't see useful patterns of connection," Poole said. "Everything and nothing correlates. We have a roster of highly educated, ambitious, efficient people, all capable of planning and executing complex operations. That's why they were selected to be sent to Ashpole. How do we separate business mentalities from homicidal ones?"

"Most of the people on your list are too young to be connected with Felix's childhood—or with Drus and his father."

"Maybe the connection doesn't go that far back. Spellman came to the U.S. from Germany, age five. Could his *father* have been connected with Drus or Schwann? Arthur Stanley and Everard Allison are Brits—could they be connected with Ashpole? We have people in publicity or advertising, in money–handling. Giorgio and Sister Louise are anomalies—they're only indirectly TransAtlas agents. Is it an outside connection?"

Amanda scribbled a note and said, "What about the village connection? You were pursuing Marie and More."

"I don't know. Damn it—we've got to talk with Stallings and Heyward!"

Amanda led Poole from her office to the suite of staff offices and the files and gun cabinet Edwards had described. "This is Sir Leicester's work space, but he rarely uses it," she said. "There's his collection."

A huge old Dutch armoire in polished, scrolled baroque design, of dark cherry. Poole examined the brass locks and noted scratches from Edwards' violation. He picked both locks and examined the shotguns, small–bore rifles and a bin of handguns, some boxed, some holstered, some wrapped in oiled paper. Each had a small tag with a date on it.

"Is there a list or catalogue of these things?"

"I haven't a clue," she said. "I was only dimly aware Sir Leicester kept some of his private possessions here."

"Why on earth would he collect all these pistols?"

"You don't understand the magpie or thimble–collector British sensibility. This house is loaded with collections—bird eggs, presentation spoons, antique artificial limbs, battle flags, toy soldiers, Regency ball dresses, old boots. No one needs a *reason* to collect things—things are their own reason."

"It's demented. In a country where handguns are proscribed, this fellow builds up an arsenal. And these aren't special weapons— just plain–vanilla handguns. Another question when I can pin Sir

Leicester down. "

He and Amanda compared notes and agreed on an agenda—a run to Inspector Griffiths' field HQ in the village and a run to Bedford trauma center. Answers seemed to beckon to them in the crazy-quilt of fields, villages and counties, awaiting patient investigation.

✧

In retrospect, Poole realized it was an insane thing to say: "I'll drive."

Amanda Evans cast a skeptical look then fetched a set of keys. "We'll take the staff car," she said, leading him to a plain black Ford Escort in the yard.

It was not the position on the road which flummoxed him but perception of space itself. On the wrong—i.e., *right*—side of the car, he could not imagine where the centerline of the road might be. It seemed all wrong to have the bulk of the car to his left. Driving from the Manor was easy—he wobbled on the empty drive with impunity. The B-road beyond the gate was also empty. Amanda sat rigid in her seatbelt, offering terse instructions.

"Look—I've got to get the hang of this. There might be an emergency. And I've driven for twenty-five years."

They moved from deep countryside toward Ashpole Norton, and Poole fought a reflexive instinct to veer abruptly in the face of oncoming traffic. *What were those assholes doing over there?*

Scrabbling for the gearshift lever with his left hand seemed perverse and unnatural. Then they reached a largish roundabout, sitting in the road like a great spider in a Bunyan-esque allegory. Poole slowed, braked, clawed at the gearshift lever to downshift then turned smartly *right* into the circle, saw a small truck approaching, lights blinking frantically. He passed the truck on the inside, slewed through the circle and shot out the other side, relieved. Then he heard Amanda saying, "You're on the wrong side of the fucking road!"

He bumped the car over the little concrete curb on the verge. "I surrender, dear." he said.

"I'll cheerfully give you learner's lessons," she said when she had taken the wheel, "but I don't think we need gamble with the grim reaper while on errands."

She hurtled the car into top gear and drove straight into the village. They stopped before a large Queen Anne house on the village green. Inspector Griffiths had erected an impromptu office in the lounge, and he sat back of a trestle table littered with papers, a typewriter, cardboard boxes of file folders and three telephones.

Griffiths was on one phone as they entered, and he acknowledged their arrival by waggling his bushy black eyebrows like Groucho Marx punctuating an epigram. When Griffiths hung up the phone, he searched the welter of business around him until he found a small cigar, which he lit with studious concentration.

"Good evening," he said. "Miss Evans said you'd appear with personnel data. If you'll put me in the picture, I'll tell you of our progress to date." He leaned toward the hallway and called, "Seward? Please take incoming calls. I'll be unavailable for the next half–hour."

Poole and Amanda did an antiphonal reading of their notes and conjectures, while Griffiths made cursory notes of his own. When they finished, Griffiths said, "You wanted information on More and Marie Winter. Constable Davies comes on shift in a few minutes. He can help fill you in there—his bailiwick. As for Stallings, we're tracing him as far as possible. We're awaiting word from Bedford on Heyward. And a lab man will be at the Manor tomorrow morning to inventory the weapons cache. Could you assist him with records, Miss Evans?"

"That's, er, private with Sir Leicester. I have no authority over his possessions."

"Nonetheless, you could smooth our way."

Amanda made a face and nodded. Poole grinned at her, and she said, "Richard and I will speak with him early tomorrow."

Griffiths sat with his hands laced behind his neck and his feet up on a wastecan, wearing a baggy grey sweater and old slacks. He seemed much more relaxed, and Poole wondered if that was an augury.

Griffiths discarded the cigar butt and said, "Your ideas are quite helpful. We'll have a team at the dovecote to see if we missed anything. Your man—Edwards—has said there were 'traces' on the wall." He stared at the wall and whistled tunelessly a second. "We're making a bit of headway. At a certain point, a puzzle like this begins to sort out—or it goes into the dead room forever."

Griffiths reiterated laboratory and medical reports and pointed to a small, untidy sheaf of papers. "My field report to date. We're tracing Stallings through University friends and family. He has only a few connections here—most of the clan has trekked to Canada. He seems to have gone invisible, but we'll find him."

"What exactly happened to Robin Heyward?" Amanda asked.

"He was knocked about and tied up in a half–witted fashion and dumped in that odd building. Whoever bashed him didn't want to kill him. I'd say it was someone who wanted a head start in a footrace. It's touchy with severe head wounds, but the medicos say he's strong and should pull through if he comes out of the coma."

There was a low knocking, and Constable Davies edged through the doorway. Glancing at Poole and Amanda, he said, "Sorry I'm a bit late, Inspector. Had to handle another call from Mrs. Villikins about her kid. "

"Ah, the inestimable Mrs. Villiers," Griffiths said. "Her youngest boy found Schwann. Suffers from nightmares and hysterics, and no wonder of it. But she's convinced his life is in danger from lurking assassins and bends the constable's ears on a daily basis."

"Too true," Davies said, switching on an electric kettle at the sideboard and sitting heavily in a low wooden chair. "The village has been at a boil for a week, and I've nearly run out of ways to quiet them."

Griffiths asked Davies to fill Poole and Amanda in on More, Marie and the village connections. The constable placidly continued tea–making, pouring boiling water into a stout brown pot and fitting it with a boxing–glove–like cozy. Then he turned and said, "Our Eliot came about ten years ago to take over the pub. His uncle had run it for years, but it went out of the family after the war. Never prospered much after that. More had worked in the hotel trade in London—a local lad but gone so long he was a stranger when he came back. People would say he'd been educated above himself."

"Is that all they say about him?" Poole asked. "What about his, er, private life?"

"People here expect publicans to act daft," Davies said. "Some joked about him being a bit of a nance, but that's just pub talk. No one really cared." Davies methodically decanted tea for them and fussed with the crockery. He continued, "Now, Marie Winter—she's a local lass right through. Grew up here with her mum, stayed around, local comprehensive school, dyed–in–the–wool villager. Pretty enough, and bright, but she's just Charlotte Winter's girl."

"Her father?" Poole asked. He was cautious in asking direct questions and wondered how police here ever got answers, with all the circumlocutious circumspection required.

"Oh, yes," Davies said. "Something of a mystery. Charlotte—Mrs. Winter—is a widow. Or no husband in evidence. She's French, you know. Came to the village with Marie as an infant. Worked a bit at the pub—a housekeeper. The story got about that she'd lost her husband when Marie was born and moved here from someplace in the north. She's worked in one of the Trusthouse places in Bicester since—goes back and forth in her funny little car, one of those Citroens made up like a whacking great pram."

Poole and Amanda left the policemen, promising to report to them and aid in assessing the Ashpole gun collection. Light was fading as they drove to Bedford, and Poole marveled at how empty the highway seemed. Day ended in Britain, it seemed, with first dark, as if the culture were still firmly attached to the natural rhythms of sun and stars. He vaguely missed the halogen–lighted artificial day of U.S. urban night, when cities and highways pulsed with flashing urgency. Then he decided he didn't miss it at all.

The hospital stood on the edge of the city, small Georgian buildings and one garishly colored main building that looked as if constructed by a witless giant from a Lego set. Britain's newer architecture seemed to Poole shabby, tasteless and insubstantial, especially as it was juxtaposed with the nobilities of the past.

The interior was like a U.S. hospital, but instead of hotel–like rooms, the patients were mainly in wards. A nurse–supervisor who looked to Poole like a nun led them upstairs to a curtained cubicle where Robin Heyward lay inert and heavily swathed. A uniformed policewoman checked their identification and spoke in a low, concerned voice: "The doctors were in an hour ago. No change and no prognosis for change. They say we can only wait, in the case of a coma after severe trauma."

Heyward was a homunculus attached to a bulky breathing apparatus, a heartbeat monitor, an intravenous feeding tube. In the white surf of sheets and pillows, he was grey and shrunken. The policewoman produced Heyward's effects when Poole asked about them. "It's all been catalogued and examined," she said. "Forensics went over them yesterday."

The plastic bag held random objects and fetishes carried by adult males—keys, papers, a battered wallet, pens, a cheap digital watch. Poole held up one odd thing and said, "What's this?"

The policewoman consulted a computer list. "They've only

marked it as 'velvet' here, with a query: 'lining material?'"

Poole and Amanda examined it under a small high–intensity lamp on the table at the end of the ward. In his palm lay a rough oval of stiffened cloth, greenish–yellow, discolored and torn at the edges.

"Where was this found?" Amanda asked.

"The forensics man was on about that, too," the policewoman said. "He said it was found in an inside jacket pocket—not part of the jacket."

"Curiouser and curiouser," Amanda said. "What do you make of it, Richard?"

"I'd say…" he pored at it with one finger to flatten it. "It fits inside something, like—"

"A small, oval box!" Amanda said.

"Did your King George the Whatsis box have a lining?"

"I don't know, and I doubt anyone would remember. Haskell, the old curator, died a dozen years ago. But if someone had used the box for, oh, jewelry or trinkets, it might well have been lined once."

"It didn't have anything inside it, did it?"

"Surely not. It had been on display for years, and Haskell wouldn't have let anything slip past his eagle eye."

They pondered the little tongue of cloth. It was as mute as Heyward, lying in his bed.

They left the hospital, and Poole breathed in the night air greedily. The pungent, aseptic hospital odor he always associated with mortality, and he felt reinvigorated, reprieved in the balmy night.

As Amanda swung the Ford from the parking lot, a magpie started from the verge of the pavement and swirled upward in a lightning–flash of black–and–white plumage. Poole had never seen a magpie before, but he knew what it was. Magpies—inveterate collectors who stole to fill their nests with everything and anything, gaudy bits of cloth, useless trinkets. He seemed to have a case of magpies—a whole flock—on his hands.

At the end of the long hospital drive, Amanda slowed to pass through a set of grand gates like those around Ashpole Manor. As she downshifted and nosed onto the highway, Poole saw a figure detach itself from thick shadow by the gate, moving away from them. It was a boy or small man, running along the brick wall that extended from the gate. Poole saw a flash of white as the figure looked back.

"Hold it," he said urgently.

He started to open his door then realized he was confined to a stiff–legged hop and cursed. "Go that way," he said.

She swung the car left, and the figure broke into an all–out run, transecting the headlights as he crossed the highway. He disappeared for a second then reappeared behind a low mass of yew hedge. The figure was in flickering, erratic motion like a bit of old movie film or a dancer framed in stroboscopic light.

As Amanda accelerated, he said, "Use your brights."

"Brights?"

"Oh, damn it—your…whatever…high beams."

When she flipped the headlights, the scene seemed to enlarge. The man, dressed in a windbreaker and corduroy slacks, threw up one hand to shield his eyes and abruptly disappeared. They stopped where he had been, and Poole realized that he had fallen or dived to the ground. An iron fence stood beyond the road. They had the runner boxed.

Then Poole saw the man on his feet a dozen feet away, lunging toward a small car nosed into a clump of shrubbery.

"The car—" he cried, "cut it off, pull in behind."

Amanda accelerated and braked behind the car, while the man flung open the driver's–side door. No—Poole adjusted his mental map—the passenger–side door. Poole opened his own door and called, "Hold it—stop where you are! Police." Did it matter if Poole impersonated a British policeman? What would they do, deport him? Should he howl, *Freeze, sucker, or you're dead meat*?

The man whirled to face them and said, "Go away, I've got a gun, I'll shoot."

Poole leaned awkwardly around his door and said, "I've got a gun too, and I'm trained to use it. Throw yours down and step forward—*now*!"

It was a frozen tableau. Poole was conscious of the empty night, his empty hands and the Ford's engine ticking over like a watch. He was also aware that Amanda was in direct line of fire. If the second swelled any larger, it would explode like a gigantic balloon.

The figure moved slowly. He stepped shakily toward them, saying, "I don't have a gun. Don't shoot me."

Amanda found a small flashlight in the glovebox and handed it to Poole, who snapped it on and leveled it across the hood.

The man walking toward them, swaying and rubber–legged, his empty hands trembling at shoulder level, was Donovan Stallings. He was smudged with dirt, his eyes rolled desperately, and he seemed to be trying to speak, to utter a single round vowel of supplication.

SCHWANN'S WAY

POOLE DROVE, WHILE Amanda sat soothing Donovan Stallings in the back seat. He had babbled formlessly for a few seconds then burst into violent sobs. Now he seemed settled in shocked stupor.

"Richard," Amanda said, "we must stop and get something into him. He's physically exhausted. We could stop at The King's Leap."

"No, no," Stallings said in a choked voice. "Please don't take me there. It's terrible. Felix died there."

Poole registered it as the voice of a man gripped by horror.

"All right," Amanda said. "There's a pub on this road, a mile or so ahead, Richard. The Blue Bull. Keep an eye open." She continued her soothing, lullaby sounds for Stallings.

In a few moments, they rounded a curve, and Poole saw inn lights. There was a primitive signboard, a blob of bovine in blue, which he pulled beneath. Amanda had Stallings out of the rear seat before Poole was around the car, and she walked him firmly toward the thatched building. Poole followed, marveling at yet another example of British wayside–inn architecture.

Each time he saw one of these low, thatched–roofed places, Poole expected an Indian–file of tiny revelers to march out singing "Heigh–ho, heigh–ho, it's off to work we go!" He held the door, and Amanda half–led, half–towed Stallings inside. Poole paused to read a sign scrawled on a bit of shirt cardboard and stuck to the door with a drawing pin :

174

LIVE MUSIC TUESDAY NITE

THE FOUR SKINS AND

OZZIE MANDIAS AND THE TRAVELERS

Poole shuddered, praying fervently it was not Tuesday. He had lost track of days in this tiny patch of the world.

A few locals inhabited the public room, with a few more wedged into a small alcove, abusing a bumper–pool game. Amanda lowered Stallings onto a red–plastic settee. More red–plastic furniture stood in clumps around the large room. Poole wondered how many naugas had died to make this place possible.

At the bar, he ordered cider for Amanda, a straight pint glass of Guinness for himself and a double vodka as a bludgeon–cure–stimulant for Stallings. The round bartender lined up the drinks, nudging the beer glass and saying "Stout fella!" Poole gazed at the array of munchies behind the bar, and his eye settled on one astounding package. He pointed, saying, "And a package of Hedgehog Crisps." He would find out what these things were by force–feeding them to Stallings.

As he set down the drinks on a teetery round table, Amanda said, "He insists he doesn't want food, but he looks positively awful."

Poole showed Amanda the crisp package, and she tittered at the label. "They're not *made of* hedgehogs, silly! It's just an advertising ploy." Poole was vaguely disappointed. He tried one, finding it only another greasy chip, with a spicy flavor.

Stallings lifted the vodka in a palsied hand and drank off half. Poole decided he would not only look awful but would be unconscious directly. Stallings looked to Poole like a drawing from an edition of *Robinson Crusoe*, in the parts before Crusoe learns to forage properly.

Slowly, Amanda led Stallings from half–articulated whimpers to a kind of coherence. He began his story:

"I found a gun. In a case of Felix's. Along with papers he was editing—those scrawls of Sir Alfred's. I was up at the Gothick Temple, working on those things. Then I found a bullet...a how–do–you say?"

"A cartridge casing?" Poole asked.

"Yes—that's it. In the pocket of my old jacket. I couldn't understand how it came there. For a bit, I thought I was losing my mind, had amnesia or was somehow doing things I didn't know about. Jekyll and Hyde—that kind of thing. Robin..."

He sat staring then shuddered and drank off the other half of the vodka.

"Robin," he said dreamily. "I killed him."

"There, there," Amanda said, "now, now. He'll be all right." Stallings grabbed her wrist, and she winced visibly.

"*Is* he? Yes—you were at the hospital tonight. How is he? Did he forgive me?"

"He's had a nasty time of it, Donovan." Amanda freed her hand and rubbed it. "But the doctors are sure he'll recover."

Stallings slumped on the squeaky plastic. "Thank God—I never meant to hit him. Not like that. But...I was frightened. It was dark and...sinister at the Temple. It's silly—girlish—but I hate the dark and the wind on that hilltop. Someone was playing tricks. That bastard Robin. But I didn't know, then. I thought it was...Felix's killer. Banging on the windows. Cutting off the mains. The mains box was outside by the door, and twice someone came by and loosened the fuses.

"And the papers I had—Sir Alfred's wartime diaries were mixed up in them, and I started reading bits. Full of horrible things, reports of atrocities. The old man was a sadist. Newspaper cuttings of death–camp discoveries. Pictures. God—the ugly pictures of endless stacks of bodies! Can I have another drink?"

Poole fetched a single vodka, evading the bartender's question about association football. Should he ask how the Oakland Raiders would do this year?

"Marie," Stallings said, as he picked up the glass. "I would have gone mad if it hadn't been for her. Called and kept me on the mark. Then the phone went out. So I went to the farm office and called her to come. But I was so afraid then. We used to meet up at the Chinese Dairy. So I told her to come there and bring the snuffbox. I knew it had something to do with it all."

"The snuffbox?" Poole said. "How in God's name did *she* get it? Did she steal it from the Manor?"

"You don't know anything," said Stallings, bitterly. He drained the vodka glass. "You two stumble around without any idea what's what. You want to know everything, but it's better you don't find out. I know—and look at me! I found out I could murder people. Just like that." He tried to snap his fingers, but nothing happened. He stared dully at his crooked fingers as if they, too, had betrayed him.

"You went to the Chinese Dairy?" Amanda prompted.

"Yes. We used to meet there, when she had days off. She didn't want me hanging around The King's Leap. She said the butcher's boy always had an eye on her and would rag her about her high-toned boy friend. "

"Butcher's boy?" Poole said.

"That's what she called More. He was always coming over her about her background, and she got back at him. I don't know exactly what she meant." Stallings seemed listless and sleepy.

"She brought the snuffbox," Poole said.

"What? Oh—yes. That's what started it. I don't know why. I went up to the Dairy, being very sure no one saw me. She came along a few minutes later. She'd slip up from the village by cutting along through the park, around the lakes. She didn't poke fun when she saw how frightened I was. She was always understanding…

"We were talking, and she was trying to explain to me about the snuffbox, when Robin burst in. That bastard. How could a friend do that? He *was* my friend, I swear it. He said he'd seen Marie and followed her. He knew we met at the Dairy, anyhow. So he started in about how everyone was looking for me, how they thought I had gone missing because I knew about Felix's death. Or Drus's. He said nasty things to Marie. He started raving about all the tricks he'd played on me—cutting off the lights, making noises around the Temple, fiddling with the telephone. He had a good laugh at how scared I looked. Then he saw the snuffbox—Marie was holding it. She'd taken out the lining to show me the writing in it. Robin grabbed the snuffbox and lining and shoved them in his pocket. He said Marie had stolen it, and he'd have her arrested. God—"

Stallings glanced around at the bar, but Amanda said, "You don't need anything more to drink. You need rest and a doctor."

"Wait," he said, "you almost know. All I can tell. So—I grabbed Robin, to get the box back. He was always stronger than me, he'd push me around like a puppy. But I was very angry. I shoved him, and he fell, against that awful statuary propped up there. I saw that he was…unconscious. I thought he'd come around again, so I took the box back and found a bit of rope. I don't know why I tied him up. Marie was crying and saying he was badly hurt, but I thought he'd…come around and follow us again. I just wanted a fair start, for once. Everyone's always run me down and c–c–caught me and made f–f–fun…"

Poole was shocked when Stallings" stammer returned—*that* was what had been missing, had made his voice seem as flat and affectless as a bad long–distance call.

Stallings flushed. He gnawed his lip then continued: "I m–made Marie go back to the village. I r–r–ran away. I always run away. I went to a dreadful hotel in Steeple Amsted at f–f–first, then I ran

178

out of m–money. Robin had said I w–wouldn't know what to d–d–do with a proper girl. He called me the g–g–Gloucestershire Gelding. But I loved Marie. I do love Marie. She'll h–h–help me." He lowered his head to the Formica tabletop. Then he straightened and said, "I had to leave Steeple Amsted. I t–tried to find out about Robin at the h–h–h...at that place. Then I saw you coming out. I don't know how long I was in the rough. There weren't any n–n–nights and days there."

He collapsed heavily back and lolled sideways. As Poole and Amanda propped Stallings and stood him up, the barkeep waddled across the room.

"Your mate been drinking elsewhere?" he asked. "He didn't come over pissed here, you know." Several people bulged from the poolroom to gape. Amanda soothed the publican, and with effort and a strain on Poole's wobbly leg, they heaved Stallings into the Escort's back seat.

"I'll see he's tucked in at Ashpole," Amanda said, "and have a doctor up in the morning. He needs a thorough exam and bed rest. Do you believe his story?"

Poole grunted. "Such as it is. But either he doesn't know a lot of things, or he can't put them together for us. You need to call Griffiths right away and let him know our wandering boy has returned."

Poole waited at The King's Leap before morning opening. He sat in the Ford on the verge of the village green and contemplated the scene. It was a beautifully clear, golden morning, with shafts of light streaming through the trees, lying flat on the green, sparkling in little gemlets on the duckpond's surface. He watched the front door of the pub, the stone lock–up in one corner of his vision. The stone jail was a sullen and (now) sinister bit in the landscape, a *memento mori*, suggesting that sin was present in the most idyllic scene: *I too was in Arcadia.* Perhaps that was why the village elders had placed it there—as a reminder against crime and folly. Poole wished decency had overmastered remorselessness. *Probably better than a pillory, at any rate*, he thought.

Then he saw Marie Winter crossing the green, head down, scarf tied tight, hands in her windbreaker pockets. The summer breeze whipped her light skirt, and Poole appreciated her legs. He caught himself thinking that perhaps she *was* too good—too much woman —for a pup like Stallings. Getting out of the car, he banged his bad ankle, which he chalked up as retribution for his uncharitable idea.

Marie started when he hailed her. One hand flew up as if to protect her face.

He asked to speak with her, and she led him around the rambling inn to the kitchen, a cramped, bright room of white walls, brick fireplace and a battery of modern stainless steel equipment. Marie puttered nervously while Poole sat in a battered captain's chair next to an open window, where bees thrummed energetically around a flowering vine.

"We have Donovan safe and sound at Ashpole." Marie, standing with her back to him, stiffened. "We fished him out of the brush up near the hospital. He looks like a starved rat, but I don't think he's badly damaged. "

Marie whirled. She held a long–bladed fillet knife. Her knuckles were white from strain, and she stared wildly at Poole.

"How did you...who found him?"

"Amanda—Ms. Evans—and I stumbled across him. He was in a bad way."

Marie tottered and collapsed into another scarred chair. The knife slipped from her grasp and slithered mechanically across the floor, as alive as the fish it was designed to hew.

Poole picked it up, idly tested its blade on his thumb and noted a small bubble of blood where he was cut. A curious old piece of culinary hardware with a fancy stag–horn handle, whose blade had been so long and carefully sharpened as to be pared to something halfway between a scimitar and a razor. He shivered as he set it on the butcher block, out of Marie's reach.

She wept soundlessly, and Poole took out his notebook and fiddled with it. In a moment, she wiped at her face with a kitchen towel and looked straight at him.

"Sorry. I've been so…worried. I hadn't heard from Donovan in three days. I thought he had done something…awful. To himself. He was almost off his head when he called last."

"Is he capable of doing something awful to someone else? I mean, has he been this way before?"

She glared at Poole. "You don't know much about him. Or me. Donovan is the kindest, gentlest man… But this business has upset him. And Robin mixed in to make it worse. That ragging and horseplay. No one took Donovan seriously. They treat him like a schoolboy. That's why he's so keen to work on those old papers. He says it will show people he has something in his head."

She looked self-controlled now, older than her years. Poole said, "He told us about the snuffbox and Robin breaking in on you at the Chinese Dairy. But I need you to fill in the whys and wherefores."

When she hesitated, he said, "It's going to come out. I'm a half-jump ahead of the police. If you tell me, I can talk with Griffiths. It may help you both."

"It's not the police who worry me. I can handle that. It's how many people will be hurt by all this…nonsense."

"Two murders and several bouts of serious mayhem don't seem in the realm of nonsense."

"That's foolish men fighting over territory. I don't give a bloody damn if they all do each other in—so long as they leave us out of it."

"The snuffbox," Poole pressed. "What's it have to do with you?"

"Everything and nothing. It was given me, if that's what you mean. I wouldn't steal such a silly thing, even if I knew how. I thought it was a...sentimental gift. A present. Stupid of me to believe he could think enough about me to give me a present."

She no longer looked beautiful and controlled. She twisted the kitchen towel in her hands and her face was distorted by long–suppressed rage.

"Who gave it to you?"

Marie looked up at him, her grey eyes steady and deep.

"Why—my father. I thought you knew."

"Your father? Who..."

She wiped at her face again, looking worn and abruptly aged.

"My father was Jan Drus. Or Dros. Or Ian Decker. Or any of a half–dozen other names."

"When did he give you the snuffbox?"

"I don't suppose 'give' is the right word. He left it for me. A fine legacy or payment or bribe. Maybe a payoff to make up for seeing that he hanged himself."

"You saw him before he went to the dovecote?"

"I met him there. He called me here—he'd never try me at home, with Mother there. He said to meet him at the Manor, that he had to talk with me. At first, I couldn't believe it was him. I hadn't heard his voice in a half–dozen years. I saw my father a grand total of perhaps six times when I was growing up." She glared at Poole. "And I damn well didn't want to see him again. He insisted he would make it up to Mum and me. He said he had a big job on but that when he finished it, he was coming back to England to stay. Did you have a father?"

"Sure," Poole said.

"Well, you're right lucky. I grew up without one, not knowing what I was missing until he'd turn up for a day or two and tip the world upside down. And then Mum having to explain to me when I was leaving school what 'illegitimate' really means. Nobody here bothered enough about me to call me somebody's lost get, a right little bastard. It might have been better if they had."

She shook her head like a dog shedding water.

"It doesn't matter a damn," she sighed. "I just want you to know why I was such a bloody fool. When I saw him hanged there, I picked up the snuffbox from the floor of that place and ran. He'd met me there, and he was all…mysterious. Like a spy or something, which is what I always remember about him. Looking around like a ferret. He told me he had a memento. That's the word he used. He wanted to talk with me about Mum. But he had to fetch something inside that pigeon house, and he told me to stand there and keep an eye out. He said he wasn't supposed to be on the Manor grounds— or even in England. He went inside, and I stood there feeling a right wally. Like someone playing a kid's game. Then I heard noises inside, and I didn't know what to do." She shivered.

"Then I finally pushed the door open and went in. God—he was hanging there and swinging around on that ladder like a toy. I knew he was dead. And that silver box was on the floor in all the dung and feathers. I grabbed it and ran all the way across the park."

Marie rose and walked to the range. She turned and continued quietly, "My mother had forbidden me to see or talk to him. Those last times I heard from him, it was on the phone—secret. He seemed to enjoy that. I know he was a…criminal, a thief. I don't know what else. I didn't want to find out. And I didn't want others to know. I don't think Mum could stand it if the whole village was twittering about Mrs. Winter's fancy man found dead at the Manor, probably did himself in, and no wonder, with that right bitch and her snot–nosed daughter. You must know the kind of thing."

"Why did you think the box was important?"

"After a few days, I told Donovan. I showed him the box, and he was very excited. He found the writing in it—engraving under the lining. Just a few words and numbers. They meant nothing to me, but Donovan started in about Sir Alfred's papers and Felix and the war. Always the rotten war. It's all you men think about—fighting and killing and all the horrible things you can do to people."

"Wait a minute—Donovan connected the box with Sir Alfred's papers?"

"I didn't understand. He said the writing on the box had to do with missions Sir Alfred directed or knew about. That the words there had to do with the things in the diaries. I didn't see how it connected, either."

Poole stared out the window. A small, cheerful bird hopped pertly alongside a hedge in the back of the garden. Banks of bright flowers swayed lightly in the breeze. He tried to shake the darkness from his mind.

"I have to go back to Donovan, and then I'll talk with you again," he said. Then the kitchen door banged open, and Eliot More strode in. He glanced at Poole and then at Marie.

"Ah, now I see why the bar has been left neglected," he said. "You have an important social engagement here in the scullery. Stupid of me not to guess it. I was under the foolish impression you were here to work for me."

As Poole stood, More beamed at him. "A first customer of the day—but most enter by the front door. Mr...er, Poole, isn't it? If you can let me have the use of my employee here, we'll see if this is a functioning public house or a sanctuary for idle chatterers."

Marie glared at More, tugged on a bar apron and exited. Poole rose and made for the door. More stopped him with: "Still busy asking impertinent questions, eh? Between you and the coppers, it isn't worth trying for a day's honest work."

Poole smiled. "I'll be back to try your best bitter again. We'll have a chat, and I can devote my attention entirely to you."

More simpered, "Oh, goody—and I thought you were wasting your charms on barmaids only. Lucky, lucky me!"

✧

After the last meeting, Poole found Amanda, looking harried and worn, but—he thought—still damned good. He thought fleetingly of chucking the whole mess, Telexing a resignation to Harvey Lewis and whisking Amanda to Tahiti with him. Poole stared at his open notebook and the scrawls therein—about as sensible as a Serbo–Croatian doctor's prescription pad. In the margin he had doodled some of his exasperation with the English and their language, after a fit of map–reading. He had invented names for hypothetical English villages: *Dagwood Bumstead, Little Richard, Belching, Clotpoll, Godfrey Daniel, Lesser Evol* and *Runcible*. He further envisioned writing a AAA tour guide for a daytrip on such a route.

Sighing, he thrust the notebook back into his jacket. Amanda was settled in a chair opposite him, a glass in her hand. They relaxed under the vast murals of the main hall, and Poole felt he had to keep hail an eye on the trains of unclad maidens racing over the ancient plaster thirty feet overhead.

"Pink gin," Amanda said, raising her glass. "Won't you join? No? Well, cheers to you, mate. I can't do without it today."

"A hard one, huh?"

"Toward the end of every conference, a point is reached where everyone and everything collapses in unison. That was today. I'm only sorry you've missed so many meetings."

Poole shook his head. "I don't know which is the bigger ordeal —suffering through those meetings or dealing with disoriented, potentially maniacal murder suspects. Either is like walking through that blasted maze again—with a blindfold on and an anvil tied around my neck."

Amanda drained her glass and set it on a table. "That reminds me: I meant to show you Ashpole's *other* maze. Well, we're right here, and you can try it out. Come along."

Poole limped grumbling after her. She guided him a few steps into the center of the rotunda and said, "This is a highly civilized maze for gentle lords and ladies—no tramping on nasty grass in all weathers. Here we are."

Poole stared around. "Some kind of mind–puzzle?"

"Look at your feet, silly."

He stared at the polished marble tiles, realizing that there was no pattern of interlocking squares here but a sweeping spiral of black and white blocks. "Follow the white," Amanda said.

Poole followed a huge circle or arc, a diagrammatic maze. "From up in the lantern you can puzzle it out," she said, "but from ground level you must walk your way through. Have a go."

Linking her arm in his, she started him. "Now—continue your fascinating ruminations or narrative, and we'll have our exercise, too. It's what the old aristocrats did when they weren't up to a hike in the long gallery upstairs."

"All right—I'll satisfy this perverse whim, but you have to listen through it all. I think I've figured most of it, but maybe you can fill in the holes.

"I figure it this way: Jan Drus wasn't murdered. Nor did he kill himself. Deliberately. He had a very bad accident. He slipped off the rung on that rotating ladder–gadget, his tie wedged itself in the crevice between the rung and axle, and he strangled. Simplicity itself."

Poole summarized Marie Winter's story for Amanda and fended off obvious questions.

"He was hung up on the old school, and then he literally hung himself by the old school tie. I spoke with Griffiths, and he cautiously bought the idea. He said the tie came from a place called Crossgates—the school Sir Alfred sent him to. Drus was fanatically proud of his English background—the school especially. Griffiths and I went over the dovecote this afternoon with the head forensics man. As Reger and Edwards said, there's a mark on the wall, and

I'm betting it's silver from the snuffbox. The forensics team didn't see it. It was across the arc from Drus's body. I think the axle must have swung him pretty violently around when he struggled. And the mark was mixed in with all that pigeon–shit. Excuse me. Guano. But Griffiths' lab boys spotted it right away when we told them what to look for. He must have reached into a pigeon–hole, where the box was stashed, over–balanced and fallen. Maybe he wouldn't let go of the box to save himself. It struck the wall, anyhow. Then he dropped, strangled and finally let it go. Then Marie came in and found it at his feet."

Amanda pushed against him sharply. "No cheating," she said. "Stick to the white path, inside the black."

"Okay, okay. I thought I saw a shortcut. Anyhow, poor Marie stood there waiting for a mysterious surprise from long–lost Daddy —and boy, did she get it. She comes in and finds him with his tongue out a yard and black as your hat. But she did take the snuffbox, thinking it was her present. Actually, I think he was going —"

"—to give her the *bracelet*," Amanda said.

"No shortcuts. Let me tell the story, and you concentrate on our trajectory. Yes—the bauble in his pocket. Now it gets interesting.

I traced the bracelet. Drus must have gotten it from Felix. Did I tell you Marcia Draper has another bracelet of the same type? I *knew* I'd seen it somewhere, but it took me a couple of days to remember. She got it from *Felix*. He told her it came from a jeweler in Aylesbury, and Griffiths ran him down. And—get this—not only did he sell Felix *two* bracelets a couple of months ago, he also did a job of engraving for him. Yeh—the snuffbox. Griffiths had to threaten it out of him, because he knew the piece was an antique and thought it was hot. When we turn up the box itself, we'll have him identify it."

"Donovan can produce the snuffbox," Amanda said. "I talked

with him this noon, after the doctor okayed him. He left it at the hotel where he stayed when he ran off. Buried in a potted palm's jar in the lobby, he says. In Steeple Amsted!"

"Ah—what else did you prise out of Stallings? How coherent is he?"

"I'll give you details later. But he seemed clear–headed. His stammer was certainly back in full force—odd, that. He referred to the snuffbox as his Holy Grail. He doesn't understand the message, but he says it is from Sir Alfred's wartime diaries. He's not sure why it would be important to either Drus or Felix. You may have to quiz Sir Leicester."

"Oh, bravo," Poole said.

"What? Oh—you've solved it!" They stood at the center of the serpentine path, and Amanda hugged Poole impulsively.

Poole looked up at the rotunda, noting the activity most frequently depicted in the ocean of mural—highly athletic foreplay. He squeezed Amanda back and nodded upward.

"That suggest anything of interest?"

She craned her neck. "Yes—but I've never had the weight or speed for Rugby football."

Laughing, they strolled boldly across the inhibiting circles of the maze toward the staff wing of Ashpole Manor.

At breakfast, members and staff were equally haggard. Poole waved to Marcia Draper, who looked flustered and smiled tentatively. Marian Halley returned his smile with a scowl. Reger and Edwards huddled in a corner banquette looking morose and chastened.

Amanda arrived a few discreet minutes after Poole, gathering her eggs and streaky bacon and a tall glass of reddish fluid.

"Carrot," she said. "And no remarks about seeing in the dark or any of that rubbish."

"I've got a lot on the agenda," Poole said as he polished off his own breakfast, "and there's—what?—two more days of the conference?"

"Yes." She looked away sharply.

"Hey—are you into full grumpy mode this morning?"

She slammed her empty juice glass down hard enough to make the monogrammed silver jump and sing. She glared at Poole.

"For a very bright man, you can be thick as a bobby's boot! Yes, the bloody conference ends in two days—and you'll pack your luggage and be off for Texas or Milwaukee or Ohio or wherever it is you go."

"Oh," Poole said.

"Yes, *oh*." She abruptly burst into tears, turning sharply away.

"Forgive me for being obtuse. It's this damned murder. I'm still a hundred and ten percent caught up in it."

Amanda dabbed at her face with the linen napkin and shook her head.

"No—it's my fault. I'm making something out of nothing."

"Aw, come on, don't go the other way on me."

"I can't go on pretending things that are only my own fantasies," she said in a low, hard voice. "Let me go on. I'm not the sort of giddy girl to be swept off her feet, and you're not precisely a dashing cavalier—or even a cowboy hero. I suppose everyone thinks ahead a bit. Even when we're supposed to be so finely tuned to the here–and–now. I just want to say that I'm not trying on a spot of emotional blackmail, however much it may seem so."

When he started to speak, she said, "Just go on with the agenda you're making, please. Tell me what to do next."

"Okay—but this isn't a closed conversation. I've got to see Sir Leicester today. Can you get him to sit still for a half–hour? He's tangled up in all this—through the memory of his dear old dad and in his own right. Griffiths will call back about the snuffbox and the jeweler, to let me know if he's sweated more out of him. Then we've got to tie the message on the snuffbox with the papers Donovan was editing. It looks as if various bits of information were trading hands, which may be the key to this confusion. Could you interpose your beautiful body with Sir Leicester and stand by to receive data from Griffiths?"

Amanda smiled brightly again, with only a little strain left in her face. "All right—but I expect a complete debriefing this evening."

Poole watched her go, chewed his lip and wished for his old pipe. "This," he said to himself in a Basil Rathbone voice, "is a half–pipe problem, Watson, and I've gone and lost my half–pipe."

Walking to the nearest tall window, he looked out at the immaculate landscape, now swathed in mild, slow rain. Everything seemed gauzed and miniaturized, as if the eighteenth–century toy kingdom were shrinking to the span of a man's hand. If only he could pick it up and carry it home with him, complete with Amanda Evans.

He sighed and turned away to find Sir Leicester Harcourt standing behind him, rolling a cosh–sized cigar in his fingers. He did not look especially happy to be examining Richard Poole at close quarters again.

In the old offices at the rear of the house, Sir Leicester showed Poole the gun cabinet. "As you see, I've rid myself of the lot. Don't know why I persisted in keeping them. Most were collected during the war. My father had a small mania about firearms. Bought them from American airmen, soldiers back from Europe, and so on. I found a fellow down in Portsmouth who keeps a museum of some sort—war memorabilia. He took the lot away, and I suppose he won't turn them loose to gangsters. For a moment, I thought I'd have them taken out to the meadow and buried under a slab next to the Lancaster's base. Seemed a bit dramatic or morbid, however."

He sat in a battered swivel chair, and Poole found a padded

armchair even less civil in aspect. Sir Leicester offered him brandy from a small bottle. When Poole declined, the old man measured himself a dose.

"Sir Leicester: I must ask about the papers which passed from Felix Schwann to Donovan Stallings. And about their contents. You, of course, aren't compelled to answer. But I am trying very hard to maintain the interests of TransAtlas here at the Cavendar Institute."

"And to manage the news of these events, I presume."

"Let's call part of my job disaster–containment. We have important staff members from many TransAtlas holdings here. We don't want a scandal that will taint many areas of the corporation."

"I understand. I have had several too–lengthy chats with Harvey Lewis in the past week. Nevertheless, you must acknowledge, Mr. Poole, that my paramount interest is in seeing that the Cavendar Institute does not come off as a scapegoat or target in your efforts to keep your particular sepulcher tidily whitewashed. Agreed?"

"Absolutely," Poole said, crossing fingers and toes and hoping the Pinocchio Effect was inoperative in rural England.

"The newspapers have been restrained and cautious thus far. No sensation–rag has seized on the, er, events. A few grey paragraphs in the *Times* and *Telegraph*, some fumbling chat in the Bucks papers. No News at Six or tits–and–bums enquiries. Nothing here nearly sexy enough for real news interests." Sir Leicester swirled his brandy and drank it off.

"About the papers?" Poole nudged.

"The literary remains of Sir Alfred. Of no real interest to anyone save genealogists, local historians and a few monomaniacs digging for nuggets about wartime intelligence. I put Schwann on the task largely to keep dog–scholars from seeking access to the papers. I thought a reasonably factual introduction to my father's tome would buy them off."

"There was nothing of a…secret nature to the papers? Nothing that could be peddled to the Eastern Bloc, for example?"

Sir Leicester stared at Poole with an expression that might have meant either annoyance or monumental indifference.

"No. Nothing 'classified,' as you people say. There were… embarrassing passages. My father should never have written down most of what's in the diaries—and if I had known they were with the papers, I would have culled them before letting someone like Schwann delve into them. My father was of a deeply histrionic bent. The war was, for him, a great history play, a chronicle in which he received his starring role. Never mind that he was actually a walk-on, a spear-carrier. Do you know the prologue to *Henry Five*? My father not only conned it by heart and recited it on every occasion. He deeply believed it all."

Sir Leicester poured another shot of brandy, saying, "My quack has been trying to wean me from this for twenty years, but he's a rascally Methodist."

"What kind of embarrassment are we talking here? Purely personal? Something damaging to the Institute? To the government?"

"You won't badger me into specifics. I think there are possibilities of all three." Without bothering to exhibit tact, he pulled out a pocket watch and read it. "I can't spend a day on ancient history, but I can tell you this: my father was in command or acted as liaison for covert operations in Eastern Europe before Overlord. There were…blunders of various sizes and shapes. War is mostly chance and mischance, and my father was never a lucky man. He lacked the grace to be lucky."

Sir Leicester swiveled his chair to look out the small window that opened to the kitchen garden and shrugged, as if to himself.

"It's been several hundred years since aristocrats were fit to lead wars. It's now the province of shopkeepers and logistics experts and quartermasters. The last time thick–headed gentry led the army, someone said, 'It's magnificent, but it's not war.' So, in my father's tiny slice of the Big War, things went badly. There were unfortunate decisions about fascists and communists as our allies and enemies. The Balkans—the Slavic edgelands—is a tangled part of the world. Concisely: there were several mass executions authorized by my father's command—or at least tacitly condoned. Russian troops— regular and irregular—met with partisan coalitions in my father's oversight. It was after Stalingrad, and the Russians were in no mood for gentle negotiation and investigation."

"How did Karl Drus fit into this?"

"He was our man on the ground. My father trusted him, and he was more a servant than a courier at times. I think my father had him cast as the perfect knight's faithful squire. But he also had masters on the Kremlin side. I imagine his part in the unfortunate actions marked him after the war. While we may convene hoards of enquiry and offer social chastisement for old soldiers proved wrong, the Russians are much more...direct in their handling. I have assumed that Karl was on a list and was tracked down in the '50s. The rest is silence. The grave's a fine and private place. And so on."

"You're saying that Sir Alfred's diaries contain personal memoirs of...what? Atrocities? A massacre?"

Sir Leicester grimaced and drained his glass. "That's precisely why I won't be precise. To reduce it to those terms is the kind of penny–dreadful 'history' I won't see broadcast. I have no special interest in defending my father. His work and life are their own testimonials. Let's say I will put a stop to niggling revisionism, as far as legends are concerned. Now—I must attend to my duties."

Poole reluctantly stood as Sir Leicester rose. He hesitated and then said, "I don't mean to push you, Sir Leicester, but in the investigations into the deaths of Drus and Schwann, you aren't ruled out as a suspect. I say that as a statement of fact, The police must consider your presence here—as an individual—as they consider anyone else's."

Sir Leicester straightened painfully and walked past Poole, leaving him to follow. He said, "I am an old admirer of British law and justice, Mr. Poole. I am confident the police will see that both law and justice are observed and completed. Now, you must excuse a hurried, harried old man…"

He walked down the corridor briskly, his back straightening and stride lengthening as he moved toward the conference rooms. Poole felt in the presence of a not–so–toothless lion and repressed an atavistic urge to tug his forelock at Sir Leicester's retreating figure.

Amanda Evans snatched moments from her schedule at tea–time, and Poole found himself sitting across from her in the center of the splendid orangery designed by William Kent and completed by Humphrey Repton, under a canopy of giant ferns, orange trees, palms and bundles of exotic flowers and fruits. The air was dense and humid, somehow reminding Poole of his Midwest, tweaking a little pang of nostalgia for heat and humidity, the scent of foliage or forage heavy in summer air.

She rummaged in her briefcase–sized purse and handed Poole a sheaf of notes on rumpled paper. "Here. I sat down and scribbled everything I could recall from talking with Donovan. And everything we got last night. I imagine you're going giddy from this unanchored data."

Amanda poured tea and distributed exotic, slightly poisonous–looking cakes, while Poole riffled the notes. He ran his fingers through his thin hair, wondering how many follicles had died on this trip.

"To sum up," Amanda said, buttering a scone with fierce concentration, "we can be sure Donovan was an innocent. He's fascinated with Sir Alfred and, to a degree, with Felix. He's mostly a cipher in the whole affair. He compounded confusion, but without criminal intent."

"I'll still need to talk with him," Poole sighed. "I wish your white lie about Robin Heyward was true—he could answer some questions if he'd drop the Sleeping Beauty act."

"Oho—your wish is my command. I forgot—C.I.D. called an hour ago. Robin is awake and talking. Griffiths sent a stenographer and an assistant to question him. Griffiths will see you tonight. He feels you both should follow up with Robin."

"Heyward just popped out of his coma?"

"Indeed. The medicos said he might, and he came out with a ferocious headache, hunger and much wrath for Donovan. He recalls things clearly, including bashing his skull on the bust of Minerva or whoever. Griffiths hopes to talk him out of pressing charges, but Robin is mightily aggrieved."

"Good—he can repent at leisure, and we'll make sure he corroborates Donovan's tale. He can't add much, except to explain the malice he seems to have vented on Stallings and Marie."

"So," Amanda said, "where do we go next?"

"The big puzzle is Felix: who killed him and why? If Drus's demise was pure happenstance, we have no connection to Felix. Who had a motive to kill him? And the opportunity at the lock-up? Who would, er, mutilate him?"

"There is a Drus connection to consider." Amanda eyed a fat bun, and Poole wondered how she could burn off calories so easily. "Remember that Schwann was a foster–uncle to Jan Drus. He must have been twenty or so when he brought young Jan out of Europe. They were something like brothers after the war, until Felix was down from University and Drus went off to his public school."

"So? Drus was dead well before Felix was killed. Are you going to pin Drus on Schwann? That would be neat, but I don't see how to prove it."

"Patience—nothing of the sort. I suggest that Felix must have left the snuffbox for Drus at the dovecote. It's the sort of place they would have known from childhood here. Perhaps Felix left messages for Jan there before. It's never locked, and no one bothers it. Felix had access to the snuffbox in the collection, and he took it to be engraved, as you've shown. But why give Drus the snuffbox? Because it has a message on it."

"Why all the charade? Why not a letter or a phone call or a microdot or whatever?"

"Glad you asked—I think I see it. I went back to the Cavendar Collection catalogue and looked at the picture and description and rummaged in our files. There is just one odd thing about it— otherwise, it's a run–of–the–mill eighteenth–century bibelot, designed as a presentation gift. King George must have handed out such things as thank–you notes for minor dignitaries who visited court or did him small favors."

"So—?"

Amanda smirked. "So, there is an *identical* snuffbox—same maker, same mark, same date—in the Hermitage collection."

Poole poured himself more tea and crinkled his forehead.

"Don't you see? The snuffbox was a message two ways: it has data engraved on it, a permanent, indelible message. But it's also a self–credentialing form of message. If you're right that Drus was going to ferry it to the Eastern Bloc, the piece itself can be verified, authenticated there by a museum curator."

Poole chewed the idea, along with a third scone. "Does that match the way Felix thought?"

"Absolutely. He loved spouting information theory, and he would have seen the device as an extension of the Cavendar Process —a sliver snuffbox becomes a messenger, with a personality of its own. Felix would have loved the notion.

"There's an irony he would have loved, too: the figure on the lid is of Hermes—Mercury. Messenger of the gods. It's like a rebus."

196

Poole said, "And you think Drus was connected with the KGB —or whatever? A high–powered spy?"

"I don't know about that kind of thing. I'd suggest he was small potatoes—but Felix may have had delusions about Drus's power and position. "

"All that Wide World has delivered suggests Jan Drus was a little operator, a freelance who mixed some profitable smuggling— jewelry, perfume, high–fashion drugs—with odd jobs for intelligence people. On *any* side. He'd probably take on an errand for Felix. Or con him, string him along."

"And let Felix think he was a big–time agent, I'll wager," Amanda said. "We've stumbled on a nest of odd birds, each one wanting to preen its feathers."

"Have you considered that this place and the Cavendar Process foster delusions of grandeur?"

"The place, yes—it was designed to convince us that human beings are demigods. But the Process is supposed to be an antidote to overweening pride."

"I wonder," Poole said. "Felix Schwann seems to have used it to spin out powerful fantasies. But that's another argument. Would you care for a stroll on the grounds until the dinner bell rings or the sunset gun is fired or whatever ceremony is on tap?"

"Mock on, mock on," Amanda said. But she took his arm, and they left the pseudo–tropical airs and graces of the orangery to walk into the natural freshness of late afternoon.

Across the largest lake, three red deer browsed near a quincunx erected in memory of Miss Abagail Hill. They saw two human beings walking with measured tread along a serpentine path between tall cedars. But the deer were not in the least curious about such unnatural creatures.

A CHAPTER TO BE SET IN GOTHIC TYPE

INSPECTOR GRIFFITHS WORE a new suit to Ashpole—or so Poole guessed. It was cut fashionably, more sporty or relaxed or human than standard policeman couture. His hair had been cut recently, and he seemed scrubbed and brisker—less focused on grey business. A policeman on a holiday, or at least on a night out.

"I feel a hundred percent better when we're in hailing distance of closing a case," he said to Poole. "My work is like fending off a debilitating disease—you go down with it, feel wholly abominable, come to a crisis and then start to come alive again. Those cases that never break make me understand the word 'terminal.'"

They sat in a small library, among ranks of dignified, buckram-bound folios and quartos and tables littered with globes and maps and astrolabes. A small double–cube room, light and airy enough not to stink of the study. They reposed in comfortable leather armchairs before a tall bookcase surmounted by a bust Amanda had identified as that of the poet William Collins, who had associations with Ashpole Manor. "Before he went mad, of course," she added.

Griffiths finished his single–malt whiskey, set his tumbler down and produced a small notebook. "It would be an immense aid if you'd help me check my findings," he said. Poole smiled and agreed.

Quickly, Griffiths summarized the Drus case, including the last forensics report confirming silver traces on the stones inside the dovecote. "We can close the Drus file unless we find startling new data. Miss Winter and her mother cooperated fully, and the intelligence services have squeezed out some tidbits on Drus's career of the past decade. He served many masters."

Poole elaborated his theories about the snuffbox, Drus and Schwann, while Griffiths strolled across the room and pressed an elaborate pushbutton near the door. In a few moments, Constable Davies appeared with Donovan Stallings, who looked less desiccated and alternated between sheepish fear and huffing bravado.

Griffiths coaxed Stallings into a chair, saying, "We need to hear more of the papers you were investigating."

"I don't th–think I should be t–t–talking without…"

"You won't need a solicitor," Griffiths said quietly. "You're helping the police with their investigations."

"I d–don't mean that. I m–meant Sir L–Leicester."

"We don't ask you to break confidences, but we feel Felix Schwann's work and Jan Drus's death are connected—and Schwann's own end."

"I would n–n–never have hurt Felix. I l–liked him. I mean, I d–d–didn't hate him."

"Yes, yes. We are not accusing you or trying to trap you into incriminating yourself, Mr. Stallings. You described the message on the snuffbox as from Sir Alfred's papers. Was it in code?" Griffiths handed Poole his notebook, open to a page headed *Written in snuffbox*. Poole read it as Griffiths continued his quiet interrogation :

7–8–43 . 750 Rs . 550 Ps

30 0 . 2.5 K. W. Pasio

9–8–43 . Genl Kurkowska . XVII

ART . 0 K.D. witness

"Our Aylesbury jeweler said he worked from a handwritten note Schwann gave him. He was told to follow it exactly, though he has no idea what it means. I presume you do."

Stallings shook his head and said, "It's not exactly a c–code. More shorthand. Sir Allred used a l–l–lot of it in his journals. Dates and p–places. I worked it out, because there were entries where he s–spelt it out, too. This m–means something about a b–b–battle where 750 Russians and 550 partisans were k–killed. Plus 30 women. Or m–maybe thirty partisans were w–women. You s–see the dates—August seven and nine, nineteen forty–three."

"What's the other?" Poole asked.

"A p–p–place. A little village in R–Rumania. Here…" Crossing the room to a big map of Europe, Stallings traced a finger across the eastern regions. "On t–two days, there was f–f–fighting. The R–Russians captured a g–garrison and a village. P–Pasio. As far as S–Sir Alfred's notes t–t–tell, a regular Russian d–d–division showed up, and there was some k–kind of truce. The p–partisans and R–R–Russian irregulars were k–killed. That meant a l–lot of the villagers, also."

"What's this about a general?" Griffiths asked.

"The r–r–regular army general was P–Polish. He's d–d–dead, killed in the p–push to Berlin. That's his d–division number. The last initials are K–Karl Drus."

Griffiths thumbed the pushbutton again and when Davies appeared spoke with him briefly.

Poole asked, "If this isn't classified information, what was Schwann's point in the cloak–and–dagger routine? The Russians must know these facts."

"Felix w–wanted to let someone know that *he* knew. He was threatening to r–r–reveal it all. M–Make a stink. It's in official h–histories—but only a f–footnote to a footnote. N–nobody cares about *that* war, Felix said. He l–left some notes."

After a low knock, Davies ushered in Sir Leicester, who looked decidedly peeved.

"Inspector Griffiths: I am happy to cooperate with you, however —"

Griffiths cut in smoothly, "And we're very grateful, Sir Leicester. There are a few matters you should understand, and you may have information vital in concluding this case."

"Concluding? May I presume, then, that you've, er, solved the crimes?"

"We're close to a conclusion, sir. Mr. Stallings has been helpful, but he feels you should be present to hear and confirm some details concerning your father."

Sir Leicester glanced at Stallings and lowered himself onto a settee. He was more than usually rumpled, and Poole wondered if his valet was trained to mash wrinkles and tucks into the expensive suits to impart a touch of careless ease.

"Very well," he said, "but my memory is thin as regards the ancient past."

As Griffiths deciphered the inscription and explained it, Sir Leicester screwed a monocle into his right eye and squinted. He looked even more like a bull terrier about to bite.

"Poor Felix had an *idée fixe*, I'm afraid." He returned the notebook to Griffiths. "He often talked about such things, but I had no idea he would concoct an elaborate fantasy."

"These deaths at Ashpole carry us well beyond fantasy," Griffiths said.

"Yes, yes. However, you must realize that Felix was interpreting documents according to his obsessions. As I told Mr. Poole, it was foolish of my father to commit this to paper, even in private diaries. Felix read redactions of redactions—incidents that fascinated or disturbed my father from a long, complex and wearying career during the war."

"This connects Karl Drus—Jan Drus's father—with your father. Was that a key, in Felix's mind?" Griffiths asked.

"Felix nurtured an immense awe for my father. He believed *literally* that my father could do no wrong. The, er, confessional nature of the diaries must have been disturbing. These incidents my father recorded later seemed to him wrong—immoral, evil. That was after the fact, out of the heat of battle. I reject the idea that my father was willingly or knowingly complicit in…war crimes."

"I make no such imputation," Griffiths said, with the air of an eighteenth–century barrister.

"However—I believe Felix felt his discoveries in the diaries were portentous—of great significance. He would have felt driven to explain them away. He would construct elaborate theories to 'exonerate' my father."

"N–Not exonerate," Stallings broke in. "From his n–n–notes, I think it was more c–complicated. He said Drus was a k–kind of seducer—I mean, that he was r–really to blame for the incident. He l–l–led your f–f–f…Sir Alfred into it. Felix had a p–plan to use the information…not just to embarrass the R–Russians. I d–don't know it all."

Sir Leicester shook his head. "I don't imply that Felix was mad —but he could develop a compulsive mania over theories. I can't guess why he would send this message with Jan Drus, or to whom."

Griffiths returned to the bell while Poole asked Sir Leicester, "Who would be most damaged by Felix making headlines with this old tale?"

"I couldn't hazard a guess. It would embarrass the family and the Institute in many ways. But Felix would scarcely need to ship data off to Moscow to do that. I doubt it would make a ripple in government affairs. But I am long removed from foreign affairs or even basic affairs of state."

Griffiths returned with Marcia Draper and Marian Halley, who looked flustered. They shot unison glances at Sir Leicester, who rose to make a slow, courtly bow. Griffiths fussed them into chairs.

"Ladies," Griffiths began pleasantly, "we have questions about Felix Schwann. We know you were both deeply involved with his work and ideas."

Marian Halley glared at Marcia Draper, snapping, "Some *ladies* were more involved than others—and must babble about it."

"We just want basic facts—no need to go into…emotional issues."

After outlining the snuffbox message and their speculations about Felix, Griffiths asked abruptly, "What was Felix doing with this information—and why?"

The two women leaned forward then hesitated. Marcia finally said, "I don't know about it all. But he…he confided he had a plan to…" She stopped and flushed deeply.

Marian shifted on the squeaky leather and grinned malevolently. "Go on—blurt it all out. He's dead and gone. You don't have to tiptoe about as if he were your sainted hermit, sleeping in the next room."

Marcia began to weep, serenely, without sobs or tremolos—tears as a footnote to grief. She spoke: "Felix had a plan to…create world peace. He said he had information that would force the superpowers—Russia and the U.S. and Britain—to meet seriously to settle the cold war. It sounds…mad. But he didn't seem that way. I mean, he wasn't fanatical. It seemed very…practical."

Marian Halley whipped her head around and growled, "You cow—you bloody *cow!*"

After a glare for Marian, Griffiths turned back to Marcia: "He told you about the snuffbox and the message—and Jan Drus?"

"Oh, no. I see that's what he meant, though. He said he had embarrassing facts about the war, that world leaders would do anything to…suppress them. I thought he meant he was in danger.

But he explained that if he could be instrumental in setting up discussions, he could…use group–process theory to help the negotiations."

Everyone was profoundly silent until Sir Leicester snorted. "Rubbish and nonsense. Even Felix wasn't that far off the ground!"

"I'm making it sound…too simple. He could be very eloquent. Persuasive. It didn't *sound* mad. Really." Her tears returned.

"Not to some," Marian said. "To anyone who believed Felix walked on water, it was true gen. I'll vouch for the content of Felix's obsessions. I heard enough of his ramblings every day. I had no idea he was…putting them into action."

"It wasn't an *evil* idea," Marcia said. "I didn't see how he could *do* it—but it was a good dream."

"It got him killed," Marian said. "And didn't he kill that Serb or Hungarian or whatever he was?"

Griffiths cut in: "No, and no. We don't believe Felix killed Jan Drus—and I begin to believe Felix wasn't killed for the snuffbox or his absurd ideas. You are not, in any event, to spread such rumors."

As he ushered them to the library door, Griffiths said, "Please make a statement for Constable Davies and the stenographer—anything you recall about Felix's, er, plans and ideas."

"You mean this will clear him?" Marcia asked.

"Felix doesn't need to be cleared. We need your sworn statements about the matters, however."

At the door, Griffiths took Marian Halley's arm. "Your malicious actions are not criminal. Miss Draper might wish to press charges on the threatening note you sent her. I don't take lightly people who impede homicide investigations. We're not sophomores, and such actions have serious consequences. So think very straight as you make your statement, Miss Halley."

Griffiths dismissed Stallings and Sir Leicester with thanks. To Poole he said, "I'd like to put my head with yours. Tomorrow at The

King's Leap, let's say, just at opening, eh?"

The policeman rubbed his hands briskly, and Poole hoped this was a portent of a neat conclusion to come—if not a happy ending for all in this corner of Buckinghamshire.

Guiltily, Poole avoided Amanda. She was winding up the last group session when Inspector Griffiths' black Cortina disappeared down the drive into a florid sunset. He walked away from the massive silhouette of the house toward the dovecote where it had all begun.

He felt chilled in the warm evening. The doves cooed mysteriously as they strutted on the little building. A wind soughed in the cedars and oaks beyond the garden. A distant church bell tolled with a muffled heartbeat rhythm. Its dirge tempo brought words into Poole's head: "The curfew sounds the knell of parting day...And leaves the world to darkness, and to me."

He circled the dovecote, trying to sort the bits of puzzle left unfitted. Donovan Stallings was the victim of pranks and hoaxes, frightened out of the Gothick Temple, left with a .22 cartridge casing in his pocket (confirmed by the lab as from the murder weapon). Marcia Draper was intimidated, jeered at, left holding a poison–pen note. Poole had been shadowed, had felled himself as he pursued Marie Winter across the meadow. He had been mauled in the maze by Reger, held up at Marylebone Station, rescued by Judy Jupiter. Stallings had assaulted Robin Heyward and left him for dead.

None of this explained or illuminated the bizarre murder and mutilation of Felix Schwann. Why that horrific violence? Nothing he now knew unraveled it.

Except by process of elimination.

Poole stopped in the rose garden, surrounded by the luminescent colors left by twilight. He walked toward a thick beech hedge and turned, when a figure reared up in the uncertain light—

205

someone in loose white clothing, head shrouded, a *thing* out of a grave or a sarcophagus or an old Warner Bros. movie. Its hands were raised in menace or imprecation or supplication.

"Jesus God!" Poole blurted.

Then he heard the words the creature formed, muffled sounds from jaws partially swathed by gauze, like Jacob Marley's ghost's bounden face : "Poole, Poole—it's me, Robin, for God's sake."

Heyward was wrapped in turban–thick bandages, an old white shirt flowing untucked from his jeans. His face was grey and grim, eyes blue–shadowed.

"Terribly sorry," he said. "I didn't mean to creep up on you. Fred said you'd ambled this way, and I wanted to see you away from the mob."

Poole released his breath and said, "You're released from the hospital already?"

"Not precisely. They probably know I'm out. I borrowed a hideous old Volkswagen from the chap next me in the ward. He was convinced I was going to a lady or a pub, so he was delighted to help me escape."

"Here—let's find you a place to sit. I'll drive you back—or find you a ride."

"Yes, I need the sit–down. Legs are a bit...wonky. I came to confess," Heyward continued, as they found wrought–iron chairs on the terrace. "I've been a shit and a hopeless jackass—maybe that's an unforgiveable combination. In school, I read your Mr. Hawthorne's *Scarlet Letter*, and I spent years trying to imagine the Unpardonable Sin. Maybe I found it.

"I want your pardon—I followed you that day you took your spill off the bloody ha–ha. I knew you were onto me, but I didn't think you saw *who* it was. I was mooning about, trying to catch Marie on a jaunt to that ghastly folly. I saw you looking sleuth-like. I thought I'd be clever and out–detective the detectives. It was quite stupid of me. Your tumble looked dreadful—I thought you'd broken your neck. But I thought I'd seem a total prannock if I waltzed out of nowhere. I saw you get up, and gentle Jock Walker was strolling toward you, so I faded away. I must have thought I was the Pimpernel—'he's here, he's there, he's everywhere.' Damned elusive, what?"

When Poole started to speak, Heyward held up a hand.

"Let me spit it all out, please. I don't want to funk it, like everything else. I spent nights making Donovan's life miserable, I said stupid things to Marie—chalk it up to jealousy, envy, loneliness, the bogies of frustration from the damned conference. I thought I'd made peace with the phantoms after I talked with you and Amanda. I was off for a spot of heavy meditation, and I saw Marie crossing the park. I knew she was going to the Chinese Dairy. Donovan said it was their trysting spot. I followed and saw Donovan lurking among all that broken statuary, looking unhinged and whingeing away a mile a minute. I had to give them a last spot of horror, so I broke in on them. You must know the rest."

Poole saw that Heyward was turned away, head bowed, a whitish blur in the dusk.

He said, "You need to see Marie and Donovan and tell them this. You're the one who's been most damaged—at least bodily. They've been so busy clearing themselves of the murder charges they haven't had a chance to be furious with you."

Heyward sighed, "I don't think I can make restitution—but perhaps they'll understand, at least."

"What do you make of the snuffbox and its connection with Felix's death?"

"Felix was a complete twit in anyone's judgment, but he was bright and capable in the Cavendar sessions. He went over the top on some subjects—hobbyhorses. He could hold forth for hours— without drinking—on how international politics could be reformed with a judicious dose of his own personal training in the Cavendar Process. He was daft on currency reform, too, but I never paid enough attention to grasp his theories. Yet, who would kill a man for being a colossal bore?"

Poole thought for a moment and said, "Maybe that's exactly the question we should ask."

In a few minutes, Poole located Fred and from him an off–duty gardener who agreed (at the drop of a ten–pound note) to ferry Heyward back to the hospital. As they left, Heyward rolled down his window and called, "Don't have all the fun here till I'm properly patched up and checked out."

As the VW's one operative taillight disappeared down the drive, Poole pondered the mysteries of personality—so many likable scamps were truly hopeless assholes but always forgivable. Heyward would never have to grasp the notion of an Unpardonable Sin.

In the early morning light, Amanda was cool toward him. He apologized for missing her, but he didn't have time or patience to try courtly politics.

"I'm meeting Griffiths at the pub—I'll try to see you at noon."

"All right. I have a busy morning. There are always a blue million details to see to as a conference ends."

Poole shuffled awkwardly. "You've been a fantastic help so far, and I need you to think it through with me and resolve some last points with Sir Leicester. We've all but eliminated the possibility that TransAtlas people are involved in the deaths. Come on, Amanda—I need your support."

She regarded him steadily and said in a sub–zero voice, "It's kind and civil of you to put me in the picture. I'm at your service as coordinator of the Institute."

He shrugged and left her. She had important needs to be met, but he was angling for a big catch now. He couldn't stop, even if he wanted to. He knew why so many of his old colleagues drank: you never had to apologize to a cold highball.

In the courtyard, Poole found the Escort and sighed at the prospect of another cautious creep down the wrong side of the road to Ashpole Norton. As he unlocked the door, he heard footsteps on the cobbles, and John Walker hailed him. He looked pale and grim.

"Before you go, I must talk with you. There are facts in Felix Schwann's background you should know. I, er, haven't brought them up. But Constable Davies talked with me last night. I gather that you and Inspector Griffiths interviewed a number of people. I hoped you would...well, I don't know if I hoped you would or *wouldn't* speak to me."

"Should we go somewhere?" Poole offered.

"No—there's no time. Plenary session in five minutes. But...I must talk with someone." He dug one elegant bootcap into the paving and assessed Poole. "I haven't been wholly forthcoming. My position—as you must have gathered—is delicate. With Felix, er, gone, I'm slated as Sir Leicester's program director. There was an ambiguity, you see, when Felix and I worked together—we were an uncomfortable duo. Maybe a trio, counting Amanda. Sir Leicester's shrewd enough to keep the power distributed among his staff. He enjoys watching our ploys and strategies. And thus we learn.

"I wasn't precisely...shattered by Felix's demise. At the same time, it was guilt–making, you see. I felt as if I benefitted from such a dreadful event. Well—I did benefit. I felt people were watching to see me gloat or preen. Do you understand?"

"I think so."

"I don't know—you're the perfectly self–contained, hermetically sealed Yank. You'd not have spent a minute in pointless navel–gazing. However, I've felt I must talk with you. Griffiths is too much the official stick."

"You have...evidence?"

"Not evidence, precisely. But you need to know things about

209

Felix that don't go into personnel folders. He was…strange, in many ways. Most of us wrote him off as just…un–English. We rationalized that he had a bloody awful time in the war, no family or roots, that he spent all his time at his work. Having compulsions is such a non–British idea. It's…*fanatical*. We aim for a grace of detachment and irony, a leavening bit of *Nil admirari*."

"Say what?"

"'Let nothing astonish you.' Dear, dead old Horace. It *won't* do to be excited, enthusiastic about ideas. But poor Felix was forever throwing tantrums, ranting like an evangelical. You saw one example. Our Felix was *always* astonished. He always had a…plan underway."

"Do you mean he was a con artist?"

"Far from it. He was the sort who is eaten by con sharks. For instance, he was involved with that dreadful Eliot More, our publican. He knew More when he was a young man first in England. He spent as much time in the village as at the Manor—it was a headquarters billet till well after the war, crawling with Army and government types. But when Felix told me he had gone in with More in refurbishing The King's Leap, I was amazed. Felix wasn't exactly tight–listed, but his economic theories made him cling to a farthing."

"Felix was More's partner?"

"Ah—I think that was the sticky part. Felix had lent More a sizable sum when he bought the pub. It was much of a wreck, and More made grand plans for a quaint hostelry, Ye Old Village Inn, which would appeal to Felix. I gather Felix parted with a considerable sum—in the tens of thousands of pounds."

"Where would Felix have gotten the money?"

"Sir Alfred made a settlement—a little legacy. He treated Felix as a not–quite–bright godson, and the money was his parting shot. I assume Felix kept his mite intact. But why he would let a rogue like

More come round him for money, I don't know. They seemed always at each other's throats—scarcely soul mates. Felix was always full of contradictions. Perhaps he felt he was beautifying the village, and so on. I...I'd like to make amends for keeping myself out of the investigation. Perhaps I could talk with you tonight."

"You've been of real help already." Walker glanced at his watch and started to move away, and Poole said, "I'll see you after the evening session, if need be."

Walker stopped a few yards away. "I can't fathom if I'm doing this out of enlightened self–interest. Being a helpful nark is yet another way to make my little light shine before Sir Leicester, isn't it?"

As Poole drove away, he watched Walker's slight figure engulfed in the massive doorway to the house. Another inmate of the prison of self–analysis.

✧

Inspector Griffiths again wore his workaday copshop special off–the–rack suit, a blue one with a faint reddish pinstripe that seemed an afterthought. Constable Davies, in full uniform, was at the wheel of the police car, looking uncomfortable in the sudden flare of English summertime. His beefy face was flushed, and sweat squeezed from the line of nearly white hair at the rim of the cap. Griffiths walked around the car, paused to say a few words to Davies and then met Poole.

"Lovely day," Griffiths said. "Cricket weather—and not long till the test matches. By then you'll be back in sunny California watching American baseball, I daresay."

"No to both," Poole said. "The only *real* place to watch baseball is some old, gritty mill town—Cleveland or Detroit or Chicago. Yeh —a Cubs game, because they only play in the afternoon. Eating peanuts and hotdogs and drinking fizzy beer that's warm before you can finish it. I wish I could explain it to you."

"We could trade reminiscences, and I'd train you up in the

nuances of cricket. What you say isn't exactly like Lords, but it might be a good county match."

They strolled from the green across the narrow street and Griffiths paused to squint at the lock–up. "Dreadful thing," he said. "I'd always regarded it as a twee tourist–catcher. I'll not pass it without a thought of poor Schwann."

Entering the quiet pub, they passed through the front room, where a bulky blonde barmaid nodded as she tested the bat–like beer handles. In the next room, Poole saw Eliot More busying himself with a long–handled feather duster, dabbing at rows of faded sepia photographs along the wall—ancient views of Ashpole Norton in the nineteenth century, with quaint gangs of locals in uncomfortably bulky clothing standing around horses or brandishing archaic agricultural implements.

More glanced at them and said, "Half a tick. You're very punctual, but I plunged into a spot of housework and won't be deflected. It's an impulse that rarely possesses me."

After Griffiths and Poole sat in a cluster of tiny chairs, More dropped the duster in the corner and said, "Can I serve you something from the bar?"

Griffiths declined, but Poole asked for a pint of house bitter, wanting to try the brew again.

"Sorry—we've run through the last of the lot. It'll be another week before we have a barrel up. Might I recommend…"

"No, no. I must break this habit of morning pub hours before I return to the States. It could lead me to crawl into a bottle and die."

"Mr. More," Griffiths said in his palest official tone, "we need to speak with you again about Felix Schwann."

More drifted to the small chairs, eyed them distastefully, finally selected one and sat. Rubbing his hands along his trouser seams, he said, "This is tedious. I believe I've gone over every detail in memory, Inspector. I doubt if I can add a single word at this date."

"Mr. Poole and I have gathered more statements about the night of the murder." Griffiths paged ostentatiously through his notebook. "You have given two statements about your last conversation with Felix Schwann. You indicate that you saw him only early in the evening. But two witnesses—John Walker and Marie Winter—have said Felix returned about closing time and that you spoke with him for some time then."

"I might have done." He continued dabbing at his trousers, as if rubbing dirt from his fingers. "I don't pay much attention to time in the evenings. One pub night is very like another, if you know what I mean."

"This is a very important night to us."

More rose and paced behind the little row of chairs. Stopping before one picture, he tentatively touched the glass. "Filth," he said to himself. "Where does it creep in?"

"*Did* you speak with Schwann at closing time that night?" Griffiths persisted.

"Oh—I daresay I did. He was in and out several times. He was forever bursting in an out, like some...*sausage*." More scrubbed at the photo's glass with his knuckles and then took out a large silk handkerchief. He polished the glass as if it were a mirror into which he peered.

"A...what?" Poole said.

"Felix, Felix, Felix," More said. "He always wanted to be the cynosure of all eyes—and ears and tongues. He got his wish."

Poole glanced at Griffiths, who smiled slightly. Riffling the notebook pages, he said, "Mr. More—did you have an argument with Schwann? Were you angry with him?"

"That's my grandfather," More said, tapping his index finger on the glass. "The particularly ugly yobbo in the second row holding the cleaver. He probably had just slaughtered an ox for the Manor. So they took his picture looking as if he's come first in the Ashpole

Norton annual drooling contest."

"Mr. More…" Griffiths prodded, but More whirled.

In a rapid, charged voice, he said, "Of course I was bloody arguing with Felix, it's all you could do with him, if you could get a fucking word in." He wrung his hands through the silk handkerchief. "More filth," he muttered.

"What were you discussing?" Griffiths asked.

"Discussing???" More barked like a fox. "You didn't know the man. Conceited, vulgar, dirty little… Felix had grand ideas to fling over you, like…filth. A great, wet web of dirty little words. Money, money, money. You'd think he was some great banker, a Rothschild."

With jerky motions, More wadded the handkerchief and stuffed it into a jacket pocket. He waved his hands as if they were wet, turned and bolted through the door to the main bar. Poole started from his seat, but Griffiths caught his elbow. When Poole looked at him, Griffiths put a finger to his lips.

Returning almost at a run, More waved another glassed, framed photograph. "Here, here—this was dear old Dad." He thrust it into Griffiths' hands, a faded color portrait of a serious–looking man in a uniform unfamiliar to Poole, staring into the camera as if it were a rifle barrel pointed into his soul.

"He was what they call a 'steady lad' all his life. There he is, all gussied up in a Home Guards rig–out. He thought it the greatest honor since the O.B.E. He wanted to be a hero, but the medicos told him he had a dicky heart, so they put him in that guy's suit and told him to guard the home front. And he never knew people laughed. He was only a butcher's boy from the village, and that was fair enough for him. He was of the sort who knew they couldn't afford aspirations."

More sat and pulled out the handkerchief again. He scrubbed each hand in turn. "He was perfectly content to work in his shop," he continued, "and send up special cuts to the Manor. He had me in hand to follow the trade, till his heart caught up with him."

With a harsh honk of a laugh, More shook his head. "Just as the bloody government was about to end the last bit of rationing, too. When he might have had a fighting chance to make his humble living. My mother found him lying behind the big butcher block, lying in the blood and offal. He still had his knife in his hand. Isn't that perfect? Priceless and perfect—he died in uniform after all, in his old white coat with grease and blood and marrow smeared on it instead of battle ribbons. "

More stood stiffly and said, "We salute you, fallen hero—*dulce et decorum est*…There's a scrap of grammar school Latin for you." He snatched the photo from Griffiths and stared at it.

Quietly, Griffiths asked, "And this has what to do with your conflict with Felix Schwann?"

More sat, putting the photo down carefully on a small table. He scrubbed one hand across his brow.

"Everything and nothing, Mr. Policeman. Felix had a thousand ways to lord it over everyone. He was so very, very *noblesse oblige*, you see, spending a few moments with a village lout like me. He had always done, since he came to Ashpole. He so desperately wanted to be a bright English lad, not a dirty–faced tramp dumped off a boat in the middle of the fucking war. So he'd hang around me —around all of us—and then trail off to University. While I learned to poleax a steer and carve a lamb."

More rose and walked in jerky steps before the hearth, his hands thrust in his pockets as if to hide them.

"It was his idea, I tell you, to sink his precious money into this place. Oh, he'd say I begged and pleaded, talked him into it. Lies. Damned lying words. Filth and offal. I had proper financing. But he said it was good for 'local money' to support the place. As if *he* were local!"

He stopped and stared at the fireplace mantel. He reached out and gingerly touched the slab of carved stone. He stared at his fingertip, saying, "Filth everywhere. It comes down the chimney. You can't fight it off."

Griffiths said, "Did you have a violent quarrel? Did Schwann return after closing?"

More whirled and grinned, a fierce rictus of internal pressure, like a valve stretching before it explodes.

"Yes, of course, of course. Don't you see? He banged in and out. He told people—whispered it about, you see—that I was homosexual. Jokes about pools and queens and fairies. He never even looked at me. Always past me, over my head, never catch an eye. He handed me a dirty great check and never saw whether I liked it or not. What's it to him? Just a dollop of grand old Harcourt money to throw to the peasants, keep them happy with their lot."

"He came back early in the morning?" Griffiths asked.

"Banging away at the door as if it were his, knocker, lock and bolt. Wants me up for a gabfest again, canceling the loan, getting accounts settled, needs the money to further the cause of world peace, a great secret mission to the East. God, how he cantered on!"

"Why was there no contract or agreement in Felix's papers?" Griffiths said. "We have no record of a loan outstanding."

More stepped from the fireplace, nearly bent double with a howl of ragged laughter. "Oh, our Felix was a right berk! He gave me money on a *handshake*! Great God, it was like a scene from a play. The lordling dispensing *largesse* with consummate ease, you see. No dirty awful papers and lawyers and seals to fiddle with. We're all gentlemen here, right? And then he wants to *un*handshake it, a few words in your pink and shell–like ear, Eliot, old dearie, and pop me back my twenty thousand quid!"

"I stood it, Inspector. Oh, I stood it like a man and a Christian, till I thought it would crush my head. Then he pulled out his popgun and waved it. Honest to Christ, with Felix about you didn't need the telly. He was that entertaining. He wants to frogmarch me to the constabulary or have me produce a sack of golden guineas from under a floorboard—or Christ knows what."

More paused and stared dully at the floor. He dragged a foot on the ancient pine board. "Filth underfoot, too. He was lying in a pool of offal. Awful offal. Blood everywhere."

"Where did you kill him?" Griffiths asked.

More looked up, for a moment foxy again. Then he nodded listlessly. "You could say I killed him. Yes, you could say that. But it was more in the nature of a random thing. We went out the door, God knows where Felix thought we were going, him pointing that little pistol like James Bond, and the silly sod slips down the doorsill. I jumped at him to get the damn–fool thing out of his hand, and it…popped. Just *pop*! And there is our Felix lying across my steps, dead as every nail in door. *Pop!*—isn't it an amazing thing?"

Poole said, "Why did you take him to the lock–up?"

More stared at him. "I ask myself and ask myself. Don't you suppose I want to know, as well? I fetched the key—it's always kept here, you know. I dragged poor old Felix's lubberly carcass across the street, and I popped him in. Popped, you see, again. It just seemed… right. Then I pushed him in there and went and found a pocket torch and looked at him. It was all wrong. He was sitting there as if he were waiting for a bus. Not properly dead at all. I thought about it—oh, indeed I did. I fetched a jimmy and locked him in there and wrenched the lock away. 'That's more like it, old sod,' I said to myself. Then I flung all the rubbish into tile pond. You see, Inspector, I can think like an oik when need be. So—that was the end of our mutual friend."

Griffiths stared and then asked, "And the cartridge casing?"

"Ah, a silly improvisation the next day. Your cohorts were

217

swarming about then, and I stepped out to show my concern. I saw the little thing lying there near the step. "Aha," I said, "an oversight." I fetched it up while I swept away at the flagstones like your average good publican. Then I saw the two varsity lads, those tiresome wankers, larking about and goggling. When one of them came up the walk, I bumped him and dropped it into his pocket. Seemed like the right thing to do, eh?" More chuckled hoarsely then looked anxious.

"But it won't go away, will it? It's never over, like Felix's talk, talk, talk. There's always a stuffy policeman banging in and out, like Felix. It *is* my place. But there are types like Marie Winter here staring at me. You know, she's just a by–blow, some foreigner's left–over. That Drus fellow Felix was so thick with. 'World peace,' Felix says. 'Negotiation on a rational basis,' he says. You'd think he'd grow up and come in out of the sun."

Poole leaned forward and said, "You've left something out. Why did you…disfigure Felix?"

More shoved himself back in the little chair, as if thrust by an outside force. "You shut up!" he said. "Just shut your horrid Yank gob!"

"Now, Mr. More," Griffiths said, "no need—"

More came out of the chair as if propelled by a giant spring, like a pilot in an ejection seat. The small table before Griffiths and Poole flipped over, and More skittered away in a running lope, through the back door to the snug. Griffiths flung the table aside and jumped after him, with Poole behind.

They plunged into a narrow whitewashed corridor, and Poole followed Griffiths' back as they burst through a doorway into the kitchen. There More scrabbled in an open cabinet drawer. Glancing over his shoulder, he reached up and plucked a knife from a wall rack. "This will do," he panted.

Griffiths threw out an arm to keep Poole behind him. He held the other hand toward More. "Come now—put the knife down, Mr. More. You don't want any more trouble."

More crouched, the knife outthrust. He wiped at his mouth with his left sleeve. Poole looked around for a weapon, but Griffiths had grasped his jacket sleeve firmly. More was only three steps from them.

"Come now," Griffiths said evenly, "it's all over now. You don't have to worry about anyone getting at you—or talking about you."

"Too true. In a moment, you won't have a worry in the world, no need to keep at poor Eliot More, poor poor More, the butcher's boy, isn't he something?—come right up in the world, I *don't* think! Wears that awful poncey cologne, enough to make you retch, smells like a field of flowers all gone rotten, don't he? You know *why*?"

In the dead silence, Poole heard bees busy in the open window behind More, going about their pastoral work as if murder and mayhem never occurred. More's breath was sharp and ragged as he spoke again:

"Because of the smell, the stench of blood and offal. Most people don't think blood smells, it just looks red and greasy and thick. But it stinks. Oh, my—what a pong! You work in it up to your elbows every day, it sticks to your shoe soles, it's worked right into the pores of your skin. Our house reeked of it, my father's clothes stank of blood and death. He wanted to go off to the war and wade in blood, but it made me gag. I swore I'd never be a butcher, I'd never be at the beck and call of idiots who never saw the animals die, walk around in bloody footprints all day. You—you two huddled there..." He began to laugh, a low giggle like a rattle in his throat. "You're ready for the slaughter..."

As More shifted forward, Constable Davies rose in the window behind him and caught the collar of his jacket, wrenching him backward. Davies grasped More's sleeve and swung the knife–hand in an arc. Hand struck water pipe, and the knife flew in a silvery parabola across the room, past Poole and Griffiths. They started forward as Davies spilled through the window and drove More to the floor in an awkward karate–football tackle.

When they reached them, Davies had More's arms pinioned and was clipping on handcuffs. He beamed up at Griffiths, with the face of a sweaty Welsh cherub about to sing in the eisteddfod.

"Well done, Constable!" Griffiths said.

Griffiths helped pull Davies and More up. More stood in a hangdog crouch, staring at the floor. He shook his head and growled, "Still blood on the floor, footprints in it, leading everywhere. You'll never soak it up with sawdust."

While Griffiths held More's arm, Davies retrieved the knife from the corner. "Is this the murder weapon, do you suppose, Chief?"

More shook his head, grinning with clenched teeth. "My business. Try to find out! It's all mine, and I'll bloody keep it, you awful little man!"

Poole said, "What did you do with the tongue, with Felix's tongue?"

More looked up at Poole, his teeth still clenched. He slowly straightened, eyes rolling up in his head. The whites of his eyes showed as his back arched, and he emitted a terrible sound, one Poole would recall on bad nights for years to come—the sound of an intelligence exploding, a soul shattering, a werewolf howl. The sound rang, then More's mouth gaped and his own tongue came out, extending and extending like a serpent, like an obscene internal organ distending, further than Poole could imagine, as if More were trying to vomit it out, spit his own tongue out in trade for Felix's.

More, back arched like a drawn bow, fell over backward before Davies could catch him. He lay in a rigid arc, feet kicking, pinioned arms jerking spasmodically, while strangled noises erupted from him.

"A fit," Griffiths said. "Constable—call an ambulance, and bring in more uniforms with it." He loosened More's clothing and rolled the stiff form onto its side. The seizure seemed to pass, but More was unconscious, face set like a death mask.

Griffiths glanced at Poole. "If you'll come with us, we can get enough on the record for an official interrogation when and if Mr. More is able to cooperate. I'll need your statement as witness."

Poole rode in Griffiths" car, behind the police ambulance, which parted from them at a roundabout and roared off toward the A-road. Griffiths looked out the side window, and Constable Davies drove with stolid concentration. Poole thought of the scene with More.

"Yes—a perfect day for cricket," Griffiths finally said.

A LONG, LONG TRAIL UNWINDING

ON THE LAST day of the conference, Richard Poole stood in the main hall of Ashpole House, watching conference members scramble to a plenary session in which the uttermost mysteries of the Cavendar Process would be unveiled, last consultant comments made, last howls of frustration voiced. The faces were anxious in a different way from two and a half weeks before. Poole wondered what the proportion of desire–to–leave with regret–at–leaving might be.

Last night, in the members' lounge, Poole had listened to tales of woe and people denying that they had learned anything of themselves and the world. The subtext had been one of loss—of friends, of the place, of the painful, exhilarating Process itself. The members were about to scatter across the earth to homes, jobs, friends and families. If Sir Alfred's theories were right, they would be touched and shaped by the experiences, would never be the same again.

Poole saw Amanda moving from her office, and he angled across the corridor to intercept her, saying, "Hey, lady—your wheels are going around!"

Her look was a few degrees less frosty than the last one he had seen. "I see you're here for the last act, at least. I suppose you're one of these people who reads only final chapters of books. But you have methods teaching that sort of thing in America, don't you? What is it?—speeding–reading?"

"Ah, come on, Amanda—unbend a little. Let's not fight the War of 1812 again."

"What? Oh, you mean that skirmish in our big war with France? I suppose you people *have* dignified it into a war. I believe we burnt your president's palace or whatever it is."

"Hey, I know you're miffed, but there's a lot to tell you. Can you meet me after the session? For just a few minutes."

They paused outside the ballroom–sized salon, filled with members in happy gabble. Poole said, "Come on—you saved my ass from day one on. I *need* you. And I don't want to lose your good opinion of me."

She laughed, "Of all the giant conceits! All right—against my judgment, I'll talk with you. But you'd better have a crackling good story for me. I've heard the authorized gossip three or four times over, and it's more sensational than any truth you might have."

Poole sat at a far end of the arc of chairs, watching faces. Reger and Edwards sat together, still looking confused and conspiratorial. Sister Louise sat serenely knitting on something enormous and bright blue. Aaron Spellman sat next to Helen Corbett, radiating possessiveness. Everard Allison was near a window, looking out at the dusk as if he wanted to take wing with the swallows. At a small, ragged cheer, Poole looked around. Robin Heyward had entered with Donovan Stallings. Heyward wore a turban–bandage and sported an aluminum cane, which he waved cheerily. Most of the staff were seated, with Sir Leicester, Amanda and John Walker in a triad.

The meeting began as Walker rose and spoke briefly on the basic Cavendar Process principles. Amanda reiterated the agenda they had followed. Then Sir Leicester gave a ponderous summation of the Cavendar Process as seen by its inventor. Marcia Draper, sitting well away from Marian Halley, spoke simply on the sociology of the group and the idea of selecting members from a single organization as large and diverse as TransAtlas. Marian Halley listed statistics about members and their roles.

Poole drifted, thinking how this was both like and unlike graduation exercises at a polytechnic university. Then John Walker abruptly asked members to comment on their experiences. After a bird's–eye rest in the concerto, members spoke, first in cacophony then in self–imposed order.

Sister Louise spoke quietly about how the conference had helped her understand the secular world and appreciate the complexity of social groups. Aaron Spellman spoke less coherently about benefits of group process training in the corporate environment. Arthur Stanley was terse and epigrammatic. Giorgio was expansive and inarticulate in a macronic language resembling neither English nor Italian.

Members congratulated themselves on surviving the rigors of the Institute, and the staff looked amused and complacent. There were gracious statements of farewell. Poole slipped out as the meeting ended and met Amanda in the members' lounge. As they settled in, Inspector Griffiths entered with Sir Leicester in tow. Constable Davies followed with John Walker.

Griffiths nodded to each in turn, saying, "Sorry to intrude further on your time, but I knew you all wanted to be briefed on the, er, events of the past fortnight. The department is grateful for your aid in concluding these two cases."

Griffiths outlined the Drus case. "A team from Scotland Yard and one from military intelligence have conducted tests and run–throughs at the dovecote. They agree that a distinct probability of an accident exists. It was a strange one–off event, but we find no inconsistencies in the testimonies of Marie Winter, Mrs. Winter and anyone else involved."

"What about Eliot More?" Walker asked. "Could he have… been implicated?"

Griffiths shook his head. "I'll outline Mr. More's situation directly—we have no reason to connect him with the incident. In fact, he has a clear alibi in testimony from numerous pub customers and staff for the time. Our report concludes that Jan Drus died as result of accident. Reconsideration of the forensic evidence in the Medical Examiner's report also points to that conclusion."

"And the snuffbox?" Amanda asked.

"That, too, comes in with the Schwann case."

Sir Leicester shifted and said, "You are not, then, connecting Drus with Cavendar Institute?"

"No. The unfortunate circumstance of the accident occurring on the grounds of Ashpole Manor is the only connection."

Leafing through pages of his notebook, Griffiths continued, "The case of Eliot More and Felix Schwann is more convoluted. I can only outline the evidence, pending legal disposition. More's mental state is deteriorating. I doubt he will stand trial for murder. He is now under institutional observation and, from preliminary reports, will remain so. "

"You mean he's crazy," Poole said.

"Mad as a hatter, as you might say. He's broken down completely in confinement—from my observation I'd say it was no sham. Diagnosis now is of a catatonic disorder."

Griffiths ran them through the connections between Schwann and More, Schwann's grandiose fantasies and the George snuffbox, visions of world peace through group–process negotiation. The listeners reacted with horror, compassion, resignation. Then Griffiths turned to Sir Leicester and said, "Can you shed any light on the information Schwann planned to transmit as part of his, er, bargain?"

The old man sighed and said, "I can only reiterate what I told Mr. Poole: Felix Schwann stumbled on fragments of narrative left by my father. Information still sequestered under the state secrets acts. Information of no real use in the present, except to embarrass a few participants still living—or to blacken the reputation of some individuals and organizations. I have placed the papers in the correct hands, Inspector. I will give you a name and a number to contact to verify the facts."

Griffiths tapped his Biro on his teeth. "I am quite sure you would not obstruct an investigation."

Sir Leicester continued irritably, "As you well know, all sides in the war conducted desperate, often reprehensible operations. My father was part of a team directing operations in a remote and inaccessible sub–war. Events in the field outstripped intelligence about them. That dreary phrase of Arnold's—'Ignorant armies clash by night'—might have been the group's working motto. I have no intention of explaining or apologizing at this remote date."

"So," Amanda said, "the memory of Sir Alfred will remain untarnished."

"I do not think I am being self–serving. For forty years, I have worked for development of the Cavendar Process, first as my father's assistant and then as his successor. No one here, I believe, wants to see the Institute damaged—perhaps dismantled—for the sake of unneeded publicity."

This seemed irrefutable. Griffiths glanced around the group and said, "That's all of the evidence I can discuss. Can I answer any questions?"

Poole said, "I'm still puzzled: what about the knife More used on Schwann? And Schwann's tongue?"

Griffiths squirmed. "Still under investigation. We located a fillet knife with a staghorn handle, but tests are inconclusive. It had been handled and used daily in the pub kitchen. As for the, er, mutilation —More has remained incoherent on the subject."

Constable Davies cleared his throat and cast a pious glance toward the heaven–frescoed ceiling: "I'll say this, in confidence to you ladies and gentlemen—I wouldn't ask for pate at The King's Leap, should you stop for the cold collation."

Six adults of diverse social standing, age and condition spent a few seconds carefully avoiding eye–contact, and Poole understood the Brits' expression, "I didn't know where to look."

Griffiths broke the silence, saying, "I'd appreciate your cooperation in keeping this as quiet as possible until legal and logistical details are tidied up."

On the sweeping terrace where Poole had first seen them, he and Amanda met Robin Heyward and Donovan Stallings. Heyward was less heavily bandaged and had regained color and vigor. Stallings seemed less agitated and querulous. Poole thought they looked like recent emigrants from Never Land, forced to grow up, lighter through loss of innocence.

Amanda and Poole sat at their table, and Amanda said, "What are your plans now that the conference has ended?"

Heyward, looking across the sweep of lawn, said, "Sir Leicester asked me to stay the balance of my internship, and I took him up. The Great Man said I had more to learn, and I believe he's correct."

Stallings said, "N–not me. While I was w–w–working with Sir Alfred's papers, I r–revived my old interests in h–history. I quite like m–m–messing about in old papers and t–tomes of forgotten lore. I've d–dug up some of my history p–papers and plan to polish them up." "What kind of history?" Poole asked.

Stallings blushed and fidgeted. "I can, of c–course, deal with the Cavendar b–bits around here. Sir Leicester said I have the r–r–run of the archives. But I was f–fiddling with Roman history in s–s–school, and odds and ends of C–Crimean war stuff."

"I came up with titles for you, old sock," Heyward said. " I forgot to pass them on. You see, he's intrigued by whatever happened to a lost Roman legion up along Hadrian's Wall. The poor, forlorn Ninth Hispana, which marched out of British history

and into the mists of time—or some such. How's this for a title?—
Blazing Sandals: The Retreat of the Ninth Hispana. Then he wants to
poke about with the Charge of the Light Brigade and that tosh.
How about *Magnificent, But Still Not War?*"

"I'll ch–choose my own titles, thank you," Stallings said. The two
young men seemed to be groping toward their earlier ragging
friendship.

Heyward said, "I'll have your fusty little tomes in paper editions,
with bosomy lasses on the covers, in every W.H. Smith's in the land.
Stick with me, laddie—movie rights are next."

They rose from the table, shaking hands all around. Poole felt
depressed at the reminder of his own departure.

Walking back toward the house with Amanda, Poole saw two
familiar figures shuffling out the front door, overburdened with
luggage. Reger and Edwards were half–wedged in the wide entry,
struggling with a small mountain of bags and grips, each draped
with a large leather golf bag in addition to the luggage. Poole
strolled toward them.

Edwards sighted him and nudged Reger. Poole waved casually
and said, "*Golf* clubs, fellas?"

"Yeh, well. Old Bob had the notion there'd be an eighteen–hole
course here," Reger mumbled. "He kept saying it was 'good cover' to
go around and keep an eye on the bigwigs."

"Be prepared for any contingency," Edwards said.

"I'll remember that in my report," Poole said.

"Now, look, man," Edwards said, "I know we screwed up a little,
but it was in the line of work. How'd we know—"

Reger held up his hand. "C'mon—we don't owe this dude a
formal apology. We've got reports to file, too."

"You've got new assignments?" Poole asked.

They glanced at each other, and Reger said, "After all that hassle
in London, your man Lewis called. You got an understanding chief

there. I think it'll smooth out when we get Stateside."

The two burly men squeezed into the back of the mini–cab, and Edwards thrust his head from the window to say, "No hard feelings, pal?" Poole, his hands in his pockets, studied his shoecaps and then nodded. "Just don't cross my path without a lot of warning." Edwards sat back with a look of relief as the cab pulled away, sagging under the burden of two large, overloaded, would–be spooks.

✧

As dusk fell across the wide vistas and artfully–placed clumps of beeches, limes and oaks, Poole lugged his suitcase and shoulder bag to the hallway. He found Amanda Evans standing by the tiled maze he had solved several days before. She had changed from her workaday severe suit to a handsome tweed skirt and soft butter–colored sweater. But she still wore her conference lapel–badge.

They walked to the portico, and Poole saw how kindly the mild light treated her. *She's made to fit this place*, he thought.

"I wish I could steal time to drive you in to London," she said. "But the next group of members arrives in minutes. There's never a gap in the work schedule in high summer."

"That's okay. I mean—I'd love to have the lift. We could talk."

"Is there more to talk about?"

"Isn't there?" She stood at the edge of the portico, and an edge of the knot–garden showed at the corner.

"Look, Amanda—you're a fine lady. I want to see you again. But you're on a treadmill here, one conference after another. I'm on another treadmill. When I get to Wide World, Harvey Lewis will have cut and sent new orders for me—for someplace halfway around the world. And I'll be off. If I'm lucky, I'll get a chance to stop over in Minnesota for a change of clothes. If not, I wind up buying a batch of Korean polyester makeshifts at an airport shop and go straight into a new assignment."

"Your point is," she said, not turning to look at him, "that you go

229

everywhere all the time, and I go nowhere ever."

"Something like that. Ah—you're in love with this place, with England. You couldn't be moved."

"A sensitive plant. Can't be transplanted or grafted. In love with…how do *you* profess to know what I'm in love with?"

Poole moved to her. Carefully, tentatively, he slipped his arm around her shoulder. She didn't move away but she didn't unbend, either—stalemate.

"I think I understand a lot about you."

She moved closer and looked at him over her shoulder. "Oh? Go on."

"You're at home here. I haven't felt at home anywhere for twenty years. I could settle down, all right, and this place—hell, I don't mean Ashpole—would be the place to choose. But…"

"Yes—the everlasting *but*. I think I've heard it before." She walked quickly away, arms crossed on her breast, head down.

Poole hurried after her, saying, "I'm trying to keep my wrecked leg intact—slow down. Listen: I'll get back to see you. Harvey owes me a few soft postings. Or I think he does. When he sees my report on the conference, I'll call in due-bills."

At the center of the porch she stopped and looked sideways at him. "I'm not extorting promises from you, Richard. You act as if I had some…power over you. I don't operate on guilt. I believe you should say and do what you actually mean."

He shook his head. "I'm trying to find out what I mean." He took her in his arms again, saying, "I mean to sort that all out, lady."

He started to kiss her, when tires clacked on the thick orange gravel before them. Cars swept around the last bend in the drive—a procession of taxis and limousines.

"Damn it—" he said. Doors opened, and a bevy of travelers spilled onto the first steps, a mob of older women in rumpled clothing. "What *is* this?" he asked.

"Our next conference—drawn mostly from your Midwestern states and from the north of England. To work." She stepped away from him.

A massive woman, thrush–bosomed and officious, stuffed into a dark–blue pants suit and with a garland of lace at her throat, pushed through the crowd, spied Amanda and said, "I've done my part in keeping them all straight. We'll need all the help disembarking you can muster. They're like…geese!"

Ascending the steps with some labor, she read Amanda's lapel tab and said, "Mrs. Evans: I'm Evangeline Shepard—*Mrs.* Shepard —from Cedar Falls. That's Iowa. I've come to your lovely country to…find myself!"

Turning to survey the carloads of conferees milling on the broad steps, she said, "I'm a practising Theosophist, but in recent years I've felt the need to expand the horizons of my soul. I hope this conference will fulfill my needs."

Evangeline Shepard examined Poole and said, "I hope you have some help with the baggage. Everyone seems to have brought much more than they will need. You're a strong–looking young man, so I suppose you'll manage."

Amanda grinned at Poole. With her hands on her hips, Mrs. Shepard hailed the multitude: "Come on, now—let's keep some order here. The staff will get us anything we need. Ah, Drusilla, darling—over here!"

A small, fox–faced woman in a suit of strongly marked plaid winced and tried to dodge the stentorian summons. "Come on up here!" Mrs. Shepard bellowed. Turning to Amanda, she muted her voice a half–decibel: "That's one of our hostesses. From Aberdeen. Scotland. We have correspondence contacts all over Britain. Drusilla. That's *Lady* Bassett–Horne, I should say. Nobility, you see."

The small woman toiled up the steps like a gillie breasting heather on a Highlands hillside, and Mrs. Shepard cooed encouragement. "This is Mrs. Evans, who will get us all settled. I look forward to a good hot shower and a long nap."

Shaking cropped iron–grey hair, the small woman said in a dense burr, "We could do with hot food, first. All day on that endless motorway!" Poole watched old Fred edge out the doorway, staring apprehensively at the mountains of luggage around the taxis.

When Poole turned to say goodbye to Amanda, he saw that the women had trapped her between them and drawn her toward the house. Poole waved, but Amanda could only make a helpless gesture. Poole lugged his bags down the steps, where a small wizened driver mopped his brow with a bandana. "Going the other way, Squire?" he asked Poole.

"As fast as possible."

He watched the grounds of Ashpole Manor shrink and recede as the cab pulled away. It was like an elaborate architect's model viewed from a distance. Memory would fix it in all its detail.

On a blank page in his notebook, Poole scribbled ROSES FOR AMANDA. It would jog his memory and—perhaps—salve his conscience.

✧

On a nearly empty train to London, Poole watched the landscape blur past—purple shadows punctuated by mercury–vapor lamps at crossings throwing weird orange rays. His smudged reflection in the train window was dim and distorted: *Now we see through a glass darkly—then, face to face.*

It was mildly blasphemous to fit St. Paul's words to his case, Poole decided. He imagined thinking back of Amanda in (say) Singapore or Indianapolis or Khartoum, saying casually, "I almost married a woman who knew all about English history…and gardens…and group–process theory."

From the tiny dot of the instant, his life appeared depressingly cyclical. The BritRail wheels clacked out a muted, genteel boogie-woogie beat: It *coulda–been*, it *almost–was*, it *never–will*… Then the train slowed and sighed into the station.

When he emerged onto the street, a small rain had begun to weep. Poole had always been a sucker for the Pathetic Fallacy and entirely approved. He looked for a cab, when a small figure emerged from the taxi rank and piped *Wotcher*!

Judy Jupiter stepped theatrically into a circle of streetlight and bowed. She stepped forward to meet him, standing on tiptoe to unsling his shoulder bag. Anyone watching would have seen a wearied traveler greeted with a hug–and–a–kiss.

In minutes, Poole had been transported to the Wide World office, seated and handed a tumbler bottomed with malt whiskey. Hugh Kennington gave him a hearty "Cheers!"

Poole skimmed a small heap of waxy Telex pages from TransAtlas and reviewed the Ashpole events briefly for Kennington. He nodded at the end of the summary conclusion.

"I talked with your Inspector Griffiths this morning. He assured me TransAtlas' involvement in the records—C.I.D. and local—will be minimized. If and when Mr. More recovers his wits enough to stand trial, you may be asked to appear as a police witness. For now, though, your affidavit suffices. I sent Lewis a communiqué this afternoon. And you'll submit your field report, of course."

Poole thanked Kennington and praised the efficiency of the Wide World operation. Kennington topped up Poole's whiskey.

"You're flying out tomorrow?" he asked.

"Yeh—late afternoon. So, I'll get part of a day in London, at least."

"You could make a quick round," Kennington said with a smile. "St. Paul's, Westminster, Buckingham Palace, the Tower—all the famous piles no visitor should miss. A dash into Harrods or Liberty's, a second to gape at the New Scotland Yard sign, a wheel past Nelson's Column."

Kennington recited the names in mock–funereal tones. Poole

imagined himself a face on a postcard, notched with a crude X. *Having a helluva time in London town. Wish you wuz here!*

As Kennington shook hands and walked him to his office door, he said, "On the other hand, if you should forego the tourist business, our Miss Jupiter has a free day tomorrow. You could lodge a semi–official request that she serve as bodyguard and escort for the next, ah, eighteen hours."

He found Judy efficiently making entries on the CRT. He shuffled his feet and said, "Hugh Kennington said... Er, you know London pretty well, don't you?"

She patted her short hair—now less orange and more strawberry, through the magic of chemistry—smiled and said, "Like the back of me bleedin' hand, as they say. Little Miss A–to–Zed. Why do you ask?"

"I have a half–day left in England. And I haven't really seen London. Hugh Kennington indicated that you...you could escort me tomorrow."

Judy rolled her eyes. "Lord, what a proper speech! I suppose you want the alpha–plus tour of great sites and historic ruins."

Poole sighed. "I'm not really into rubbernecking. I get enough sights in my work to hold me forever."

"Ah. So—no guided tour. What else could we do with half a day? And the balance of the night?" She smiled sunnily.

"You going off–duty soon?"

"Yes. Yes, indeed. And then it's home to sleep in a wretched Zed–bed in Mum's flat. My sister's down from Birmingham for the week, you see, and good old Judy is assigned trouper's lodgings."

"And I have to find a hotel," Poole said gloomily. "Probably a small, cramped room in the back, facing an airshaft. Maybe a nice bed, though."

"That's a pleasant thought."

"Maybe—" Poole said, as if inspired, "maybe you could escort me to a hotel? And check it out. My life has been in danger a few times here. Who knows—I could be waylaid by paid assassins. The room might be booby-trapped."

"So I could write this up as line–of–duty? Put in for hazardous duty pay?"

"I don't think it'll be *that* dangerous."

"Don't I just know! Still and all, it's a smashing idea. I'll sign myself out to 'field duty' and leave Hugh to sort it out. And I'll have the car, if we...if you should wish to venture out for a spot of gawking and gaping."

"I think that's a remote contingency," Poole said.

She gathered her bulky purse and snapped off the desk lamp. As she stood adjusting the lemon–yellow and abbreviated dress she wore, a kind of modified shimmy–skirt–blouse, which accentuated her trim 1920s figure, Poole thought fleetingly of Amanda. *Not even faithful to you in my fashion*, he thought. Ah well: *Live in the here-and–now!* A principle, he decided as Judy took his arm, not nearly as irksome as Moses' first injunction.

They descended the steep, shabby stairs, and Poole said, "Don't you think we all should try to live in the here–and–now? I mean, not spend time on regrets about the past and worries about the future?"

"Me—I'm on the side of the lilies of the field, mate."

"Amen," Poole said.

In the car, Judy asked the name of the hotel. Poole reached for the sheaf of papers in his jacket and then thought *To hell with field ops guidelines.*

"Pick one. Take us to a really nice hotel, one you've always dreamed of staying in."

Her laugh was a little rill of amazement, and Poole thought *Let's burn our bridges before we come to them!*

Harvey Lewis, he calculated, would be stirring in his soft

suburban bed in a house a dozen miles north of Pittsburgh, about to rise and commute back to reality. Half a world away and seeing the sunrise.

Judy pulled the car out of the alleyway and into an empty street, and Poole said, "'Though we cannot make our sun stand still, yet we will make him run.'"

"Yes, indeed," she said.

About the Authors

Bill Schafer was, up to his death in 2009, professor of English at Berea College in Kentucky, where he held the Chester D. Tripp Chair in Humanities. He taught English and humanities courses there beginning in 1964. He has written extensively on African–American music, Appalachian and Southern literature, and modern American fiction for periodicals and reference works. Bill's wife and co-author, Martha, still lives in Berea, Kentucky. She and Bill traveled extensively in England, and studied group processes there and in the United States. Process of Murder is their first published novel.

www.ingramcontent.com/pod-product-compliance
Lightning Source LLC
Chambersburg PA
CBHW050034180626
46810CB00002B/708